Exterior View of the Great Coliseum, designed

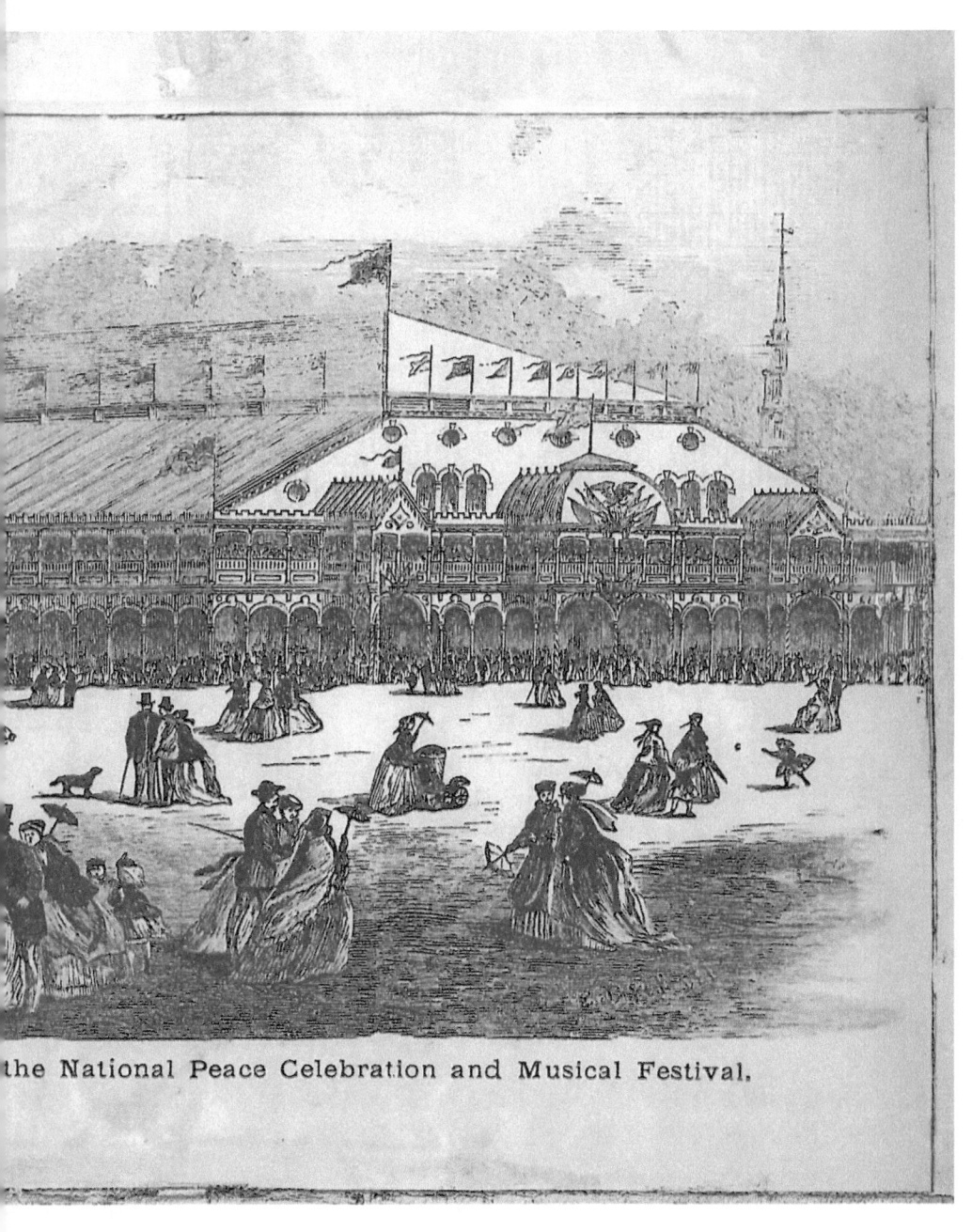

the National Peace Celebration and Musical Festival.

The Great Coliseum in Boston (engraving) by John Andrew & Sons, 1869.

LAYERS

LAYERS
Uncovering Confederate Treasure and an
Attempt to Assassinate President Grant

Written by
PAUL E. BOLIN

ISBN: 979-8-9905013-0-0
Library of Congress Control Number: 2024911848

Paul E. Bolin, Author/Educator, LLC
P.O. Box 131
Wellborn, TX 77881
www.paulebolin.com

First Edition | College Station, Texas | 2024

This book is a work of "historical faction" in which parts of this novel are based on fact and others fiction. Many of the locations, events, and individuals in this account are well documented within the record of history. However, the thoughts and actions of individuals in this novel are fictitious, being products of the author's imagination.

Names: Bolin, Paul E., author. | Price, Lori A., editor & book designer.
Title: Layers
Subtitle: Uncovering Confederate Treasure and an Attempt to Assassinate President Grant

Images:
1858 Remington Percussion Cane Gun (image) by Seth Hamman, Courtesy of Cisco's Gallery.
The Great Coliseum in Boston (engraving) by John Andrew & Sons, 1869.
Grand National Peace Jubilee and Musical Festival (monthly bulletin) by George Coolidge, 1869.
1851-O Three-Cent Silver Coin (image), Courtesy of Professional Coin Grading Service (PCGS.com).

Thank you, Jane,
for your unwavering belief in me
and my work on this book.

A NOVEL

Layers is a work of "historical faction" in which parts of this novel are based on fact and others fiction.

It may have happened,

   it may not have happened,

      but it could have happened.

   -Mark Twain-

Overlooked objects, like the past itself,
may divulge the most unexpected finds.

Tuesday Evening, August 22, 2017
Before the Beginning

This fake driver's license has served me well. It's been my go-to pass lots of times in the last five years. At first, I used it for entry into bars and clubs in my early college days, before turning 21. Since then, this phony license has been my ticket through so many adventures. The photo on the license—fortunately a bit grainy—still captures my likeness pretty well: five foot-six, 130 pounds, light brown hair, dark eyes, firm jaw, and slightly dimpled cheeks.

And the made-up name and date of birth on the card always make me smile: Emily Elizabeth Wilson. DOB: 9-19-1991 (easy to remember, nine-one, nine-one, nine-nine-one). Who would suspect my favorite book character as a kid, Emily Elizabeth from *Clifford the Big Red Dog*, and the volleyball Wilson from the movie *Castaway* would one day meet up to be my invented name on a forged driver's license. It's never let me down.

Seeing my license on the table after a trip to the safe deposit box in the bank this morning, I'm taking a few minutes to write this introduction to my account of what's happened to me in the last three and-a-half months, which I've recorded in the pages that follow. It's quite a story!

I've learned some valuable lessons about keeping a journal over the years. The first of these came when I was 13 and my nosy brother 9: hide your diary well.

A second important lesson I gleaned about journaling is that if you're going to write one, do so with much descriptive detail and from the depths of your heart. It may save your life. I learned this by way of my father and brother a few years later when both were killed in a car crash. My mom and my journal—but mostly my journal—carried me through that horrific time.

A third lesson about keeping a journal I've gained through experience is, never start writing on the first page. Always leave a few blank pages at the beginning. These may come in handy later to give space for a reflective lead-in to the writing that follows, or they can be used to add a sketch or colorful collage to help start things off. It's difficult to introduce a journal without space to do so up front.

If it turns out the first empty pages are not needed, then you can remove them. Like life, when the journal-writing journey begins, you never know where it will take you in the days ahead. It's best to be prepared, with options.

By habit, when I began writing this journal, I left the first few pages blank. I'm glad I did, as I am filling those pages here with this reflective lead-in to the incredible story of what has happened in my life these past few months.

I do ask myself why I would write an introduction to a record of my own thoughts and happenings? It's a good question, and one for which I don't have a completely satisfactory answer. But I believe that doing this helps me process and maybe better understand what I've already lived through and recorded.

In one way this journal is different from any other I've written. I knew from the start—about 15 weeks ago—that someone else would be reading it. My writing here began on May 10th as a record of my summer internship activities, to be handed in to my professor as a university course requirement. It was supposed to be a straightforward record of my work in the university's Civil War and Reconstruction History Museum. That purpose changed dramatically, however, just four days later. My formal internship ended abruptly, and my life almost did as well.

The writing in this journal changes from that point on. Since the events of May 14th, it is written for me, not a course grade. It's a record to help me remember in vivid detail what I've lived through and discovered in the months since then.

It's hard to grasp that people have been killed and my life in jeopardy by events told in this story. Why, then, am I keeping this account if I'm in danger through it? Perhaps it would be best for me to destroy this journal and let the incidents of the past months diffuse like ripples across a pond over time, hoping I've hidden the trail of my life well enough so those in pursuit won't find me.

But this is the chance I take in keeping this remarkable account. I feel an immense responsibility to do so in honor of unknown women in the past—those written about in the pages that follow—who years ago generated my recently discovered record of hidden United States history unveiled here. I have an overwhelming desire and heartfelt responsibility to give voice to their previously untold story.

However, a cautious approach is taken when recording this account. I'm currently living in hiding and plan to do so for the next few months. As I learned from my little brother years ago, no journal is completely safe from uninvited eyes. For this reason, in the account that follows I reveal enough information so that the main facts presented here can be confirmed by anyone who may read this journal some day, but not so much that I or anyone else mentioned throughout the pages that follow are purposely situated in harm's way.

Wednesday, May 10, 2017
My Summer History Museum Internship Experience

This journal is written to record my university internship activities this summer. It's supposed to be straightforward and objectively descriptive, an approach unlike my usual journal writing that's much more emotionally charged and personal.

This written document is "required" for my Museum Internship course grade. But I'm told it's no big deal. Just make it "a concise record of what you're learning and doing," which I'm expected to submit for a grade at the end of summer term. It seems pretty direct: "easy-peasy japanesey," to quote Brooks Hatlen from the award-winning *Shawshank Redemption*, a favorite movie of mine.

My professor told me not to sweat it. He described the journal as being written to document my internship experience in case some university administrator wants to know what I did for my summer internship grade. He added that it's very likely no one will ever ask to read it.

So here I go. This summer internship is a great opportunity for me. As a 23-year old female graduate student in the American History Department—studying the US Civil War—the museum provides immediate access to Civil War era objects while fulfilling my university required internship experience. And to top it off, I pretty much get to work on my own. There's a lot to do, but I think I'll enjoy this!

The only drawback is I don't get paid for the work I do in the museum this summer. However, the museum does pay my summer school tuition, which this term is only my internship credit. To support myself financially, I work a few hours a week at the local hospital delivering linen and towels to patients' rooms. It pays the bills.

Dr. Donaldson, director of the museum and professor of history, offered me this internship position a few weeks ago. I was thrilled when he asked if I was interested in sticking around town this summer and working at the museum, mostly cataloging and storing Civil War and post-Civil War era items donated to the museum from people in the area. I gladly accepted the position.

This is a great chance to work directly with Civil War objects. My university classes involve learning about the War from a distance, to experience it through books and lectures. Don't get me wrong, I enjoy that, but here in the museum I'm able to encounter history firsthand, to touch the War, literally.

There are a number of recently acquired Civil War artifacts to be cataloged and placed in museum storage. These items possess life-stories of a time long ago. My job in the museum is to care for these objects, and to research and tell their stories. I give voice to silent physical traces of battle and life, helping them to become animated for visitors to the museum. This is why I love what I get to do!

Professor Donaldson—Don, as people often call him—will be away from campus and the museum most of the summer. This is Don's regular schedule, as he spends two or three months each summer where he grew up in rural Arkansas.

The museum here is somewhat small in size, but well organized. Its focus is centered primarily on preserving and displaying artifacts from the Civil War and the Reconstruction era, and serving those on campus and in the surrounding community. Students, faculty members, and some locals from the area are the ones who use it most. For this reason, with few classes in session during the summer, the museum is closed to visitors from mid-May to mid-August, except by appointment. And appointments are made through me. No one has contacted me yet about visiting the museum this summer. The Professor told me not to expect many visitors.

Professor Donaldson is gone this weekend, speaking at a Civil War history conference in Atlanta. This is not uncommon, as the Professor is an expert on various aspects of the Civil War and often attends and delivers lectures at Civil War history meetings.

Before leaving for the weekend, Professor Donaldson passed along my first internship task. Don said he recently received a letter from a woman named April Jones who will be moving from the area soon. Ms. Jones indicated she has two large trunks containing Civil War and Reconstruction era items for donation to the museum.

Don gave me instructions to drive to her house, retrieve the trunks, and bring them back to the museum. My job will be to inventory the objects from the trunks into our electronic database before placing the items (including the two trunks) in the secure storage room in the basement of the museum. It's the straightforward type of cataloging I've done in my class work and some volunteer experiences here at the museum.

I'm headed to pick up the two trunks tomorrow afternoon—to arrive at 4:00 p.m. sharp, Don said—and then return to begin the object inventory and storage process. The Professor didn't leave any specific information about what the trunks contain. That, I guess, will be my surprise tomorrow.

Thursday, May 11, 2017

I can't do this! I read over my first journal entry from yesterday and it just isn't me. I've been keeping journals on and off since junior high school and I have my own way of writing them. Making an objective record of what I do each day and learn through the process is not my approach to journaling. I'll do my best, Professor (and anyone else who might read this someday), but there may be more rich descriptive language and picturesque storytelling in this journal than you expect or want to read. But as you say, Professor, it's likely no one will ever read it. So, here's what took place today, written in my style:

The travel app on my phone showed the trip would be about 60 minutes. This alone time provided a chance to relax, roll down the windows of my old red somewhat beat-up Ford pick-up truck, catch my breath, and enjoy the ride through a blossoming Virginia countryside. Classes for the academic year are over, and my entire focus for the summer is now directed toward the museum and its collection. I feel good.

The Professor will leave soon on his annual summer trip to Arkansas. He was born and grew up there. I know a few things about his family and early life, but not too much. These summer excursions aren't talked about, except to say he spends them mostly deep in the Arkansas woods, and often by himself or with one of his longtime buddies from the area.

Don told me these trips are his time to take off his academic-hat and spend weeks hiking and camping in the steamy-summer backwoods of northern Arkansas. It doesn't sound like much fun to me, but he must enjoy it.

My GPS (as well as pencil sketched directions provided to the Professor by April Jones) led me through the quiet rolling hills of rural central Virginia. The cheerful mid-May afternoon drive from the university carried me to a brushy, nearly hidden turn-off road that veered to the right from the main highway.

I navigated the sweeping bend slowly and continued on. The narrow dirt and rough stone roadway leading to a distant farmhouse held two car-width parallel strips of deep-pitted sunbaked potholes. There were too many to avoid, which produced the feel of my pick-up truck bounding along the jagged spine of a large stegosaurus.

Few vehicles would have braved (or survived!) the trip. I was glad to be driving my dependable 15-year-old pick-up. The necessarily slow-going bounce-along led me toward a large two-story wood-slatted farmhouse. I could see it standing stark and rigid in the distance, partially hiding a tree-spotted hillside.

The divot-strewn roadway arced slightly back and forth in the quarter mile drive off the main road to the farmhouse. Slowing near my destination, I could easily see the wrap-around porch of the early 20th-century multi-gabled residence. A small outbuilding was situated in the back, which earlier had been obscured by a vine-infested grove of willow trees.

Arriving closer to the house I could see it needed work. Several coats of once white paint were pealing in brittle agony from what was probably in earlier days a majestic residence now silhouetted against a darkening Virginia sky. If this was April Jones' house, it was plain why she wanted to leave it soon.

A few overgrown red and yellow flowering shrubs skirted the farmhouse, but the view between the house and entry road was mostly wide open. It would be difficult for anyone to approach the residence from the road unnoticed. A fact I soon learned firsthand.

A woman, perhaps in her 80s, appeared to be waiting for my arrival. She wore a long blue and white striped linen dress, with her shoulders and upper torso covered by a white full-sleeved sweater, which seemed a bit out of place for a pleasant yet cloudy Virginia afternoon in May. The woman rose slow and stiff from a well-worn wooden rocking chair positioned on the front porch. Watching her stand, I'm not sure which teetered more, the chair or the woman.

I parked, stepped out of my truck and approached the porch, climbing the three rough wooden steps in rapid succession. I introduced myself and held out my hand in a warm yet professional greeting.

The woman, who I assumed was April Jones, did not reciprocate. She eyed me silently for a long moment—like a fish suspended in watery focus behind the aquarium glass—before speaking to me in short sentences, evoking attention through her rolling southern accent: "Who are you? And where is the Civil War professor? He said he would be here to get these trunks, and pick them up at 4:00 this afternoon," she drawled, pointing at the two large wood-constructed and metal-hinged trunks resting on the somewhat sagging wooden porch.

I replied that the Professor was called away to Atlanta for some business and had asked me, his assistant, to drive here and pick up your two trunks. Her silence continued, but she did shake her head slightly in affirmation, indicating that she understood my words and perhaps accepted my explanation.

The trunks looked heavy. About the time I made this observation, a middle-aged man wearing blue work overalls and a narrow-rimed straw farm hat approached around the corner of the house. While also somewhat stiff in manner and movement, he did seem a bit more relaxed and pleasant than did the older woman. From his features and actions, I couldn't tell if he was a relative or hired hand, helping with chores. It didn't matter much either way. His assistance with the trunks was needed and appreciated.

With little conversation the man helped me lower the tailgate and load the two large trunks into the back of my truck. I was correct in my observation: they were heavy. Once the trunks were covered with a thick canvas tarp and tied in with a length of rope kept in the truck, I secured the tailgate and thanked the quiet and wary couple for their donation to the museum.

Before leaving, I told them Professor Donaldson would be in touch when he returned, to thank them himself. With a brief hand-wave and a glance in my rearview mirror at the two individuals on the porch, I headed back toward the main highway. It's hard to know for sure, but all parties seemed pleased—or at least satisfied—with the completed transaction.

Except for the expected jarring ride back to the main road, my return trip to the university was uneventful. I drove to the museum, backed my truck up to the loading dock, retrieved a hydraulic dolly from storage, carefully slid the two trunks out the bed of the truck and on to the dolly, moved them inside, and placed them in the workroom of the museum. It was an interesting afternoon for my first day on the job. I'm curious about what's in the trunks, but looking at my watch I saw it was now past dinnertime.

Leaving the museum, I headed back to my apartment and made this journal entry before going out to enjoy the evening. I plan to get an early start on unloading and inventorying the contents of the two trunks tomorrow. I do wonder, however, what I'll find?

Friday, May 12, 2017

I'm glad I scheduled myself out of my hospital job for the weekend and this coming week. I had a feeling there would be a lot of inventory work to do in the museum, which appears to be the case with the need to unload and catalog the contents of these two heavy wooden trunks.

Bracing myself for a pull, I carefully took hold of the smooth metal handle on one end of the trunk. Pulling hard, I slid the first of the two identical wooden chests around the end of the table for easier access to its contents. I was curious to see what the trunks contained. The central metal lock on the first wooden trunk was easy to open. I slid the metal lever to the right and the lock yielded with a distinctive click.

I slowly lifted the trunk lid and surveyed the top item. A woman's white linen smock was folded neatly and resting on what appeared to be a full container-load of items. The work of handling, classifying, and documenting objects for the museum can be time-consuming, especially if the objects grab your interest. It's easy to lose track of the day and get caught up examining objects from the past. A particular old book or document, intriguing antique farm tool or household implement, or curious item of clothing or jewelry can seduce you for hours of imaginary reflection and story-construction unless one stays focused on the ever-present documentation task at hand.

The Professor has offered useful advice on how to keep from getting sidetracked early in the inventory process. He believes the best way to undertake the cataloging of items into the museum is to first put on a pair of white cotton gloves. Then, item by item, lay out all the objects to be cataloged on the large worktable in the center of the room. Once this is accomplished, it is wise to arrange the objects in groupings of similar items, if possible, before starting the process of recording an electronic description of each individual object to be placed in storage as part of the museum's permanent collection.

Even though the Professor instructs his students not to spend too much time looking at objects early in the unpacking process, it's often difficult to follow his advice. It's exciting to see what things appear as the trunks are unpacked. Each object removed from one of the wooden chests has a life-story of its own, with questions surrounding it calling to be investigated.

My initial read of the trunks' contents lead me to believe the owner was likely a female schoolteacher. This is because both trunks contain a few dresses and a couple pairs of women's shoes. From my university study of antique fashion, they appear to be worn in the second half of the 19th century.

The trunks also held a vast array of reading, spelling, arithmetic, history, drawing, and geography primers from this same time period. Included are two very nice hand-carved wooden chess sets, an assortment of maps of the world and the United States—printed in the 1870s—as well as a world globe from that era. As tantalizing as it is to dive into close inspection of these objects right away, I'll wait to study them more carefully once I complete the inventory process.

However, I just had to investigate one very curious object I unpacked. This is a finely crafted stiff light-brown leather tube, about 6 inches in diameter and 40 inches long. It fit neatly at the bottom of the second trunk I unloaded. Removing it from the wooden chest, I carefully unlatched the top leather strap of the cylinder and slid off its small cover.

With hesitation, I reached inside. Gently moving my fingers around the interior top of the tube and slowly tipping the open end of the cylindrical container to the tabletop, I carefully slid from it five walking canes of various dimensions, materials, and handle decorations. They range from a stunningly intricate pearl handled wooden cane, to one displaying a handle in the shape of a dark colored dog's head. I look forward to giving them a close examination in the days ahead. I returned the canes to their container and secured the leather top to its case. I have such interesting work ahead of me!

All the contents of the trunks are now organized on the large table in the center of the museum workroom. It took me longer than anticipated to unpack these objects from the trunks and spread them out. It's hard not to spend time studying each item for at least a few minutes. But I keep reminding myself that I have all summer to investigate them.

With that said, this seemed a good place to stop my work in the museum for the day. I had some errands to run around town this afternoon. I'll begin my inventory of the items first thing tomorrow morning, even though it's Saturday. I can't wait to explore more carefully what I unpacked from the trunks today.

Saturday, May 13, 2017

This is the day my world changed! I left my apartment about 8:30 a.m. and headed to the museum. Nothing out of the ordinary for a Saturday morning in mid-May. There were few people around town and even less on campus. I parked my truck in the museum lot and entered the building through the back door—for employees only—set my backpack down and looked over the array of objects I removed from the two trunks yesterday.

I drew a long and thoughtful breath before beginning my inventory work. Since I had arranged the items in groupings on the table—books, maps, chess sets, kitchen and sewing utensils, some hand-tools, a couple small light green line-stitched blankets, some women's clothing, a world globe, and a variety of other objects—I began my inventory with the trunks themselves.

My first observation of the trunks was that they are heavy, even when empty, and solidly made. I remember how difficult it was to load them into the bed of my truck when picking them up from April Jones on Thursday. Both trunks are constructed of wood with metal casings and clasps, along with three large metal hinges connecting the body of each trunk with its flat top lid. The two trunks appear the same in design, size, and construction.

The only marking I see is a very faded white five-pointed star, about four inches in size, painted on the outside in the middle of each trunk lid. No other design feature is visible on any side, top, or bottom of either trunk. I'm not certain of the wood, but I believe it is oak. The trunks presented a pretty easy inventory job so far.

To complete my documentation of the trunks, I made a detailed measurement of their dimensions, inside and out. I recorded my findings into the spreadsheet on the museum tablet and labeled it:

April Jones Trunk 1, accessioned May 13, 2017.
Exterior: L42" x H26" x W24"
Interior: L40" x H24" x W22"

There's a 2-inch difference in the length, height, and width dimensions between the inside and outside of the trunk. The inch thick wood used for all sides, top, and bottom of the trunks make them very durable, but also quite heavy.

Resting nearby on the floor, its twin looked the same dimension. My initial inclination was to duplicate the entry for Trunk 2 into the tablet, as it was easy to see they were the same size, with an identical faded white star painted on each lid. However, something the Professor instilled in all students who work in the museum is to observe each item individually and carefully, not to assume anything, and to record accurately all features of the object studied. "Take time to get the details recorded right," was a recurring mantra in his instruction to us.

Don's words paid critical dividends here. I dutifully stretched my tape measure across the dimensions of the trunk in all three directions, both inside and out, and recorded the results on the tablet:

April Jones Trunk 2, accessioned May 13, 2017.
Exterior: L42" x H26" x W24"
Interior: L40" x H21" x W22"

It took me a moment to realize my error in measurement. I'd recorded the interior height of the second trunk to be 21 inches instead of 24, as was recorded for the first trunk I measured.

But then I caught myself. I know the measurement on the cloth tape I stretched up the inside wall of Trunk 2 read 21 inches. I could see the number 21 in my mind's eye. I measured the interior height of the trunk again. Sure enough, the tape measure showed the inside distance of the chest from the bottom panel to the top edge to be 21 inches.

I thought this discrepancy odd, so I inspected the trunk more closely and measured its interior depth at all four corners. Each time the tape measured 21 inches. It was clear that something was amiss in this second trunk. With some struggle I lifted the trunk off the floor and positioned it on a lower worktable. Doing so I realized it was a bit heavier than the first empty trunk, which I'd placed on the floor after recording its measurement. It was time for a flashlight and closer inspection of the second trunk.

The beam of light focused within the trunk's interior did not reveal much—at first. Closer scrutiny and a few knuckle taps on the inside bottom panel displayed something peculiar. In places, my solid raps evidenced a hollow sound. Working my hands back and forth while pushing on the bottom panel brought out the fact that there were actually three pieces of quarter-inch thick wood, set side-by-side with nearly matching wood grains, making up a false bottom of the trunk. The craftsmanship was excellent and purposeful in its disguised intent, and it appeared something of weight was concealed in the hidden compartment below.

Pressing down on the wooden slats at the bottom of the trunk and sliding them sideways back and forth ever so carefully, I was able to maneuver them from their set position. As I slowly removed the three finely prepared pieces of wood one-by-one, what met my immediate gaze were four brown-colored flat packages resting side-by-side in the opening at the bottom of the trunk.

I anxiously removed the four brown bundles from their previously hidden location and placed them on the worktable in the middle of the room. Each package was covered with light brown soft leather, folded around with no tie string.

The other objects on the table, which minutes before held my rapt attention, now faded in significance to the four brown leather bundles. The weight and size of the wrapped objects, although secured in their leather covering, gave the feel that each package contained a book.

The first leather wrap when unfolded revealed, indeed, a sturdy black hardbound volume. I attentively laid the book flat on the worktable and gently turned the first stiff-leafed pages to reach one with its title in large block font: *History of the National Peace Jubilee and Great Musical Festival: Held in the City of Boston, June, 1869, to Commemorate the Restoration of Peace Throughout the Land*, with the author being Patrick Sarsfield Gilmore and a publication date of 1871. Moving delicately through the book, I turned to its final page, numbered 758. Yes, this is a large volume. Its thickness, with leather wrapping, barely fit within the hidden space at the bottom of the trunk.

The second package I unwrapped was thinner and lightweight. It is a softcover black and white pamphlet, typeset, with a dramatic cover displaying a winged angel blowing a long trumpet and carrying a flowing banner with the words LET US HAVE PEACE centered at the top. In large script the title of the booklet read *Grand National Peace Jubilee and Musical Festival*, with a printed date of May & June 1869. On the back is an engraving of a large two-story building. The dimension of the printed pamphlet is approximately 7" by 10" and about a quarter inch thick.

I carefully laid the pamphlet aside on the table and reached for the third leather-covered bundle. Unwrapping it brought to light an austere black-cover King James Bible with height and length dimensions similar to the other two books, but well more than an inch thick. The first few pages I attempted to turn were brittle and stuck together in places, so I didn't take time now to examine its assumed content.

One wrapped leather package remained to be opened. The findings I made so far were exciting, but pale in comparison to this final book found in the concealed bottom space of the trunk. This book is similar in size to the pamphlet I unwrapped second, but this one has a stiff leather cover. Much like the Bible, however, it appears many of the pages in this document are stuck together and delicate to separate.

Beyond that, this book isn't like the other three hidden in the bottom of the trunk. Those are typeset volumes. This book is handwritten. It's a 19th-century account, composed by a woman named Mary Moore, from Franklin, Virginia. It's an amazing historical document, but it's the story the diary contains that is truly astonishing.

Taking this handwritten personal journal to a bright lit reading table across the room, I spent the next couple hours gently plying brittle pages apart and working my way through the writing line by line. I caught my breath multiple times as Mary Moore's story unfolded.

Deciphering this 19th-century journal, word by word—sometimes a letter at a time—is hard work. In places I'm forced to use a magnifying glass. There are pages and pages to the story, but skimming ahead through parts I'm able to read it appears this journal tells the dramatic and compelling account of an unsuccessful attempt to assassinate the President of the United States, Ulysses S. Grant, during his attendance at a huge celebration known as the National Peace Jubilee and Great Musical Festival, held in Boston, Massachusetts in June 1869. This is the event described in the large black book written by Patrick Gilmore and the smaller pamphlet, both included in the space below the false bottom of the trunk. These books are an unbelievable find, introducing me to an incredible piece of overlooked American history.

My first thought after I examined the handwritten account for a few hours was to contact the Professor and tell him about this discovery. But I hesitated. What if Mary Moore's written diary here is a fake, some forgery arranged in the trunk as a trick, maybe even by the Professor himself. Perhaps this is his sly attempt to see if I am, indeed, thorough in my documentation and record keeping of objects brought into the museum. But would he really plan all this to find that out?

I don't think so. The more I examine the document, the other books surrounding it, and the way they were hidden, I increasingly believe this 19th-century written account concealed in the false-bottom trunk is authentic. The pages are thin, brittle, and difficult to separate. It appears no one has examined these books for a very long time.

Once carefully pulled apart, the black-ink handwritten pages are hard to read. In places, the ink from one side of the page has bled through to the other side. This slows my reading, but each line I decipher is thrilling.

I couldn't contain myself. I had to tell the Professor what I found. Rather than give him a phone call out of the blue, I sent Don a text asking him to call me when he was available to talk. He would know it was important, as I sometimes contact him through text, but never when he's away on business.

About 45 minutes later my phone lit up. I could tell by caller ID that it was the Professor. Hitting the accept button, I cut through the small talk and immediately blurted, "I picked up the two trunks from April Jones on Thursday, like you asked me to do. While going through the trunks and inventorying the contents, I found something you are not going to believe!"

I paused to catch my breath, but then continued, "One of the trunks contains a false bottom. Hidden in a concealed compartment inside the trunk are four books. One of the books is a handwritten personal diary telling the story of an assassination attempt made on the life of President Ulysses S. Grant. It happened at an event called the National Peace Jubilee and Great Musical Festival, held in Boston in June 1869. Have you heard of it?"

Without waiting for an answer, I told the Professor that I went online and googled this Musical Festival. Yes, it did happen. And the facts written in the parts of the journal I've read so far match what I've been able to learn online regarding this 19th-century musical event in Boston. Two other books hidden in the trunk tell about the Peace Jubilee and Musical Festival. The 4th book is an old black Bible.

I finished my part of the conversation and Don was still silent. After what seemed like a long minute taking in and processing my words about finding these books, the Professor sounded simultaneously captivated yet flustered by my revelation to him regarding this handwritten document. As we continued to talk, Don couldn't hide his enthusiasm to see these four books, especially the diary. He asked me to take a couple pictures of it with my phone and send them to him.

After finishing our brief conversation, I used my phone to take three pictures of pages from Mary Moore's diary and quickly sent them to the Professor. He responded with a text about 10 minutes later, thanking me for sending the photos and asking that I put this handwritten journal on his office desk. Don said he was very interested in seeing the diary and would do so first thing when he returned to campus on Monday morning. I replied with agreement in a text.

It was well past lunchtime and I hadn't eaten the peanut butter sandwich I brought with me. The adrenaline-rich excitement of the day was wearing off and I felt the need to head home, but not without taking Mary Moore's journal with me. I put the three other books on the worktable but gently wrapped the handwritten document in its leather covering, placing it in my backpack and taking off for home. I wanted to spend time reading it more carefully before leaving it for the Professor tomorrow evening. If what I've read so far is true, then this will undoubtedly change American history and likely my life as well!

It's Saturday evening and I've had some dinner. I just finished this long journal entry, but the thrill of having this handwritten diary in my apartment is too much. I've decided to record in my own journal the exact words found in Mary Moore's diary, to make a complete record of what Mary writes, telling her story using her own words. It will be an amazing historical account to possess, and to transcribe it word-for-word along with my thoughts as I do so. I want to get started tonight.

By the hand of Mary Moore of Franklin, Virginia, June 16, 1889.

This is not a legal document, but I am writing it as such. Today I am putting to pen and paper an account that should have been transcribed many years ago. Since I am the only one here to tell the story, and it is now 20 years to the day of when this event took place, I feel the act of recording this deed first-hand is now left to me.

The story begins, however, long before June 16, 1869, when the horrific event of this writing occurred. It is on that date—exactly 20 years ago—at a vast event known as the National Peace Jubilee and Great Musical Festival in the city of Boston, Massachusetts, that I participated in a plan to kill the President of the United States, Ulysses S. Grant.

This failed assassination attempt has been hidden from history for far too long and is recorded here as it is clear I am now nearing the close of my earthly life. But rather than to give a cursory account of the attempt to settle the score with this Northern Butcher, it is important that I present a more full record of events leading to that June day of 1869 in Boston.

It's late, but I just had to get started on this transcription. I can hardly grasp what I've read so far. I'm headed to bed now but will pick up the recording of Mary Moore's journal first thing tomorrow morning. I hope I can get some sleep.

Sunday, May 14, 2017

I'm up early this morning. With one cup of coffee down and one in hand, this is how Mary's diary continues.

Writers of history generate many untruths. Sometimes these are penned by accident, other times not. As much as these historical inaccuracies (and very often lies) gnaw inside me, most times I turn away in ire but let them settle into the standard of the day.

But sometimes I cannot do so. And this is one of those occasions, particularly since I know for certain the untruths being told. Patrick Sarsfield Gilmore's tome about the Musical Festival in Boston is an incomplete record and unrigh-

teous fallacy. It must be regarded for what it is: a celebratory tribute to ongoing northern tyranny, and the whitewashing of Southern slaughter and devilish destruction.

I am writing this account to set complete the historical record of the musical jubilee in Boston and in it reveal the attempt to bring revenge on then President Ulysses S. Grant, the indiscriminate Butcher of the South.

I was born near Franklin, Virginia in 1822. I have not married, nor have I birthed any children, and was the Primary and Grammar school teacher for pupils in and around Franklin beginning in 1841.

The story that culminates some 20 years ago— on June 16, 1869—had its beginning years earlier. I can still see their young bright faces, even today.

From 1841 I taught dozens of young sons and daughters of the South. They came to me from proud hardworking families. Some left school and Franklin to pursue occupations elsewhere, but most stayed to carry on life in the footsteps of their fathers and mothers. The children of Franklin—and I taught most of them at some point—are important to this story, but none more than the Lees.

There were three children in the Lee family, two boys and a girl. Gideon and Samson were separated by two years. Deborah followed a little more than five years behind the younger brother, Samson. As teacher of the village school, I kept a record of the birth dates of all students in attendance. The Lee children:

Gideon Lee, born March 4, 1845
Samson Lee, born June 9, 1847
Deborah Lee, born July 1, 1852

The three Lee children were close to one another in comfort and care. The older boys looked after their sister, especially when their father—Joshua—first lost his leg in a farming accident, and then died of infection a few months later in the winter of 1860.

The young Lee boys carried on the workings of the farm the best they could. Neighbors on the next agricultural tract, Mr. and Mrs. Duke, periodically sent two of their slaves—Noah and Josiah—to assist the boys with their farming responsibilities. But it was a struggle for the boys to overcome their station, especially after the passing of their mother Ruth about a year thereafter. The physician said her dying was from pneumonia, but I believe it was from a broken heart. She loved her husband Joshua very much and is with him joyous in Glory now.

But before that crushing time the Lee family was a sunny feature of our little community. Ruth Lee took care of the house and family, and Joshua looked after their small peanut farm. The boys helped their father tend their crop and even enticed the help of their young friends from time to time.

Little Deborah displayed the radiance of the sun! She was a delight to her mother, helping with chores and often rescuing young animals and birds in need of care and healing. She was quick to learn, often staying after the school day was complete to see if there was anything she could help me with in our little schoolhouse.

Young Deborah took great delight in conveying to others the origin of her given name, as well as those of her brothers: Gideon and Samson. A recounting where these three names were drawn shows that Deborah's parents were endowed with a playful sense of religious humor. Joshua and

Ruth Lee were strong in Christian spirit, both being named for characters and books from the Holy Bible: Joshua the sixth book of Scripture, and Ruth the eighth. Between them rests the Bible's seventh book: Judges.

When it came time to select names for their children, Deborah told me—through high-pitched laughter—that her parents believed, "It was only right they select names for their children that were found in the Holy Scriptures between Joshua and Ruth." Hence, their three biblical names were from the book of Judges, chosen as needed: Gideon, Samson, and Deborah.

Deborah confided to me that she is not sure what names her parents would have selected had more daughters been born to the family, as Deborah is the only woman judge listed in the book of Judges. She is also glad her parents did not use the biblical judges named Jephthah, Shamgar, or Ibzan. Deborah didn't think these names would be appropriate for any Virginia Sons of the Confederacy.

~

Engrossed in my experience with Mary's journal, I've suddenly realized it is now into the evening. I want to leave the handwritten diary on the Professor's desk, as he had instructed, so Don can examine it as soon as he arrives on campus tomorrow morning. I'm also looking forward to telling the Professor what I've found and recorded so far from Mary's writing. If this story is true, then it will alter the historical record of the United States. And to think this is just my first week on the job. I'm headed to drop off the book at the Professor's office now.

Events of late Sunday, May 14, 2017
(written on Monday, May 15th)

I'm recording the date in my journal as Sunday, May 14th, but I'm writing this on Monday, May 15th. It will probably take me quite a while to put on paper all that happened to me yesterday evening when I went to the university to leave Mary Moore's diary on the Professor's desk. It's been a dramatic blur since then, with no time for writing until now. I want to take today to record the details of my experience yesterday, as it is recent and raw.

To save time yesterday evening, I drove to the museum even though it was only a few blocks away. I parked my truck in the employee lot and entered the History Building through the back door of the museum, which is my standard operating procedure.

Unlocking the door, I went inside and put my backpack on a nearby table. I took the still leather wrapped journal from my backpack, handling it carefully. Even from the small parts I've read so far, I had a stirring inside me that I was holding something very special, a book that truly would change American history. I could not wait for Dr. Donaldson—a name I used formally—to have a look at this diary.

By now it was past dinnertime, and I was hungry. With keys in hand, I headed out the inside door from the workroom down the hall toward Don's office to drop off the diary. I noticed at the end of the hall that the overhead light was on in the Professor's office. This is strange, I thought, as Don told me he wouldn't be back in the office until tomorrow morning.

The cleaning staff shouldn't be working at this time of night, especially on a Sunday. As far as I know Don and I are the only ones—other than the cleaning staff—with keys to his office. Perhaps the Professor returned early, I thought, which is great. I decided a surprise was in order, and I was excited to be able to pass the diary to him myself and see his reaction to what I'd found.

Walking silently down the hall to reinforce the surprise, I heard voices coming from the Professor's office. The door was ajar. Before entering the slightly cracked-open door, I listened quietly to the conversation from outside his office.

One voice belonged to the Professor. The other I didn't recognize. However, the words spoken by this unknown visitor were distinctly southern—almost Cajun. The speaker was male, yet with an expression that was particularly high-pitched and squeaky. His words to the Professor sounded strained and officious.

I listened in hushed darkness at the doorway as the Professor declared, "You and I have spent years looking for that journal, even though we weren't 100 percent certain it actually existed! It looks like it is real, and we now have it!"

"Well, Don, let me clarify that," the other man spat, "You have the diary, but I want the diary—now, please, hand it over! We both know about the few hazy stories surrounding its contents, how the book contains an account that will re-write an important piece of American history and possibly hold clues to a fortune in Confederate treasure."

I caught my breath in perplexed confusion. "What am I hearing?"

"But it's not here!" the Professor replied, "As I told you on the phone last night, I only heard the diary was found and was sent three photos of the first pages. It looks genuine, and I was expecting the book to be here in my office when I arrived. That's why I contacted you, returned early from my trip, and told you to meet me here."

"If the diary is not here, Professor, then where is it?" the high-pitched voice asked angrily.

"I don't know," the Professor replied, "Perhaps a janitor or maintenance worker picked it up from my desk, while cleaning."

"Not a chance, Don!" the man declared in raised volume, "Especially not on a Sunday night. No one cleans campus offices on weekends in the summer. That won't do, Don! Who has the diary? Who sent you the photos? Who are you protecting?"

Silence hung on these questions for what seemed an eternity, knowing that a truthful reply would lead a trail directly to me. "Tell me Don, or I'll use this," the high-pitched voice resounded with increasing anger as I heard the preparatory click of a firearm. Because I couldn't see into the office, it was only then I froze completely, realizing the seriousness of the Professor's situation.

"I will not give you a name," the Professor replied.

"I think you will," was the quick coarse but high-pitched response. "Professor, we both know I've used this weapon distastefully in the past, and I'm not one to play games. Who contacted you and sent you those photos of the diary? That person must have the book. I'm running out of both time and patience."

"There's no need for violence," the Professor replied, "I can get it for us very soon. Be patient and it will be ours."

"Wrong on all counts, Professor," the distinctive voice hissed. "Us, patience, and ours are no longer part of the equation. I can solve this riddle myself. Give me your phone!"

There was a momentary pause and then a body-hurling frenzy erupted in the Professor's office. Books and objects crashed to the floor. The fighting continued as the Professor choked out: "Not my phone! You can't have my phone!"

A pistol shot then reverberated through the Professor's office. There was a deep-throated gasp, the sound of a body smashing to the floor, and silence then surrounded my horror.

I gathered my composure and knew I had to escape the hallway outside the Professor's door as fast and quietly as possible, or I would likely be next in the line of fire. Especially since I held the diary in my hand.

In my anxious retreat down the darkened hallway, I stumbled and fell over a large metal trashcan placed in the corridor. It went sprawling, noisily spilling its contents far and wide. It was now or never. I had to make a run for it!

Jumping to my feet, I fled down the hall toward what I knew was the closest exit. I managed to hold my footing and turn the corner to the right as I heard the penetrating crack of a gunshot. A bullet tore through the decorative oak corner molding just above my head!

It was nearly pitch dark in the hallway, which was my only possible advantage. I knew the layout of the History Building as it had been my second home this past year, but I had no idea if the shooter was familiar with this space as well. He had the weapon, however, and was clearly not reluctant to use it.

Although the building and campus were nearly deserted on a Sunday night in mid-May, I hoped someone had heard the gunshots and alerted the authorities. My cellphone was in my backpack stowed in the museum storage-room. Without it I had no way to make a 911 call, even if I wasn't running for my life!

I was on my own. Rushing down the hall as fast as possible in the dark, my mind flashed on an appropriate response to my desperate situation. Slowing purposely, I grabbed the dark silhouette of a fire alarm handle I'd seen in the corridor countless times and pulled down hard, just before reaching the double door exit from the building.

The screeching sound of the fire siren tore through me! Reaching the exit, I pushed down on the metal bar door handle and rushed through the opening just as another pistol shot whistled past my ear and struck the wall to my right. I was outside and alive, with the still nighttime air surrounding me.

The alarm siren shrilled loudly. I hurriedly zigzagged down familiar sidewalks and around buildings. No bullets registered in the area. In their place I heard the piercing sounds of approaching fire engines and emergency vehicles. I felt both safe, yet vulnerable.

I faced a dilemma. On one hand I needed to report the details of what I'd just experienced to the police, but I also knew that whoever pulled the trigger toward me twice, just minutes ago, would have my name from the Professor's cell phone. This meant the man with the high squeaky Cajun voice and firearm could readily search the university's online directory and gain access to information about me as well as my home address.

Time was of the essence. I needed to get to my apartment as soon as possible, grab some things from it and find a place to hide. If I delayed too long in reaching my apartment the shooter could be waiting for me outside. Damn, if only I hadn't sent that text and those photos to the Professor, and instead waited for him to return from Atlanta, then none of this would have happened! Why did I do that?

The gut punch came when I realized it was this action that set in motion events that led to the Professor being shot in his office. I had to erase that thought from my mind right now. There was too much at stake in this moment to dwell on the past.

Glad I still had my keys in hand, I headed for my apartment to gather a few clothes and essentials and make it back to talk to the police as soon as possible. My residence was only four blocks from here. I figured the shooter would likely need more than these couple minutes to locate where I live—at least I hoped that would be the case.

I rushed down the street to my apartment. With the sound of emergency vehicles echoing in the distance, I cautiously turned the key, opened the door, and tiptoed inside. Grabbing some clothes, a pair of shoes, and small travel case, I stuffed them into a shoulder bag and returned to the History Building within 20 minutes of fleeing campus.

Arriving, I could see the attendants were bringing a body on a gurney out of the building. My heart was crushed by the scene, but then immediately buoyed. The attendants were rushing to an ambulance. The person on the rolling stretcher was being attended to feverishly. The Professor was alive, or at least it seemed that way from the actions of the medical attendants!

Taking a deep breath, I approached a young policeman standing beside one of the patrol cars now parked near the museum. The officer was suspicious of my admission that I was involved with events that had unfolded in the History Building just minutes before. I drew his increasingly full attention, however, as I recounted to him details of my experience in the building: a single shot that took place in Professor Donaldson's office, a tipped over trashcan in the hallway, another shot striking the right-side corner molding in the hallway about six feet up, and someone pulling the fire alarm in the corridor.

I told the officer that detectives would find another bullet hole in the right-side wall by the door at the end of the hall near the fire alarm, if they hadn't encountered it already. He placed a phone call to someone in the building to check on these facts. Some parts of my story were confirmed as new information, giving support for the truthfulness of my account.

Soon after that I was ushered inside the building and brought into a meeting with two suited detectives who listened intently to my story. They asked me questions as I recounted events that had just unfolded in the History Building, but with a few selected omissions.

I informed them about the man I heard in the Professor's office, and his distinctive high-pitched squeaky southern accent. There was not much else I could offer, along with the fact I saw a light-colored sports car speed from the parking lot soon after I left the building. But I wasn't sure if the vehicle had anything to do with the shooter. I did not reveal to the detectives any specific information concerning the conversation I overheard in the Professor's office, or about Mary Moore's 19th-century diary I now had stashed in my overnight bag.

By the time my discussion with the officers was complete it was close to 10:00 p.m. I learned from them the Professor was alive when medics took him from the building, but he was in critical condition. I gave the officers my address and phone contact information but told them there is no way I'm going home after this ordeal. They could call my cell phone if I was needed.

A police officer walked me to the back entrance of the museum. Using my key, we entered, hastily retrieved my backpack, and upon leaving the museum I got into my pickup truck. With a sincere thank you to the officer, I gave a quick wave, and my truck and I headed down the driveway from the museum.

I drove around town for half an hour. This was done both to collect my thoughts about where to go from here, as well as make sure no one was following me. What had just happened? What would be my plan for tonight? What about the future?

After many turns and glances in my rearview mirror, and now fairly certain no one was tailing me, I decided it was time to find a place to stay the night. None of my friends from graduate school are in town for the summer, as they are off involved in their own internships at various museums around the country.

My options were then limited. I headed to the edge of town to locate an out-of-the-way motel. Spying one that looked like it would be both secluded and safe, I drove in, parked my truck far in back, entered the front door, and rang the small metal bell at the registration desk.

A woman, perhaps in her late-50s, emerged from the back room. Fluffing her matted gray hair as she made her way to the front desk, the woman seemed a bit annoyed I had interrupted her early-nighttime sleep. However, when she saw I was alone and needed a place to stay the night, she became a bit more pleasant.

Wanting to be as anonymous as possible, I used my forged, yet always reliable, Emily Elizabeth Wilson driver's license as ID. It's never let me down. I paid the woman in cash for two nights, with an understanding that I may want the room a bit longer. She said that would be fine. It didn't appear the rooms here were in high demand.

Locating room 112, I inserted the key and turned the handle. The beige metal door was heavier than I expected, but opened with some encouragement from my shoulder. It had been a long time since I encountered a motel room with metal key access.

I tucked the single key into the front pocket of my jeans. Entering the small out-of-the-way motel room, I immediately felt the caustic touch of a long-shuttered space. It was apparent no one had crossed this threshold for quite some time. I tossed my shoulder bag on the bed.

Switching on the outdated black-box TV, I surfed the local channels to see if any mention of Professor Donaldson made the news. I paused a few minutes at a couple local stations, my standard sources for TV-based information. No news about the Professor. Further clicks of the remote brought me to another local news channel. Even in the tenseness of the

moment I smiled recalling my graduate school friend Amelia's thorough-
ly rich description of this station's news broadcasts: "Bimbo thighs and
bald-faced lies! Thighs and lies, for short!"

There was no mention of Professor Donaldson, yet.

Monday, May 15, 2017 (evening)

I was right about how I began my journal entry this morning. It has
taken me most of today—with some snack breaks—to get caught up
recording in my journal what happened to me and to the Professor yesterday evening, and how I ended up in this out-of-the-way motel room.
I'm tired and headed to bed. It's hard to believe what's occurred in my
life since Saturday! I'll work on figuring out a plan in the morning.

Tuesday, May 16, 2017

Events in my life keep getting stranger. This morning, the local television
stations reported an update on the shooting of the Professor on campus
Sunday night. Fortunately, the police haven't revealed any witnesses to,
or motive for, the shooting. I felt a bit relieved in this, but still anxious
that by now the shooter likely knew my name and local address, and
possibly my pick-up truck license plate number as well.

After catching up on my journal entries and having a fairly good
night's sleep, there were two things I planned to accomplish right away.
I weighed in my mind which to do first. One was to undertake a visit to
the Professor and learn his condition, beyond what is being broadcast to
the news outlets. I have a plan for doing this.

And second, I wanted to pay a return trip to April Jones and see if I
could get any information about the history of the two trunks and the
belongings located in them. Although my heart wanted to learn the Professor's condition first, my mind told me to return to the farmhouse for
a visit with April Jones. The Professor said Ms. Jones would be leaving

the area right away, so it was important I try to contact her as soon as possible.

For that reason, a return trip to visit April Jones was my first choice. After a long shower and thorough clean up from the chaotic events of Sunday and writing about them yesterday, I pulled on a pair of blue jeans, white T-shirt, and some brown hard-soled lace-up shoes, and thought carefully about what I wanted to accomplish in a visit to April Jones. I also decided to bring along Mary Moore's diary, as I didn't want to leave it out of my sight, especially in this motel room.

After collecting my thoughts, I headed down the hall to the motel office and paid for two more nights. I had enough cash stashed at my apartment to cover this cost. I'm glad I grabbed it in my hurried flight. Any more nights beyond these would likely mean the use of my credit card, which I didn't want to do. Credit cards can be traced if someone is searching for you. It's not so easy to do with cash.

Looking over my shoulder more than once, I hurried from the motel office to my pick-up truck. I'm glad I parked as far out of sight as possible. Climbing inside and reaching for the seatbelt, I checked my surroundings carefully. Things looked clear. Rather than drive around town to see if I'm followed, as I did last night, this time I took the first road out of town but spent more time looking in the rearview mirror than I did through the windshield. I journeyed down a few country roads, taking switchbacks to make certain I wasn't followed, and eventually wound my way to the highway toward April Jones' property.

My drive through the Virginia countryside was filled with thoughts about what I hoped would be a revealing conversation with the elderly Ms. Jones. My plan was to initiate our meeting with a question about whether she'd heard news of the Professor? I rehearsed my lines from there: The Professor told me you were leaving the area soon, and I didn't want you to think he forgot to thank you himself for the gift of the two trunks and their contents. Because he isn't able to do this now, I made the trip today to again thank you personally for your contribution to the museum and to see if you had a forwarding address, in case we need to contact you.

That was my introduction. It was a bit cheesy, but my real line of conversation would be these questions: Is there anything you can tell me about the two trunks and their contents? Who had they belonged to? Was the person who owned them a relative of yours? Did you pack the trunks yourself, or know what was in them? Where have the trunks been for the last few years? I figured these would be enough questions to get me started, and I'd ad-lib our discussion from there.

This time the 60-minute trip to the farmhouse went fast. I saw the turnoff road from the main highway and soon found myself bouncing over the same heavily rutted dirt road I'd been on just days before. Not much had changed from my earlier visit, except for a couple things. First, the late-morning sun in a cloudless sky now made the old house seem even more drab and dilapidated. And second, April Jones and her rocking chair were not waiting for me on the front porch.

Absence of the rocking chair and greeting by April Jones or the man with her did not strike me well. My arrival at the farmhouse would likely be seen by anyone on the property, so failure to gain the attention of someone as I arrived increased the likelihood Ms. Jones and her companion had already moved from the house.

I parked my truck near the aging farmhouse and climbed the steps to the still sagging front porch. Even from the outside the house looked and felt deserted. I rapped hard on the screen door and waited for a response. None came. A repeated effort brought the same result. Shading my eyes from the sun's reflection I peeked through a couple of the front lower windows. Drab cotton curtains obstructed my view inside. The screen door could be opened, but the main heavy wooden door into the house was locked and felt solidly secure.

Stepping off the porch I circled the house to see if anyone was in the backyard or perhaps in the work shed out back. Doing so, I saw a small wooden three-step porch leading to a single back door. A solid pound on the door produced no results, except some smarting knuckles.

I retreated down the steps and peered into the shed. "Anybody here?" I called out. The empty outbuilding replied with silence. It appeared April Jones—and the man with her—had, indeed, left the area.

Returning to the back door, I found that it didn't seem as heavy and firm as the one in front. This time I tried turning the doorknob back and forth a couple times while pressing my body weight against the door as I twisted the knob hard. There was, to my surprise, enough give in the old lock mechanism that the door first creaked and then lurched open. Fortunately, doing so did not damage the door casing or leave a forced entry mark on the wooden door jam.

I was in. I'm not certain why, because no one seemed to be here, but I cautiously stepped inside the farmhouse and called out, "Anyone home?" before quietly making my way across what appeared to have once been the residence's kitchen. It was completely empty of any appliances or furniture, as was every room I entered on my journey through the first floor. The only noise was the reverberating hollow tap of my hard-soled shoes as I stepped across the uneven planks of what I'm sure had been a fine wooden floor.

Every piece of furniture was removed from the house. And beyond that, it needed a lot of cleaning! A layer of dust filled every corner. Cobwebs clung to interior doorways. No wonder April Jones wanted to leave all this behind!

I visited each room on the lower level of the house and then headed up the stairs to the floor above. Exploring through the empty second-story rooms, I wondered about the life April Jones had lived in this house. Contemplating the residence and its history, I pulled back the window curtain in one of the front rooms upstairs and peered down at my truck parked outside. Indeed, I was correct. A drive from the roadway was completely unobstructed and would allow at least three or four minutes of viewing an approaching vehicle before it arrived, a fact for which I became at that moment very grateful.

Looking from the window I was startled to see another vehicle slowly negotiating its way over the potholed roadway. It was now not far from the farmhouse. In quick gazing horror I realized I had little time to flee the house before the car and its unknown driver arrived.

Closing the curtain and dashing across the room, I hurriedly descended the stairs and tiptoed quickly through the kitchen. Quietly pulling the door shut behind me, I walked down the back stairs outside as nonchalantly as I could, straightening my hair and my composure with each step.

I figured my best approach was to address the situation straight away, rather than try to delay contact with the newcomer. Taking a deep breath and rounding the corner of the house, before I could speak I was greeted loudly with the words, "Are you looking to buy?"

Caught off guard by this question, I replied somewhat hesitantly, "Well... I'm just looking it over."

Beyond this question, the man asking it startled me a bit more. He was uniformed—likely in his late-50s and a bit overweight—and headed my way, carrying both a holstered handgun and a suspicious look.

Fortunately, he led the conversation. "Hello, ma'am. My name is Billy Bullwright. I'm the sheriff for this area of the county. Is there anything I can help you with?"

Given his initial question about possibly looking to buy, I played along, hoping to carry out my ruse. "I heard this place is for sale, and I thought I'd stop by and check it out. It's quite a house, but it and the road to get here could use a lot of work."

Once the sheriff saw he was dealing only with one person, and that I didn't seem out of place or menacing, he volunteered more information, some of which was shocking and I'm still trying to process.

Sheriff Bullwright's next words drove straight through me: "Yes, this whole property needs a lot of work, with little upkeep lately. As you probably know, being a potential buyer, no one has lived in the house for about three years. I check on it every so often to make sure there hasn't been any vandalism or anyone squatting on the property. When I saw the truck parked out front, I thought it best to drive over and take a look."

I didn't show any emotion, but my mind reeled in response to the sheriff's words! In the silence of my mind, I questioned: "This place has been abandoned for three years? That's not possible!"

Gathering my thoughts and attempting not to sound too inquisitive, I pressed the officer on what he had just said: "I'm not too familiar with the history of the house, but you say no one has lived here for three years?"

"That's correct," he replied, "As far as I know, no one has set foot in this house since the past owners—the Sullivan couple, who were in their 90s—passed away within days of each other nearly three years ago. Their kids came and cleaned out the house and put it on the market soon after their parents died."

"And you're telling me that no one has lived here since?" I offered, but quickly continued, not wanting to raise any suspicion with the sheriff: "I guess that explains why there's so much work on the property to be done."

"That's right," the sheriff laughed and continued, "I understand there've been a few inquiries about the property over the years, but no serious offers."

I wanted to ask the sheriff about April Jones, but decided not to pursue that line of questions, at least not then. I thanked him for his time and information, and we walked together to our vehicles. The sheriff handed me his professional business card and told me to contact him if I needed any information he could help me with. We shook hands and each drove off. He followed me to the main highway where I turned left and he went right.

By then it was afternoon, and I was hungry. I stopped at a small diner on my way back to town and ordered soup and a sandwich. Sitting in a high-backed booth for an hour or so, I wrote this account of the day so far in my journal and contemplated what had occurred in my conversation with the sheriff at the Sullivan farmhouse. I'm trying hard to make sense of what he had just revealed to me.

Tuesday, May 16, 2017 (evening)

The trip back to my motel room from the diner was uneventful but filled with questions from my conversation with Sheriff Bullwright. How could it be that he didn't know April Jones? She lived in the house and was sitting on the porch, rocking in the rocking chair, when I arrived. Who was the man who joined her and helped me load the trunks into the back of my pick-up truck? This was their house, wasn't it? How could it not be?

Pondering these and other questions about my initial visit to the farmhouse, I tried to recall the specifics of my arrival and conversation with April Jones. How long was my meeting with her? Maybe 20 minutes. Thinking through this time with Ms. Jones, it dawned on me that I didn't see her or the man in the straw hat and overalls actually leave or go into the farmhouse or any building.

April Jones was sitting in her rocking chair on the front porch when I arrived. The man came from around the back of the house just when I needed help loading the trunks, and I saw them both standing on the porch through my rearview mirror as I drove away. Neither of them entered or exited the farmhouse during the time I was there.

Something was amiss, either in the story presented by April Jones or that told by Sheriff Bullwright. Questions always lead to more questions. My head hurts.

I did some circling around town in an attempt to throw off anyone following me. I feel somewhat safe now parking and staying in this secluded motel. Local TV news broadcasts indicated no change in the Professor's condition or in bringing a solution to his assault. I'm finishing this journal entry and thinking through my idea for visiting the Professor tomorrow. I don't know if my plan will work, but I'll give it my best try.

Wednesday, May 17, 2017

I stayed inside the motel until late afternoon, snacking on a few things I brought back from the diner yesterday. I used my day inside to first check on whether there's a local sheriff named Billy Bullwright, and if the old Sullivan house is for sale.

A few clicks of my mouse brought up on my laptop an image of the sheriff (albeit from a few years—and pounds—earlier). His biography matched the self-description and contact information he passed along to me.

It took a little more digging in some online real estate sites—but not too much—to find the Sullivan house for sale. Photos of the residence and property on the real estate website matched my mental image of the farmhouse and surrounding landscape. More and more, April Jones and the man with her appear to be the ones in question.

This motivates me to spend time with the contents of the two trunks that are in the workroom of the museum, including the diary and the other three books. Perhaps these items contain more clues to help solve the mystery of things hidden in the trunk. There are lots of questions to pursue, but not until I'm certain no one is following me.

I've received four phone calls and a text from the other five graduate students who are doing their history museum internships in various locations this summer: Jessica in Knoxville; Kirstin in Washington, DC; Clare in Chicago; Amelia in New York City; and Douglas in Los Angeles. They had heard about the Professor being shot and wanted to know firsthand, understandably, what is going on.

By returned phone calls and texts, I shared with them the Professor's condition as best I knew. I didn't, however, volunteer any information beyond that. I told them I'd be back in touch as soon as I learned anything more about the Professor.

I spent the rest of my time until an early dinner working with Mary Moore's journal and preparing to visit the Professor in the hospital later this afternoon. I want to see for myself how he's doing, but the timing of my visit needs to be just right.

It takes some effort and I'm still not very good at it, but I am getting better at reading the pages of Mary Moore's flowing handwriting. It's difficult to decipher in places, especially when the words from one page have bled into the opposite side of the next page. But that's not the only puzzle I've been trying to figure out.

I'm not much of a Bible reader. However, I'm familiar with the name Gideon from the Bible, and in my art history classes I've seen Gothic and Renaissance paintings and sculptures that depict biblical stories from the life of Samson. But in reading where I left off in the diary a couple days ago, I've no idea who Deborah is referring to in Jephthah, Shamgar, and Ibzan.

Those three names have bugged me since my last day working with Mary's diary. Who are they? Fortunately, Google comes through again, so I have at least a little understanding that these three men were judges in ancient Jewish history, recorded in the Hebrew book of Judges. I now understand Deborah Lee's joke about those three names not being appropriate for any Virginia Sons of the Confederacy!

I remember seeing in my motel room a maroon Bible in the drawer of the nightstand by the bed. This book was placed there by the Gideons; how ironic—the Gideons. Deborah's story recorded in Mary Moore's diary said that Judges was the seventh book of the Bible, located between the two books of Joshua and Ruth (the names of her parents). Thumbing through the pages of the Bible, I found the book of Judges near the front and looked these three Jewish judges up to see what I could learn about them. Interesting reading. All three of them did some crazy stuff!

With that name-riddle solved, I'm continuing now to record Mary Moore's description of events leading to her involvement in the plot to assassinate the President of the United States, Ulysses S. Grant.

With the passing of both Joshua and Ruth, the little Lee family struggled. Gideon and Samson worked the peanut farm as best they could after the death of their father. It was then, when their mother's health waned, that Deborah began spending more time with me. And when her mother passed-on the next year, young Deborah joined to live with me full-time. Deborah's brothers did all they could for her, but it was hard for them to tend the farm as well as take care of their young sister. It was best for everyone that Deborah was with me.

*A change to all this came in early October 1862.
This is when the War descended on our little village of Franklin. At this time the two Lee brothers
were 15 and 17 years of age. Deborah was with me
that day—October 3—as I was preparing for studies to begin in our little schoolhouse. I assumed
the Lee boys were at the farm working the recently harvested peanut crop. They were not.*

*It was early in the day that shelling and rifle
fire commenced. I could hear it from my place
at the school. The young children under my care
were frightened but curious of what they heard.
No such sound of continuous deep booming can-
non explosions and weapon-fire had ever before
reached their ears.*

*After all the commotion had ceased later in the
day, I learned that three Union boats had maneuvered up the Blackwater River from Albemarle
Sound, and at Franklin they engaged some of
Virginia's finest. The Unionists were sent dashing,
with casualties. The young Lee brothers, while
they did not take part in the fighting, ran to the
river and watched wide-eyed from their hiding
place on the hillside above the water as the battle
was fought around them. It was the brothers' first
direct experience with war, and I could tell from
their declarative description of the gunfire, can-
non blasts, and fighting that it would not be their
last.*

*The boys' excitement for what they saw and
felt that day delivered my anguish. It was clear
from their words, countenance, and expression in
their large fiery eyes that they had encountered,
first-hand, the sights, sounds, and taste of battle.
Young men are drawn to it. I knew they would
be on to the fight soon—far too soon. And like so*

many young men before them, death—along with my tears and those of their dear sister—would be their recompense.

~

Wow, what a story! Finishing this journal entry, I had a quick dinner and am heading off to the hospital to try and see the Professor.

Events of Wednesday evening and Thursday, May 17-18, 2017, written on Saturday, May 20th

Charles Dickens opened *A Tale of Two Cities*: "It was the best of times, it was the worst of times." These words capture my life now.

I always keep an extra set of hospital work clothes—scrubs—in a duffel bag in the back seat of my truck in case I'm needed for an on-call shift at the hospital. I brought them with me into the hotel room the other day to use now in my attempt to visit the Professor. I put them on and stashed a couple cloth surgical booties in my pocket. The lanyard holding my name card and electronic personnel badge for employee entrance to the hospital was slung around my neck. This device can get me into most areas of the building without raising any questions.

I was on edge as I made my way to the hospital. The trip there should take about fifteen minutes, but I doubled that for safe drive-around time. Becoming my common approach, I made a few extra turns and checked my rearview mirror regularly. A sports car, perhaps like the one I saw speeding from campus the night the Professor was shot, passed me going the opposite direction. Apart from that, nothing seemed out of the ordinary. I parked my pick-up in the employee lot, which got me close to the hospital workers' entrance.

Although they're not my close friends, I'm familiar to most of the employee door attendants and those stationed behind the security desk.

This evening was not my scheduled time to work, but those who permitted me access to the hospital had no idea I was there for something else.

It was an easy entrance. Since I wore my scrubs, as do many arriving workers, the door attendants assumed I was there for work. I had waited until nearly dinnertime to enter the hospital, when I knew there would be lots of personnel coming and going in the hallways. My presence there would for sure not raise any questions.

I gave a smile to those passing in the corridor. Pushing the down button of the service elevator, I waited a few seconds before the red indicator light flashed, bell sounded, and the shiny aluminum door in front of me slid open. The lift was empty as I entered. Pushing the B button on the panel to the right of the door, I was carried down the short ride one floor to the Basement. This was my familiar home base in the hospital.

My work begins each shift with a report to the laundry area in the basement and registration with a swipe of my ID badge in the electronic ledger. I then select a white metal rolling cart filled with neatly folded bed sheets and towels of various sizes. Following that, I identify on the workstation's computer screen a set of rooms where I'm to distribute the needed towels and linen. I then head off to complete my rounds on various floors and wings of the hospital. It's an easy job. Most evenings in the hospital are a nice break from classes and studying.

Tonight was different. I ran through my regular initial duty of selecting a linen cart, but this time without checking-in using my electronic ID badge. The heavy cart filled with linen and towels was the prop for my ruse. I was using it to help me circulate, unquestioned, to any floor and area of the hospital I desired. The Professor's room was my intended destination. I wanted to find out his condition for myself and see if I could make contact with him.

I figured the Professor was in the critical care ward on the 3rd floor. I donned the gloves, mask, and surgical booties brought with me and rode the same elevator this time to floor number three. Two doctors joined me on the ride up, but I didn't recognize or make conversation with them. The Professor's room—number 333—was identified by a peek at an admission chart during my quick stop at a nurses' station after leaving the elevator.

Negotiating a turn in the hallway with my fully loaded linen cart, I proceeded past the nurses' station and through two heavy metal doors. I was now in the critical care ward. The hallway was intentionally dark and silent as I made my way down the corridor toward the Professor's room. I pushed my linen-filled cart passed several closed doors as rooms beginning with the number 3 increased from the teens into the twenties. Continuing, I figured room 333 was about eight doors ahead, on the left.

Drawing closer to the Professor's room I saw a figure in a dark blue uniform seated on a chair outside room 333. Moving my cart ahead slowly I could now recognize this individual as a police officer with a protective sidearm. I figured he was positioned to guard the Professor's room from any unapproved visitors.

In keeping with my usual manner of introduction, I thought it best to engage the officer first, before he spoke to me. I greeted him with a warm yet professional, "Good evening," which he returned in a some-what similar tone.

"How are you this evening?" I inquired.

His reply was formal. "I am doing well, thank you."

"Any activity in this end of the building?" I questioned.

"Not much," he returned, "And that's just the way I like it."

Although I already knew the answer, I asked the officer who he was guarding?

His response was an understandably vague, "Someone I am charged to watch."

"Okay," I replied, not wanting to push the issue. "I'm here to drop off some linen to room 333."

I showed the policeman my name badge. He glanced at my security ID but didn't look at it too closely.

With the officer's help holding the door open, I rolled my heavy cart forward and made my way into the Professor's darkened hospital room. I paused as my eyes slowly adjusted to the opaque space.

What I encountered was far more electronically intense than I anticipated. I could hardly make out the prone form of the Professor because
of the many medical instruments—with blinking lights and low-hum-
ming monitors—that surrounded his bed. There were multiple colored
plastic tubes emerging from the Professor's nose and mouth, and his
head was mostly covered with a cloth wrap. His eyes were closed. It was
clearly a view of the Professor I'd never seen before, and it pained me
so much.

It was obvious I wouldn't be able to hold a conversation with the
Professor and likely he would not even know I'd visited his room. There
was nothing for me to do but stand and gaze for a few moments at the
immobilized form, which until now I knew only by his sincere interaction with students and love of history. It didn't take long to tell myself
I'd seen enough.

I laid some towels and sheets on a shelf by his bed. As I maneuvered
my linen cart around the tight space and prepared to leave the Professor's room, I heard the police officer stationed in the hallway talking with
someone. I paid little attention to what was said until I neared the door
and could take in the conversation more clearly.

What struck me immediately was not the words being said, but the
voices of those speaking. I was now a bit familiar with the policeman's
professional expressive cadence from my brief conversation with him a
few minutes earlier. But I didn't expect to recognize the other voice. Yet
right away I knew I'd heard it before: Cajun, high-pitched, and squeaky!

I stopped rolling the linen cart at the closed door and listened more
carefully to the conversation taking place just outside in the hallway. I
knew that unique squeaky-pitched voice. It belonged to the man I heard
talking with the Professor in his office last Sunday night! I paused to take
in what was being said. No question, Don's assailant, the man who also
tried to kill me, was just outside the door talking with the police officer.

This can't be! Just then, as I was ready to leave the Professor's room
and head into the hallway, the door opened and a man in a white doctor's jacket with a stethoscope slung around his neck held the door wide
open. He greeted me with a high-pitched squeaky southern, "Hello,

young lady how are you this evening?" Without question, this man was the shooter, and he was now waiting for me to exit the Professor's room so that he could enter it, alone!

With the door held open, I used both hands to maneuver the bulky linen cart out of the Professor's darkened room. I had to act fast! Rage kicked in! Instinctively, and with as much force as I could muster on the spot, I rushed the laundry cart ahead and rammed its front right corner directly into the man's crotch. Responsively, the man's head, with eyes bulged, lurched forward while his body jerked back in excruciating pain and complete surprise!

"It's him!" I screamed. "He's the one who shot the Professor!"

The man in the lab coat staggered backward into the hallway as his stethoscope flew end-over-end off his shoulders behind him.

Righting himself somewhat, the man pulled a small gray handgun from a concealed location in the waistband of his pants and pointed it in my direction as he tried to regain his balance.

A split second later a pistol shot reverberated through the hospital hallway and a streak of hot blood coursed across my face. I fell backward. In shock, it took me a few moments to realize, however, that the heated blood trail I felt on my cheeks was not my own!

The man with the squeaky southern voice and wearing a white doctor's jacket now lay sprawled across my linen cart, the side of his head nearly disintegrated. In horror I floundered back into the Professor's darkened room and collapsed to the floor.

My screams reverberated off the white cinder block walls!

The policeman in the hall had reacted in quick and masterful fashion. He shot the assailant in response to the gun the man in the lab coat had drawn and aimed at me. If the officer hadn't stepped in with such instantaneous speed and accuracy, then I likely would not be writing this.

The next few minutes are fuzzy to remember. But I do recall that within seconds the hallway and the Professor's room were filled with a rush of police and medical personnel. In this activity I was ushered from Don's critical care room down the hall to a vacant hospital lounge for some rest and a bit later discussion with a police officer.

In my conversation I revealed to the policewoman that I was the one who was outside Professor Donaldson's office at the university when he was shot last Sunday night, and who was chased and fired at twice in the History Building on campus moments later. This fact brought about a call for the original detectives I spoke with the night the Professor was shot.

Within 30 minutes these detectives arrived at the hospital room where I was staying. Answering their questions, I told them the story of how I came to be in the Professor's hospital room this evening, and about hearing the distinct high-pitched squeaky Cajun voice of the man talking with the police officer in the hallway. I explained that there was no question: the armed man who was killed by the policeman in the hospital corridor little more than an hour ago was, indeed, the man who shot the Professor and fired at me twice while on the run in the hallway of the History Building.

When my conversation with the detectives was complete—at least for now—I was told the hospital had arranged for me to stay the night in one of their rooms, if I wanted. I took them up on the offer.

I was informed the next day that the man with the high-pitched voice was named Johnny Painter. He was also known as "Squeaky." Johnny Painter was a self-made business investor with a questionable reputation and seemingly far less employment and stock market success than his accumulated wealth would show. While in college, Squeaky studied historic preservation with an emphasis in civic building restoration, but apparently had done little with his degree after graduation.

Johnny Painter had a few dark spots on his criminal record, but seemingly nothing that would lead him to attempted murder. Yet, the facts tilted in that direction. A search of Painter's personal effects revealed that Squeaky carried the gray revolver as well as a 5-inch serrated blade knife, which was folded into the handle and hidden in the pocket of his pants.

Painter had made his way into a hospital physician changing room and stolen a doctor's white lab coat, stethoscope, and ID badge. It was also determined through analysis of the spent bullets and cartridges early this morning that the gun used to shoot the Professor and discharge at me in the hallway of the History Building was the weapon Painter carried and was prepared to use in the hospital before being killed by the police officer. Taken together, these facts confirm that Johnny Painter was, indeed, the man who fought with and shot the Professor in his office on Sunday night. What an incredible last few days this has been!

I'm ending this entry now. I'm exhausted. I'll take my mind off the Professor and the deadly incident in the hospital by getting some much-needed rest. If I feel up to it, maybe I'll spend some time reading and deciphering a bit more of Mary Moore's diary.

Sunday, May 21, 2017

Today I'm trying to focus on something other than the Professor and the shooting of Johnny Painter in the hospital by transcribing a few more pages of Mary Moore's diary. It's likely slow going, but a useful distraction.

After that early-October day in 1862 when Union boats invaded our town's waterway and thwarted by Virginia's finest, things in our little town were never the same. Strong young Southern men, one-by-one or a few at a time, left their wives and loved ones behind to join local Virginia infantry and cavalry brigades. We were proud of their actions going into battle, but our hearts torn by the likely consequences of them doing so.

The two Lee boys worked their peanut farm as best they could through the next year, but news from the war continued to draw them closer to entering the fight. Letters sent to wives and families by those on the battle lines did not deter the boys' interest in experiencing the conflict first-hand. In fact, tales of the war and descriptions of the fighting—recounted mostly by men who passed through our town—captivated the brothers and stoked their desire to join the fray. Southern determination was in their blood.

Then came the spring of 1864. News told of increased fighting, and it drew closer to home. I could tell that both Gideon and Samson were itching to trade their farm implements for those of battle. I wanted to dissuade them from doing so, as I had seen too many young Southern men leave home and not return. But I knew my words would not keep them here. Their sister was steadfast in my care, which eased their departure for the fight. The cause of the Confederacy was their induce-ment. General Grant was their provocation.

In early June, word circulated that Grant and his forces were moving toward Petersburg, 50 miles north of Franklin. This military action was the hot ember that ignited the burning flame of war within the two Lee brothers. On June 15, 1864, Samson and Gideon gathered some provisions, two Springfield rifles, ammunition, and the family horse Colonel, and headed north on the road to-ward Petersburg.

Prior to their departure, Gideon and Samson had made arrangements to have Mr. Duke look after and work the Lee family peanut farm—as much as possible—while the brothers were away in battle. Mr. Duke assured them that he, along with Noah and Josiah, would care for the land and small Lee homestead as best they could until Gideon and Samson returned.

Their actual time of goodbye was somewhat brief. Deborah delivered hugs and shed tears for Gideon and Samson, and perhaps just as many for Colonel. She loved all three, dearly. The two brothers—Samson riding Colonel, and Gideon leading—strode, shoulders upright and heads held high, toward the edge of town. Both brothers looked over a shoulder to give a brief wave and tip-of-the-hat nod, and then turned back toward the weighty task before them.

What struck me soundly in that moment of farewell was that they were now no longer sandy-haired, blue-eyed Virginia farm boys. Taking these few steps toward the battle that lay ahead, the two Lee boys had now become the two Lee men. This realization does not lessen the pain, even as I write these words 25 years after their departure, that as their silhouettes faded down the road to the north it marked the final time I ever saw the two Lee men.

More information about Johnny Painter emerged today. The police continued their investigation of Painter's background and learned that, among many things, he and the Professor were originally from the same small town in Arkansas. The Professor was a decade older than Johnny, but they had known each other. As it turns out, however, Squeaky's current and longtime residence was in New Orleans.

The authorities have not been able to learn what Painter was doing in the Professor's office that Sunday evening, and what caused him to fire his handgun at Don. Even though I possessed the key to unlock that part of the relationship puzzle between the two men, I kept it to myself. At least for now, I want to keep secret information I have about Mary Moore's journal and what I'm learning through my efforts to decipher and record its contents.

The biggest change for me personally has come in the realization that with the death of Johnny Painter I no longer feel in danger. The man who tried to kill me is now dead, and I can begin to get back to a more normal and safer lifestyle.

After spending one night in the hospital immediately after the horrendous events I encountered there, I then went back to stay at my apartment. Before doing so, however, I returned to the motel and collected the things I'd left there overnight. The calming difference for me is that I no longer spend time looking over my shoulder and peering intently in my truck's rearview mirror. Some parts of my life may be shifting back closer to the familiar.

Monday, May 22, 2017

Even with all the traumatic things that have happened to me this last week and weekend, I can say without question that none of them is more difficult than enduring what I learned today. The Professor is dead. He succumbed to the injuries received from Johnny Painter's gunshot.

I'm devastated! As time went by after the shooting, I expected the Professor to improve and recover from his wounds. The longer the Professor was alive, I became increasingly confident he would heal and life would return to normal.

I looked forward to showing him the diary and the other books I found hidden in the heavy wooden trunk. I was excited for the two of us to explore the trunks' contents together, as I'd share with him the story I've been able to decipher from Mary Moore's diary. But now this dream is over. The Professor's injuries were more severe than doctors let on to the public.

The local news media picked up the story, especially the dramatic death of Johnny Painter in the hospital hallway. The account was even circulated through some national news outlets, but the gruesome demise of Painter seemed to close out this story. There was little to keep the attention of reporters. They soon rushed to cover other newsworthy events.

My own circumstances don't allow me to easily move forward from here. What is my plan for the future? I came to this university and to this History Department to study with Professor Donaldson. I'm the Museum Intern this summer and planned to be his Teaching Assistant again starting in the fall. But now all this is over. Without him here, should I stay or move on to study Civil War history somewhere else? There always seem to be more questions than answers. However, an unexpected invitation from the university bought me time to sort out some direction ahead.

There are no family members to contact about the Professor's death. It was not a surprise to me that Professor Donaldson had no known relatives. In my frequent conversations with him throughout the past year—occasionally over an on-campus lunch—I learned a little about his background. The Professor's parents died in Arkansas some time ago, and he was an only child. He never married, although I sensed there were a few possibilities for that over the years. His life revolved around the university, and especially the museum. The only break he took was to spend time hiking and camping in the Arkansas wilderness each summer.

The Professor left notarized papers with an attorney in town that upon his death he desired no funeral or memorial service. He was not a person who sought fanfare, even in death. His monetary assets were in two bank accounts in town, which he directed at his death would be combined and then divided into three equal shares. One-third would be allocated each to the museum, the Department of History, and to the university library.

Although I never saw it myself, I understand the Professor lived in a sparsely furnished apartment. His life was simple, with a few pieces of antique furniture and a limited number of historical objects and photographs sprinkled through the residence.

Information Don left with his attorney requested that his household goods be placed for sale at a local second-hand store or sold outright. All proceeds from their purchase were to help fund the museum. The disposition of his assets and effects was well planned and simple to carry out, which is in keeping with how the Professor lived.

The Professor also left instructions with his attorney that he be buried in a small cemetery on the outskirts of town. A plain headstone displaying his name—with birth and death dates—was to mark his resting place. This stone marker was also to contain the inscription for which the Professor was well known among his students and colleagues: "The captains are the key."

This phrase was Professor Donaldson's Civil War mantra. A class session rarely went by—and certainly not a week—without him pausing to share this passionate belief about how best to study and understand the "War for Southern Independence," he sometimes called it.

Most authors and history classes approach the Civil War through the writings and actions of Union and Confederate Generals—Grant, Meade, McClellan, Sherman, Longstreet, Lee, Jackson, Pickett, Beauregard, and others—and their various strategic battle campaigns. Professor Donaldson's approach was different from this. His strategy was to present and analyze the War through the perspectives and insights of the military captains, both from the North and South.

Captains were the officers directly in charge of the soldiers who fought the battles. Who were these military captains and what did they think of the war? What was their training? Did they take orders and follow them well? How did these captains rally their troops and prepare for battle? What connection did they develop with men under their charge, and what was their approach to conducting a successful military mission?

These questions were at the heart of the Professor's work. Answers to them and other similar questions provided an uncommon lens through which to view the Civil War, giving opportunity to explore how "the captains are the key" to understanding how it was fought. This often-shared phrase from the Professor will forever stay with me, and I'm sure many of his students over the years would agree.

But now the hard work begins. Since the Professor had no known relatives and I was listed as his Teaching Assistant for this past year and next, as well as his summer Museum Intern, the university asked if they could hire me to clear out his office and distribute the items located there into three groups, as also designated in the Professor's will: (1) Civil War books, photographs, and artifacts such as bullets, a sword, some maps, a bugle, and a drum were to go to the permanent collection in the museum and the museum's research library; (2) Books on other subjects were to be donated to the university library for shelving there or sale, with any profits split evenly between the library and the museum; and (3) Any remaining items without value to the university were to be sold, donated, or discarded.

Because I'm familiar with the Professor's office and things in it, the university's offer seems reasonable and the job manageable. The pay for doing this means I don't have to go back to work at the hospital. That's fine with me. I'll start my job disassembling the Professor's office when I feel up to it in the next week or so.

Monday, May 29, 2017

I've done practically nothing for the entire last week. This includes no personal journal writing and no transcribing Mary Moore's written account. My heart hasn't been into either one. One Netflix binge has slipped into another, and another.

It's hard for me to get past the Professor's death. And I keep telling myself that it's my fault. If only I hadn't texted those photos of Mary Moore's diary to the Professor when he was in Atlanta, then he would still be alive today. Why? Why? Why? And, to top this off, I'm preparing to begin work in the Professor's office tomorrow. I told myself I would start there the day after the Memorial Day holiday, which is today.

I did have some communication with the outside world. The other five graduate students enrolled in their museum internships this summer contacted me during the week. I'd sent them each a short text at the end of last week, saying that the Professor had died from his wounds. Each of them communicated back to see how I'm doing, which I appreciate very much.

My graduate school friends also told me that a representative of the university had been in touch with each of them to tell of Professor Donaldson's death. The purpose of their call was also to find out how each of the Professor's summer internship students is doing emotionally with this news, and to encourage them to continue in their internship and assure them they would receive credit for their work. Each student said they would follow through in completing their internship. The fall semester is in question for some, including me. But there will be time ahead to sort that out.

I requested that any trace of the fight between the Professor and Johnny Painter be removed from the office before I start my work there. I was told this was done during the past week, so I'm building up the courage to begin cleaning out the Professor's office tomorrow.

Tuesday, May 30, 2017

I knew it would be hard, but sorting through the Professor's office today was more difficult than I anticipated. Taking apart his office in the place where he had been shot was painful enough, but I didn't expect the collection of things in his office—and the stories about them that the Professor had told me—to stay so heavy on my heart. As I picked up objects from his office for consideration of what to do with them, Don's animated words about so many of them echoed back to me.

In a conspicuous place on his desk was displayed the first Civil War bullet he found in the Arkansas woods many years ago. The Professor told me the inch-long lead cylinder had been encased in the trunk of an old oak tree his father had felled. As a boy, the Professor's job was to cut and split tree trunks into logs for firewood, and the lead slug was embedded in a tree trunk he pieced with his axe. With much enthusiasm, Don told me how finding this bullet started him on a life-long search for Civil War artifacts. I'll find a special place for this object in the museum's permanent collection.

In a fine wooden box on a shelf in the Professor's office rested a well-worn velvet bag housing a Remington .44 caliber revolver. Don showed this long-used firearm to me in his office once before, and let me handle it carefully, and without wearing gloves! He told me the gun had been used in the Civil War by his great-great grandfather, and that the Professor sometimes brought the revolver out into the light just to grip it as his elder Donaldson relatives had done throughout the years. The family story told over generations was that this firearm was used to kill dozens of Yankees in various battles of the Civil War, but there is no way to verify any truth in this. Such is the way of many family stories.

The revolver would also now become part of the museum's permanent collection. My sadness was in recognizing that even though this firearm would be well kept in the museum for years to come, the Professor's story about his great-great grandfather's weapon would likely be lost through time.

There was one object currently found in the Professor's office that eclipsed all others in its uniqueness and monetary value. It was rarely removed from the pristine most secure basement storage room, but it so happened the Professor had this object in his office at the time of his death. It's a cloth Battle Flag of the 3rd Arkansas Infantry Regiment, which the Professor acquired in his home state many years ago.

The Professor donated the hand-stitched battle flag to the museum, where he knew it would be well cared for. The flag was in the Professor's office in preparation to be photographed for use in an article Don was writing for a Civil War history journal.

The flag looks very much like the well-known Confederate Battle Flag, with a blue X and thirteen white stars situated on a blood red field. Don told me there are only a handful of such Civil War-era regional battle flags known to exist. For that reason, it will be one of the first things I place back in the permanent collection storage room.

Next to his office desk is a two sliding-drawer gray metal file cabinet. The Professor never mentioned what it contained. And I never asked. Today was the day to find out.

Feeling very odd doing so, I sat in the Professor's chair and braced myself as I took hold of the metal handle, pressed the unlock button, and pulled open the top drawer. The contents, while intriguing, were not as exhilarating as what I uncovered in the false bottom of the old trunk in the museum a few weeks ago. This metal file drawer housed several manila folders containing lecture notes and pages of ongoing historical research the Professor was working with.

The bottom drawer held still more teaching and research notes along with a box file containing numerous grainy black and white photographs from the Civil War. Most of these images were military portraits. Close examination brought back memories from class lectures the Professor gave throughout the year. The photographs were of soldiers, both Union and Confederate, which the Professor had shown during class.

The Professor was an excellent teacher. In his lectures, Don often told that generations of his family hailed from the South—rural northern Arkansas mostly—and many of his "rebel-tives," as he called them, spilled their blood and died in the War Between the States more than 150 years ago. Grinning at the memory of the Professor's word play, I wondered if some of these fuzzy photographs were, indeed, images of his Civil War "rebel-tives."

I think this is a good place to stop for the night. I do miss his smile.

Friday, June 2, 2017

My work in the Professor's office this week is moving along, slowly. I find myself pausing, often, to read a research note he wrote to himself or examine some small trinket tucked away in a drawer of his desk. I wonder why he kept many seemingly insignificant objects, and I'm curious about the stories surrounding each of them. It's hard to do sometimes, but most of these story-less objects—a key chain with a peace sign, a small white agate stone, a signed Christmas card from someone named Maggie, a picture post card from Hawaii with a short "wishing you were here" note signed Kaela, and a faded and torn ace of clubs playing card—I'm forced to discard in the trash as their significance in the world is lost with the death of the Professor. I am, however, making headway cleaning out his office, but there's still quite a ways to go.

I'm finding that time spent in my apartment deciphering and recording Mary Moore's diary is another place of difficult work, but a useful distraction from my thoughts of the Professor. There are still lots of pages from her diary to transcribe, but with each one I'm gradually uncovering a truly fascinating story from nearly 150 years ago.

~

I came to learn after the Lee brothers left for Petersburg that they did not depart alone. Two other young Franklin men joined them on horseback up the road in their journey north to defend the city: William Harris and Charles Wild. As their teacher, I saw young Willy, Charlie, and the Lee brothers grow up together. It did not surprise me to learn they rode as one, north into battle. Willy, leaving his parents and their farm behind, brought an extra horse for the Lee brothers to ride. This sped the quest to fight at Petersburg. However, little Charlie was the only member of this Franklin Four to return home sometime later and offer the abhorrent and heartsick account of the deaths of Gideon and Samson Lee, and Willy Harris.

On his return from battle, Charlie told me the following tale. After a 3-day ride north, the four young men from Franklin arrived at the outskirts of Petersburg early on June 18, as fierce fighting took hold in the area. Unable to join any formal Confederate unit because of the ferocious military action around them, Willy, Charlie, and the Lee brothers took up arms in battle as best they could.

Brave in heart, the four young men entered the action immediately. However, being untrained in military strategy, and without any uniform and indicating military colors to display, the young men were left to fight the Federals as they saw fit.

*Sadly, their engagement with the Northern ene-
my did not last long that day. The four heroes of
Franklin were soon outnumbered, out-skilled in
battle procedures, but not out-shown in bravery.
They fought hard, but young Gideon, Samson, and
William were soon out-maneuvered and overrun
by the older war-hardened Union troops. Charlie
saw his three friends fall in battle. Their young
lifeless bodies were never recovered.*

*Charlie, separated from the three other Frank-
lin sons during the battle, made his way into
dense foliage and took cover until the fighting
subsided and he could officially join a Confederate
infantry unit two days later. Colonel and the other
horses fled wild-eyed during the battle and were
not seen by Charlie again.*

*The continued crush of sadness, even through
the years, does not permit me—nor is it necessary—to record the details young Charles shared
with me about the slaughter of Willy and the Lee
brothers. Out of love, I kept the full description
hidden from the mind and memory of young sister
Deborah.*

The account recorded in Mary Moore's diary gives me chills. The slow
process of figuring out certain words and sentences draws me in to not
only read and re-read the story carefully, but also feel her raw emotions.

I'm taking the weekend off from going through papers, books, and
objects in the Professor's office. I'll continue work there on Monday.

Monday, June 5, 2017

My first action today was to return the Arkansas Battle Flag to its secure location deep in the recesses of the museum's basement. It's one of the institution's most prized and valuable possessions. The flag is stored flat in a gray archival box, designed and constructed to house this unique and precious object. With gloved hands, I carefully laid the outstretched flag in the large low-sided box and gently smoothed the treasured cloth from the center outward in all four directions.

With the lid positioned tightly in place, I attentively carried the box from the Professor's office down the hall to the museum. Carefully navigating the entryway, I headed toward the interior workroom and stairs that led to the secure storage room in the basement.

I was caught off guard as I walked through the workroom on my trip to the basement. It was there I realized that the contents of the two trunks I'd unloaded a few weeks ago were still in the same location I left them. I need to document and store them in the museum as soon as I'm done with work in the Professor's office. I have a lot to do!

Venturing down the stairs to this deep interior part of the archival storage room was a fairly new experience for me. I'd been there a couple times to enter the museum's most protected space behind a large, locked metal door. Ironically, however, the key to this secure room hangs on a hook just outside the door. But only those with Don's authorization would even be in this area of the museum, so it's helpful and safer to have this single key accessible to those needing it. Being in the room a few times, I'd never stopped to examine any of the thousands of objects stored in pristine containers housed on rows of shelves. It's a vast repository of the past, shrouded in dark silence.

Storage containers in the large room are neatly stacked on metal shelves and identified by coded letters and numbers displayed on the outside. These alphabetical and numerical indicators coincide with the master list of archived items recorded on the electronic spreadsheet accessed on the museum tablet. It's all very organized, clearly the thought-work of the Professor. Without taking time to open each container and access the comprehensive record of their contents, it's hard to know what specific prized and valuable objects are stored here.

Recognizing more and more the amount of work needing to be completed in clearing the Professor's office, I knew it was best for me not to begin investigating the objects in this secure storage room today. Perhaps there will be time for that later. Work in the Professor's office is calling me now.

Turning to exit the room, my eye caught view of a curious feature on the room's back cement wall. Something I couldn't quite recognize was in the shadows between two large floor-to-ceiling storage shelves. I picked up the flashlight resting on a small table by the metal door where I entered the room and clicked it on to investigate what had just drawn my attention to the back wall.

Shining the light into the dark recesses of the room, I could now easily make out what I'd seen in the shadows. Situated between the two tall storage shelves in front of me were the facades of two metal safes built flush against the room's concrete back wall. They were positioned about chest high, one safe above the other. The metal facing of both safes was identical, black in color and about 15 inches square, with a large rotating numbered dial used to unlock the safe located in the middle of each metal front.

The Professor never mentioned anything to me about two safes in the museum basement. But there's probably a lot about the museum I don't know. I tried the handle of each safe, but neither moved. I didn't expect they would. I easily spun the rotating dial of both safes, wondering what was housed behind the metal facing and how I might get each one open. Finding these safes, I'll for sure look more closely at what's in the Professor's office desk. Perhaps the combination to these safes is recorded somewhere in his things.

Making sure the box containing the Confederate battle flag was returned to its rightful place, I set the darkened flashlight on the table, switched off the room light, and stepped out of the secure storage room. I pulled the metal door shut behind me. It locked with a solid click. Placing the room key back on the hook and ascending the stairs, my mind shifted from what I had just encountered in the basement to taking on the afternoon tasks ahead.

I returned to the low gray file cabinet by the Professor's desk. As I thumbed through some of Don's lecture notes I was reminded that he was an impassioned teacher. Whether in his class or office, his desire was to unlock a student's curiosity about the world.

A favorite lecture I remember was based on a question the Professor asked students in class one day near the end of this past semester: "Do you know that nearly all coins minted in the United States over the years are filled with references to American history?" Most of the students had never stopped to look closely at the coins in their pockets or purses, so they had no idea what the Professor was even talking about.

Receiving curious looks from his students, the Professor started class by saying that changes in United States coin designs give keys to the birth-years of two of the nation's presidents. The Abraham Lincoln 1-cent piece (first minted in 1909) and the Washington quarter (first minted in 1932) were initiated to commemorate the 100th anniversary of the birth-year of Abraham Lincoln (1809) and 200 years after George Washington was born (1732).

The opposite occurred for the dime and half dollar. Franklin Roosevelt died unexpectedly in 1945. To honor him, Roosevelt's likeness was placed on the dime the next year, 1946, and has been there ever since. The same happened for John Kennedy when he was assassinated in 1963. His likeness was first situated on the US half dollar the following year, 1964.

During the next hour the Professor unpacked for the students a continuous stream of intriguing facts and stories about the designs and symbols found on US coins. In doing so, Don related his discussion of coins to issues of censorship, feminism, racism, politics, world wars, art, artists, symbolism, and metallurgy. It was a fascinating detailed and diverse look at United States history, and students loved it!

The Professor finished class that day by saying there are four things always found on United States coins. First, the country can be identified, as the phrase "United States of America" is situated on all US coins.

Second, the year the coin was minted is imprinted on the coin. Third, there will be some indication of the coin's denomination: 5 cents, 10 cents, 1 dollar, etc. And fourth—perhaps most important—everything placed within the design of a US coin has symbolic meaning. Nothing is included by random happenstance or for decoration.

"This is what makes the study of numismatics so intriguing," he concluded. "All coins are filled with symbols to investigate and, sometimes, concealed designs and hidden meanings to be solved."

We all left class that day with an expanded sense of intrigue about, and appreciation for, the many overlooked layers of history that surround us.

The Professor's class lectures were always captivating and informative, but conversations in his office were most memorable. I miss them so much! One I remember clearly followed right after his lecture on US coins.

Don's approach in discussion was rarely to answer a question directly. He often started conversation with a question, which to my response would lead to more questions directing me toward an answer he knew but wanted me to figure out on my own.

I asked him in the office after class that day what he meant by saying that US coins are sometimes "filled with symbols to investigate" and "concealed designs and hidden meanings to be solved"?

The Professor paused, as if deciding how to respond to this question, or even if he wanted to answer it. Finally, after a few seconds of silence, he questioned, "Do you know there are clues to a treasure embedded in the design of a United States coin?"

"No way!" I responded.

"Yes, there is," he countered, "but I'm not going to tell you directly what the treasure is or its location. If it's a hunt you want to pursue, then I'll give you questions and clues to help you perhaps figure it out. I'll get you started. But before I do, I want you to promise that the search for this treasure will be yours alone, with my help—and online and printed sources—only. If I learn you've involved any other person in the investigation, and told them what you are doing, then I'll discontinue the hunt immediately. No hard feelings, but that will be the end. Is that understood? If so, come and report to me what you find in your search, and I'll let you know if you are on the right track and give you more clues to investigate. Do you want to take the challenge and abide by these rules?" he asked.

"Of course!" was my enthusiastic response.

To that he replied, "This is where I want you to begin."

The professor slowly pulled open the top right-hand drawer of his office desk. From deep in its recesses, he retrieved a 2 x 2-inch thin clear plastic container holding a small circular metallic object sandwiched between the two clear sides. The encased object appeared to be a tiny coin, the size of a small button, but not one that looked like any coin I'd ever seen.

"What is it?" I asked.

"You tell me," was his response.

That is so like the Professor, I thought. No direct answers.

"Tell me what you see," he said, and handed me a magnifying glass.

The Professor continued, "Start with the basics. What about the object, which indeed is a coin, strikes you first?"

I picked up the plastic holder with the coin in my left hand and the magnifier in my right. "First," I said, "is the coin's size; I've never seen a coin this small. It's so tiny."

"This means you'll have to look closely," he advised.

"What's the date on the coin, at the bottom?" the Professor asked. "Can you see it?"

Squinting at the coin through the magnifying glass, "1851" was my reply.

"Excellent! That's a good start," he offered. "What more do you see? Begin with one side of the coin and inventory what you see on that side. Then turn it over and do the same with the other side."

"I'll start with the side that has the date," I said.

"Good choice," was his response. "What else is there on that side?"

"Circling the coin across the top are the words The United States of America," I replied.

"Okay, we know now it's a coin minted in the United States in 1851. Remember, that takes care of points one and two that I said in class a few minutes ago. Now for point three: Do you see a denomination—the monetary amount of the coin?" the Professor asked.

"Not yet," I replied. "Maybe it's on the other side."

"Before turning it over, what else do you see on this side?" he prodded.

"The only thing left on this side is a six-pointed star with what looks to be some kind of shield positioned inside the star."

"Good work," the Professor answered. "Now let's try the other side."

I turned the coin over. "Wow!" was my response. "This doesn't look like anything I've ever seen on a United States coin. It doesn't have an image of a person—perhaps one of the presidents—like we have on coins today. There's no portrait shown on the coin at all, on either side."

"You are correct," the Professor countered, "but what do you see? Again, begin with what is most evident and work from there."

Starting with the outside edge of the coin, I responded, "I see some stars circling around the coin."

"How many?" he questioned.

"13."

Again, his response was, "Good. Go on. Inside the stars, what's on the inside?"

Before I could answer, the Professor told me to wait. Seeing that I had my laptop, he asked me to turn it on, pull up Google Image, and type in the words, Three-cent silver, 1851-O. "This will make it easier," the Professor offered.

And it did.

On the screen now was a greatly enlarged image of the small coin I had been looking at. Touching the screen, I was able to grow the image even larger until all details of the coin were easily seen.

The large coin image on the screen made it much clearer to view, but not necessarily easier to understand what I was looking at. Staring intently, I saw positioned in the center of the coin was a large C with what appeared to be a Roman numeral III in the center opening of the C.

The Professor agreed heartily with my observations.

"Do you see anything to the right of the C?" he asked.

I peered more closely at the screen and answered that it looked like a zero or the letter O.

He supported my inspection of the coin, and acknowledged that the circle shape was the letter O.

With this accomplished, the Professor continued: "Given what you've seen so far, do you want to continue the search?"

Without hesitation, I replied with an emphatic, "Yes!"

"Enough for today," was his response, but he continued, "Stop by my office tomorrow and I'll have some information about the coin and a list of questions for you to investigate as you begin your quest for the treasure."

He made it sound so exciting!

The next day I stopped at the Professor's office. There he handed me a manila envelope containing some sheets of paper: typed information about an 1851-O three-cent silver coin and a list of questions to investigate in starting my hunt. There were also some electronic links to information related to the coin.

Sadly, this conversation with the Professor took place just days before he left for the Civil War conference in Atlanta. Johnny Painter shot Don that Sunday evening after he returned. I haven't had time to search out answers to the questions the Professor gave me to investigate, but maybe I'll look into them when things slow down and I finish my work in his office and transcribing Mary Moore's diary.

With all the excitement in life since then, I must admit I'd forgotten about the search for treasure involving the 1851 coin and the envelope with the Professor's questions for me to answer. They should still be in my backpack. But urgent always seems to win out over the important. I have the Professor's office to sort out and his many shelves of books and Civil War objects still to catalog and distribute.

I'm continuing to work through transcribing Mary Moore's diary a few lines at a time. It's an intriguing evening activity, especially for a self-labeled "history nerd" who's experiencing life more positive these days without feeling danger lurking around me.

For the next year, fighting continued. Grant's army surrounded Petersburg, inflicting an embargo that stretched from weeks to months, during which the proud city spoiled from the inside. In April 1865, General Lee pulled back his Southern forces from Petersburg, leaving the remnants of the city to be overrun by Union marauders.

This action marked the Confederates' stagger toward surrender, as Lee bent his knee to Grant at Appomattox Courthouse soon thereafter. It was a sad day for the South, but also a time for many brave Southern sons and their long enduring wives, families, and mothers to reunite. The War was declared over, but the anger still seethed. Unremitting hate, like a wounded serpent, will conceal and regenerate below ground. In time it will emerge from its dark lair with savage strength to roil and recoil, bearing deadly fangs to strike again.

Mary does have a way with words.

Wednesday, June 7, 2017

Then there were the books. Three of the four walls in the Professor's office were filled nearly floor to ceiling with 19th- and 20th-century published volumes. Two of these massive bookcases contain texts on various features of the Civil War. It looks like the bookstore at the Gettysburg Memorial Battlefield, only bigger! The third wall of his office houses volumes related to his other love: things—objects from the past and present—what scholars call the "material culture" of our lives.

The Professor confided to me early in my time as his Teaching Assistant that a few years ago he had to move his desk toward the center of his office to give more wall space for his expanding library. Don loved his books!

The fourth office wall, however, was the one that always drew my attention and that of most other students who visited his office. Instead of floor to ceiling books, the wall to the right of his desk was filled with grainy black and white photographs from times long ago, many of them actual photos—or daguerreotypes—from the Civil War. This was his passion: to collect not just words but artifacts and images of people and settings from the Union and Confederate conflict.

These photos, the Professor told me, were of Civil War captains from both the North and South. Ten identically sized framed photographs were hung in the Professor's office in support of his frequently stated belief that, "The captains are the key" to studying and understanding the Civil War. They were situated on the Professor's wall behind and to the left when facing his desk, for all his students to see when they sat and talked with the Professor.

I paused, read, and wrote down the name attached to each photograph as I removed them from the wall. Carefully wrapping them in packing material one at a time, I placed them in a large wooden crate for storage in the museum basement. These were the captains:

- John Gregory Bishop Adams (Union)
- John T. Burgess (Union)
- Joseph Raphael de la Garza (Confederate)
- William Walter Leake (Confederate)
- Andrew Mahoney (Confederate)
- Adolph G. Metzner (Union)
- Francis T. Moore (Union)
- John W. Torsch (Confederate)

- Henry F. Young (Union)
- Manuel Rodriguez Yturri Sr. (Confederate)

The stories of these men's lives, and their battles fought—those won and lost—were at the heart of the Professor's work and life. He shared dramatic and vivid accounts with his students that taught us not only about times past, but also provided considerations for each of us to ponder about ourselves and the world today. He made history personal and gripping, and we loved that.

Not all the photographs hanging on the Professor's wall were rustic black and white depictions from the Civil War. To the far left were photos—some in faded color—of the Professor's family-members, tracing back to the early 1900s. Children pulling young friends in wagons, pubescent boys struggling to hoist weighty stretchers of fish proudly displayed on a sunny afternoon, and outdoor scenes of what I assume to be rural Arkansas serving as the backdrop for portraits of people from his past. There was even a slightly sun-bleached photograph of a 10-member basketball team the Professor coached, with the label "Boys Club District Champions, 1970," which the Professor said was from some town in Arkansas with a name that didn't register with me.

Ten boys, most with short crew cuts—wearing even shorter shorts—were positioned in a single slightly concave row. Their coach, an earlier echo of the man I knew as the Professor, stood at the right end of the row. Each of the three boys situated near the center of the group wore the letter C on his jersey, signifying the position as a team captain. I studied the picture closer, focusing attention on the much younger version of the man I often watched captivate a full class of 20-somethings with his rousing stories of the Civil War.

Don could make the conflict come alive! His protruding distinct nose and chin, and penetrating blue eyes held our rapt attention, yet in this photograph these features didn't yet possess the experiential wisdom captured in the face of the far more mature man I knew. My tears soon took the photo out of focus.

Drying my eyes, my gaze shifted to the boys in the photo. They were then—nearly 50 years ago—possibly in their early-teens. Some of the players were tall and lean, straddling the cusp of manhood. Others carried the rounded shoulders and somewhat flabby weight of yet-to-be-developed maleness. They were, however, a team, and a championship team at that! The Professor had proudly pointed out that fact to me, at least twice.

I wondered where these boys in the photograph are now. What lives had they lived? What were their successes and failures in life? Had any of them stayed in touch with the Professor over the years? I was curious about whether the Professor had influenced their lives in ways similar to how he directed thousands of young men and women after this time as their basketball coach?

But there was one other piece of photo detail that caused me to pause. I played on sports teams in high school: a little softball and basketball. I wasn't very good at either one, but they helped keep me in shape. In no sport that I ever played, especially on a team with 10 members, were there three captains. Often there were two captains, and sometimes one, but I never encountered a team with three designated captains wearing the letter C on their jersey. I wondered why that was the case here?

The three captains in the photo were a bit taller in comparison to the rest of the group. They faced directly at the camera in stoic athletic poses and wearing their blue and white numbered jerseys: 10, 30, and 42. As I stared at this photograph, a hazy assortment of jumbled thoughts swirled through me in perplexed motion. However, instead of these wonderings spiraling away in diffuse direction, I found them drawing together and intensifying toward some significant yet unrecognized conclusion.

I continued to scrutinize the team captains. Keeping that intensity, my gaze shifted to the face of the Professor. I remembered him, my time in his classes, and the words he so often shared with us throughout his many lectures and conversations: "The captains are the key." Those words now tumbled over and over in my mind. I had to pause and sit down.

I needed to think. Could this phrase the Professor so often used in his lectures—and also had placed on his headstone—have a more obscure and manifold meaning beyond the Civil War? Was the Professor conveying his beliefs about the importance of captains within the history of the Civil War, and at the same time revealing some sort of secret message to be discovered? He was a man of riddles.

Peering intently at the photo, something I had passed over many times as insignificant jumped out at me that moment: the numbered jerseys of the captains standing in a row, 10-30-42. Could the uniform numbers they wore, indeed, have significance? Might they even be the key to solving my dilemma of the two locked safes I had encountered in the museum basement a short time ago? I likely needed three numbers to open each safe, and there were three numbers on the jerseys of players wearing a captain's C in the photograph.

This is crazy, but I had to investigate! With these three jersey numbers in mind, I hurried out the door of the Professor's office, through the hall, into the museum and its workroom, and down the concrete stairs to the secure storage room in the basement. I unlocked the metal door and entered the large interior room. Picking up the flashlight from the table by the door, I approached the back wall where the two black safes were set flush into the gray concrete.

My palms were sweating as I paused and looked at the two safes in front of me. Choosing the top one first, I briskly turned the large dial of the lock a few rotations. This attempt at opening the safe needed to be made carefully. I slowly spun the dial first clockwise to the right, stopping at number 10. Resting there momentarily, I carefully turned the dial one full rotation to the left, pausing at the number 30. Completing the three-step process, I moved the dial ahead 12 digits to the number 42. I gathered my breath and moved the large silver handle of the safe downward, not sure if it would do so but hoping the handle would respond to my forceful request.

It did not click open. My heart sank. "Maybe this is just foolishness," I muttered. But I tried the three-number sequence again in case I'd been off the mark the first time. The safe handle didn't budge this time either. I attempted the three numbers on the safe dial a third time, only now I ran them in reverse order. No success.

There was still the other safe to try. I went through the same steps in attempting to open the lower safe, pausing with a deep breath as I reached out and took hold of the handle after rotating the dial through the three numbers—10-30-42. I pushed down on the handle. To my astonishment and excitement, this time the lever in my hand dropped down with a firm clink!

The door to the safe swung free with surprising ease. Breathlessly, I pivoted the door all the way open to let in as much light as possible and permit access to anything perhaps stored in the safe. I directed the flashlight beam into the opening in the wall. Even with a high air of anticipation I was not prepared for what my eyes encountered as I peered into the now gaping steel cavern.

I flinched as the beam of the flashlight reflected back in my eyes from the contents of the safe. What was I seeing here? It couldn't be what it looks like, could it? Wrapped in clear plastic were three shiny gold bars, each about eight inches long. I reached into the safe and slid the packages closer to the front edge and flipped the gold bars over for closer inspection. They felt heavy and solid.

Reaching deeper into the safe I slid toward me two canvas bags containing what seemed to be coins. I reached into a bag and pulled a handful out. Yes, I was correct. They were gold and silver coins minted in the United States and Mexico. The few in my hands were dated between 1821 and 1867. Deeper in the safe were wrapped packages of US currency, in designations of 20, 50, and 100 dollars. This is beyond belief!

Next to the gold bars and bags of coins was a small notebook. I took it to a worktable where the light was better. With shaking hands, I opened the small booklet and read the following handwritten entry.

Greetings! I'm not sure who is reading this, but I—Professor Thomas Donaldson—hope it's my Teaching Assistant or Museum Intern. If so, this likely means you solved the riddle I've been sharing with my

students for many years: "The captains are the key." I update the names in this notebook with each new Teaching Assistant and Museum Intern I hire. Your name may well be at the bottom of the list of names on the next page.

I paused my reading and flipped a page in the notebook. Sure enough, my name was written at the bottom of a long list of names—all those many others before mine crossed out—whom I assume to be the Professor's former graduate student Teaching Assistants and Museum Interns who worked with Don since the 1970s. The writing in the Professor's notebook continues.

For this reason, you should be proud of yourself for recognizing the clues embedded both in class lectures and in my basketball team photograph and putting these leads together to solve the riddle of how to open this safe. With this being the case, then it's highly likely I'm now deceased or somehow incapacitated and you are reading this as you sort through the effects of my office and the museum. Congratulations on a job well done! I do hope I've not left you with too much sorting work to do in my office.

I'm sure you are far more perplexed now than you were before encountering the contents of the safe. It's here I'll tell you a more complete story and leave you with the results of your riddle-solving success.

First, let me begin by saying that I have a hidden past, darker than you realize, which will likely be a surprise to you. Second, the bars residing in the safe are real gold, each weighing about 4 pounds. The gold and *silver coins in the bag are authentic as well. And third, behind the gold bars and coins, if you have not found it already, is $50,000 in cash.*

All the contents of this safe belong to me and are yours now, if you want them. There are, however, some considerations you need to be aware of as you decide whether to take these items. What you see in front of you is half of a large hoard of Confederate coins and gold bars, which my treasure seeking partner and I have retrieved over the years during our summers spent in the backwoods of Arkansas and other locations in the South.

The second half of this cache is housed in the other wall safe, placed there by my treasure hunting partner, Johnny "Squeaky" Painter. He and I have been searching for treasure and Civil War artifacts together—as associates but not friends—for many years. His part of the cache is also held here for safekeeping. Just so you know, he is number 42 in the Boys Club championship team photograph you likely used to solve the lock combination riddle and open the safe.

We split our annual treasure findings 50/50 at the end of every summer. Some hunts are more productive than others. Each of us has a safe housed in this wall, but we know only the combination of our own safe—or so Squeaky thought. He never knew the combination to my safe (even though his basketball uniform number was part of the 3-number sequence), but unbeknown to him I figured out the 3-digit dial code used to open his safe.

One night after Squeaky had too much rum, I asked him to tell me the combination of his safe, to use in case I needed to get into it for some reason. He refused to give me the three number sequence, of course, but did offer in his inebriated state that the three-number code for his safe was related to, "The best day of my life, ever!" Knowing Johnny as I do, it didn't take long for me to figure out the three-number combination to his safe: 11-26-02. A little sleuthing of court records revealed this to be the date his divorce was made final: November 26, 2002. Johnny is that kind of guy.

Be aware. Johnny will definitely want his half of the cache. Moreover, he will probably try to figure out how to get a hold of my portion as well. He has a notarized letter I signed, stating that upon my death or incapacitated state, Johnny Painter would have one-time access to the secure room in the museum basement for a period of no longer than fifteen minutes to retrieve items he has stored in a wall safe there. He will likely be stopping by with his letter giving him access to the secure storage room soon, if he hasn't done so already.

After Johnny completes his visit, please take the notarized letter from him and destroy it so that he's not able to try and use it again. Have one of the museum guards or a police officer escort him to the basement and back, and make sure he takes things only from his wall safe and doesn't exceed fifteen minutes in the museum basement.

This is my caution to you. If you decide to take what you find in this safe—and especially if you leave with Johnny Painter's portion of the treasure now that you know the combination to his safe—he will certainly come after you. And he is ruthless. He may not seem like it at first meeting, but Johnny Painter has killed before, which I know firsthand.

Now that you have succeeded in finding the treasure, it appears you have three primary options: (1) Leave the gold, silver, and cash hoard where it is and walk off with just the story I've told you here; (2) run away with my portion of the treasure you've discovered in this safe, with the expectation that someone may follow you and try to take it; or (3) flee and hide very well with what you take from both safes, knowing that your life will certainly be in danger if you do.

I paused from reading the Professor's words. Johnny "Squeaky" Painter was the man who shot the Professor in his office and tried to attack me in the hospital and was killed by the police officer in the hallway. Of course, the Professor wrote these words before knowing Johnny is dead! Johnny Painter is out of the picture now. He won't be after his half of the treasure or that portion owned by the Professor. I caught my breath, taking in the significance of the information and valuables the Professor left in the safe. Incredible! Still shaking, I went back to Don's writing.

There are two other individuals included in this venture from my hometown in Arkansas. They are the Smith brothers—longtime friends of Johnny—and were also members of the Boys Club championship basketball team. In the photograph they are the other two captains: uniform numbers 10 and 30. As you have figured out, the numbers on their jerseys are also part of my safe combination, but like Johnny Painter they never knew that feature of the story.

I call them Tweedledum and Tweedledee, a bit rotund now, right out of Alice in Wonderland. *They are not in any way involved in hunting and finding the caches of Knights of the Golden Circle coins and gold bars hidden throughout the wilderness and other secure locations of the southern United States—which is what this treasure is—but they are the ones to whom Squeaky and I sell the coins and gold bars that we find. Johnny and I have sold a lot of gold and silver to the Smith brothers over the years, and they know we have quite a bit more 19th-century Confederate treasure stored in the museum.*

These two Smith brothers, Mason and Dixon—I'm not making up these names—are highly regarded and very successful coin and gold bullion dealers. One owns coin shops in various US cities, mostly out west. The other travels the entire country buying and selling large quantities of gold and silver coins and bars. The brothers also purchase and sell rare Civil War artifacts. They have been the source for a number of items now in the museum's collection.

But the honesty of the Smith brothers is only skin-deep. Like Johnny Painter, both brothers are friendly on the surface but have blood on their hands and no remorse in their souls. Trust no one when it comes to gold, and with me out of the picture all these individuals may think the entire cache should now belong to them.

There are others who will want these gold bars and coins as well. These include Knights of the Golden Circle sentinels living throughout the southern United States, who have been charged with guarding these treasure troves for many generations until Johnny Painter and I made off with the gold and silver they were sworn to protect.

In addition to the sentinels there is the US government who will want its cash cut as well. If they ever find that it was Johnny and I who discovered and dug up much of this treasure on private and government land, then they will certainly want it back.

If you're perplexed about the Knights of the Golden Circle sentinels mentioned here, go back and read your class notes. I discussed the KGC in one of my lectures early in the first semester. I always make sure to do this in hopes that this information about the KGC may eventually be useful to one of my students, which perhaps is the case here.

You can also check out the Knights of the Golden Circle online, as well as through several books about this clandestine Southern organization, active before, during, and after the Civil War. My point is this: the treasure trove in this safe is yours, but there are others who may lay claim to it. If you choose to remove the contents of this safe, and especially Johnny Painter's portion from his, then I want you to know that your life will very likely be in danger.

There's one other piece of information I want you to know. The cost of my Teaching Assistant each year and Museum Intern every summer is paid by my part of Confederate treasure Johnny and I have retrieved over the years. Many of my extended summer travels to Arkansas and elsewhere in the South have been very lucrative. I'm the anonymous donor who has supported the museum for the last number of decades and paid it ahead quite a few more. Congratulations on your work here, and best of luck!

—Don

~

I have to let this settle.

Saturday, June 10, 2017

It's been three days since I made the incredible discovery in the basement of the museum. Even now, it's hard to take in all this information about the valuable coins, gold bars, and cash found in the two safes.

Before leaving the basement last Wednesday, I tried the three-number code, 11-26-02, on the dial of the safe used by Johnny Painter. Sure enough, the handle moved downward with the same solid click registered by the Professor's safe.

Taking quick inventory of the top safe's contents, apparently Johnny Painter did more business than the Professor selling gold bars and coins to the Smith brothers. There was only one four-pound gold bar and a handful of gold and silver coins in the safe that belonged to Squeaky Painter. However, his safe contained a little more than $200,000 in cash. This is amazing! For now, I left it all there for safekeeping.

My mind is doing back-flips! Beyond experiencing the shock of the fortune found in the two safes, I'm still not certain what to make of the Professor's "dark side" revelation, and that he has been hunting and "retrieving" gold bars and gold and silver coins in the backwoods of the southern United States for decades. And to do so with a known murderer who later shot and killed him. This description is hard to reconcile with the man I thought I knew so well. I guess it just goes along with the rest of my life that doesn't make much sense right now.

Since writing my last journal entry I've been developing my ideas for the future. It's helped my planning that the university has decided not to open the museum back up at the end of the summer, which has been the usual practice when the Professor returns from his summer travels. Given the Professor's death, university administrators have decided to instead keep the museum closed to visitors at least until the new calendar year. This will give the administration time to decide on a course of action for the museum and select a new director to replace Professor Donaldson.

The Professor indicated in his writing that all the valuables stored in his safe—and that of Johnny Painter—are now mine, if I choose to take them. While this may be true, it still raises questions for me about the ethics of ownership and how he came to possess them. The Professor and Johnny Painter were involved in questionable, and even illegal, activities in acquiring at least some of these coins and gold bars. However, Don doesn't leave any details about who, specifically, had previously owned these valuable items, and when and from where Johnny Painter and the Professor took them.

Also, it appears these coins and gold bars were never formally accessioned into the museum. For this reason, they are not actually part of the museum's collection, so they don't really belong to the museum. Don and Johnny were only storing these valuables in the museum basement, so I would not be taking for myself objects that are owned by the museum.

I have no way of returning these coins and gold bars to their original owners, so I'm at a loss here. I'll give this more thought, but until I find some specific way of giving them back to whoever owned them, I'm going to follow the Professor's third option from his writing left in the safe. I'm taking what I found in both safes, knowing that Johnny Painter is out of the picture.

The Professor did write that there likely would be others who will want the gold and silver that he and Johnny acquired, including the Smith brothers, the US government, and possibly Knights of the Golden Circle "sentinels" (whoever they might be). I'll watch my steps carefully, but with Johnny Painter dead and me perhaps taking some time away from the area, I think I will be fine.

I'm told that my priority is to complete work in the Professor's office. This is fine with me. Learning that a huge treasure is now mine, locked away in two safes in the museum basement, gives me motivation to finish disassembling the Professor's office and to consider my own direction for the future after work here is complete.

The History Department has also granted me the option of taking a leave of absence for this coming academic year. I'll decide in the next few weeks if I stay here or move elsewhere in the fall.

With increasing purpose, I'm making headway through the Professor's office. The sorting of Don's books is nearly complete, and almost all his Civil War objects have been relocated to the workroom. I'll begin inventorying these items once everything is out of Don's office.

There is one object from the Professor's office that will not make its way into the museum's permanent collection. While going through Don's desk, deep in the back I came across the 2 x 2-inch thin clear plastic container holding the very small 1851-O three-cent silver United States coin, which the Professor told me possessed symbols related to hidden Confederate treasure.

Like the gold, silver, and cash I found in the safes, I don't believe this small silver coin is part of the museum's collection. Instead, I think it belonged to the Professor. For this reason, I don't feel bad in keeping it for myself. I think Don would want me to have it. I'm not sure when I'll get to investigate the mystery surrounding this coin, but I'm keeping it to help in that search, whenever I get the chance to take it on.

One piece at a time, the Professor's office is becoming a shell of the space I knew very well only a few weeks ago. It now strikes me as hollow, and sounds that way, too. Walking through the room, the haunting echo of his once familiar voice is replaced by the sound of my footsteps on the gray linoleum floor. For my own well-being, I need to finish this job in the Professor's office soon and close the door one final time.

Monday, June 12, 2017

My evenings are filled with deciphering Mary Moore's diary. Some of these sessions spent recording her writing are more successful than others, but with every entry I'm increasingly amazed by the story that is unfolding. Let's see what I learn tonight.

> *Deborah did not remain the same young girl after learning the death of her brothers. And her beloved horse Colonel was gone now, too. A sullen spirit engulfed Deborah as she accomplished her best to endure the coarse ridicule of death that surrounded her: first Deborah's father and mother, and now her brothers and Colonel. They were gone. Deborah was alone, and she felt it. I did what I could to console the young girl—and there were times when she covered her deep pain quite well from those around her—but many nights the thin wall separating our two bedrooms was not enough to veil the tearful sobs of her lonely, anguished soul.*
>
> *She did, however, appreciate that I had taken her in. For not this, Deborah had no place to go. School days came and went with little fanfare or heart, for Deborah as well as for the other children of Franklin. The War continued to rage and tear at the remnant of our little community. News*

told of death and increasing Southern defeats, and over time fewer war letters were received by families back home.

When the end came—the surrender of the South—our pride was bent but not severed from its soul. Franklin, like many towns in the South, was shredded of its citizens but its saddened spirit remained unbroken.

The next few years of my life do not play importantly in the events that took place in Boston on June 16, 1869. It was not until early May of that year which requires my record here.

I have a sister, Martha, three years my senior. Unlike members of the Lee family, Martha and I were not close siblings. Most of the time it was just the two of us. Our father and mother died at an early age, when Martha and I were in our teen years. Our little brother Henry passed from cholera in the summer epidemic of 1832, at age seven.

Martha was a free-spirited young woman with a wanderlust approach to all she did. She read books about life in New England and wished to see that part of the world for herself. This she did. After working in the local dry goods store for some years and then teaching the school children of Franklin for two more, she left our town for New England in 1840 at age 21. I filled the void she left behind, as her departure signaled the beginning of my time teaching the school children of Franklin.

Martha moved to Massachusetts to study pedagogy through the instruction of Massachusetts' educator Horace Mann. She was drawn—like the call of the mythical Siren—to Mann's views on education by his writings that made their way south, to us. However, it was clear to me that Mann's ideas about children and schooling were intended for bookish Northerners and not for the practical-minded children of the South—the ones I love most.

I had little time for Mann's words, but not so with Martha. Captured by their lofty sentiment, Martha left her Southern life behind and traveled north to Massachusetts. She took up residence in the city of Chelsea, near Boston, exploring and teaching out the beliefs of Horace Mann to school children there.

Few were the times I heard from Martha in the years after she left. Silence fed the estrangement between us. When I did receive correspondence from her, it was brief with little care or emotion. My notes returned to her read much the same. In a letter dated June 3, 1847, I learned Martha had married. Her husband—Alfred Lovell—was a recognized teacher of drawing in and around Boston.

Martha did not share many details about Alfred or their life together. They bore no children, at least that her limited correspondence revealed. Martha, who had been a teacher of drawing as well, gave up her formal instruction position and taught, instead, independent classes in sketching and drawing out of her home in Chelsea. From that point on correspondence between us remained infrequent and of little bearing.

This matter changed dramatically on May 1, 1869. That was the day I received a small paper-wrapped parcel addressed to me from my sister Martha.

Even though it's an exciting and inconvenient place to pause my transcribing of Mary Moore's account, it's late and I need to get some sleep. I'll pick up my recording of her diary tomorrow evening.

Tuesday, June 13, 2017

I finished cleaning out the Professor's office today. In doing so I made another incredible find! The job of taking apart the Professor's "campus home" has been difficult, but I'm glad to be the one making sure all items in his office are sent to their proper locations, as the Professor requested. Most of his books are now in the museum or university libraries, with a few duplicate volumes donated to the local city library.

I'll start cataloging the Civil War objects intended for the museum next week. All of them have been moved into the workroom of the museum now. But it was in my final stages of cleaning out the Professor's office today that I came upon something breathtaking, which still has me baffled.

Completing my work in the Professor's office, I slid the now empty bookcases a few feet out from the wall to sweep away years of collected dust and cobwebs. With each bookcase resting on short sturdy legs, I found that without much effort the empty sets of shelves could be slid, one at a time, a few feet across the smooth linoleum floor. Moving the closest bookcase, I caught a glimpse of a small dark rectangular object resting amongst the accumulated grit on the floor near the wall. Picking it up, I realized the object to be a dust-covered smartphone.

My inspection of the phone revealed that a thin plastic cardholder was attached to its back. This tight-fitting holder contained three cards. The first is a credit card registered in the Professor's name, Thomas Donaldson. The second item is the Professor's Virginia driver's license. I stopped to stare at his picture for a few moments. I do miss that man.

The third item in the thin plastic holder is one of Don's university business cards.

The name F T Henry is hand-printed in black ink on the back of the business card. I have no idea who that person is. But more important, these items indicate that this is the Professor's cell phone. I'm not certain how it got lodged under the bookcase, but it likely ended up being dropped or thrown and slid there during the fight with Johnny Painter moments before the Professor was shot.

This explains why the police were unable to locate the Professor's phone in their search of his office, and thinking the shooter took it as he fled. Finding the phone under the bookcase makes me wonder if Johnny Painter ever saw the photos of Mary Moore's diary on Don's phone, and if he was able to use the phone to learn my identity. If not, then hiding out in the secluded motel for a couple nights was not needed. But that's water under the bridge. I had no way of knowing that possibility until now.

Instinctively, I pushed the phone's activation button. Of course, the phone didn't power up after four weeks under the bookshelf. The glass face is badly cracked, probably shattered in the fight. However, the Professor's phone is the same model as mine, so I have it plugged in and recharging now as I write this journal entry while sitting in my apartment. Though damaged, I'll see if it will recharge.

The last thing I removed from the Professor's office today was the gray two-drawer metal filing cabinet located alongside his desk, which contains his lecture notes, research material, and some Civil War photographs. I kept the cabinet and its contents as is and used a hand-truck and the elevator to move it to general storage in the basement. Someone, likely not me, will have the opportunity to go through the files carefully and catalogue these papers and photographs for future use. My focus in the days ahead will be on recording and archiving the Civil War items themselves, which are now assembled—along with the objects from the two trunks—on the large table in the workroom of the museum.

With mixed and muddled emotions this afternoon, I prepared to close the door to the Professor's office one last time. It seemed a bit odd to lock the door, as there is nothing left in his office but an empty desk, three wooden chairs, and three walls of completely cleared bookshelves. But hearing the click of a lock brings finality and closure, something I need very much in my life right now.

Before shutting the door and giving the key a final turn, I paused and gazed slowly around the vacant room. In its stillness, I listened for the Professor's voice. Silence, however, was his purposeful reply. It was then I whispered softly to the empty room the words that have changed my life and will forever stay fixed in my memory: "Yes Professor, indeed, the captains are the key." With that I turned off the light, shut the door, inserted and turned the key, and heard the distinctive click of the Professor's office door lock one final time.

Even before opening the small paper-wrapped parcel, I knew it was delivered from my sister. Martha's flowing handwriting carried with it qualities that only she possessed. This arrival to me, however, was different. Previously, Martha sent only short notes and letters. I had no idea what would come to me from her, wrapped in an overlay of stiff coarse paper.

I carefully unwrapped the small bundle one fold at a time. In front of me on the table now lay a small softcover booklet with the title Grand National Peace Jubilee and Musical Festival *dated the month of its arrival, May & June 1869. The cover showed the illustration of an angel blowing an immense trumpet and carrying a flowing banner with the words LET US HAVE PEACE in large letters centered at the top. Tucked inside was a folded piece of paper with the name MARY inscribed in large, graceful letters, my sister's handwriting.*

My pulse raced as I transcribed these words of Mary Moore into my journal. The pamphlet she describes here appears identical to one of the books I found in the hidden compartment at the bottom of the trunk, along with this diary, the King James Bible, and the large book about the Musical Festival written by Patrick Gilmore. I'll check on this first thing tomorrow morning, but I'm betting that the booklet written about by Mary Moore here in her diary, and the one now sitting on the table in the museum—both described similarly and dated May & June 1869—are one in the same!

Wednesday, June 14, 2017

Yes, I'm as certain as can be! The softcover pamphlet titled *Grand National Peace Jubilee and Musical Festival* described in Mary Moore's journal and sent from her sister Martha looks to be the same small book I found hidden in the false bottom of the trunk and is now in the museum workroom. Even though this realization raises many unknowns, it does establish an intriguing connection between Mary Moore and the two trunks I picked up from April Jones—or whoever that woman was—on the farmhouse porch five weeks ago. Each thing I learn in this search leads to another layer of perplexing questions!

I've spent so much time reading, deciphering, and recording Mary Moore's diary that I've barely looked at the other books I found hidden in the trunk. Now, with this connection between Mary Moore's writing and the contents of April Jones's two trunks donated to the museum, I plan to examine this pamphlet and the other two books and explore all the items from the trunks even more closely. This is good timing. Now that my work in the Professor's office is complete, my next task is to catalog all the objects I unloaded from the two trunks a few weeks ago.

Thursday, June 15, 2017

The Professor was a complex man. Even at 70 years of age (I know this now from his driver's license) Don had a gamesome spirit of young boy innocence. He liked word and number problems, riddles, games, and searchable questions. Yet, information learned over the past few weeks has taught me that along with his boyhood wittiness the Professor possessed a somewhat dark and thievish past. Knowing this hidden and nefarious part of his life as I do now, it was good to encounter Don's familiar-to-me side of life as a playful puzzler once again today.

To my amazement, the Professor's screen-splintered cell phone eventually powered up. I soon learned it was, however, pass-number protected. Similar to my phone, the user must enter six pre-programmed numbers into the phone to unlock it. But I had no idea what six numbers made up the code on his phone. My previous experience with unlocking his safe in the basement of the museum using basketball jersey numbers showed me that the Professor liked to play number games.

I wondered if the pass-number for his cell phone also had some hidden mystery. I tried combining the three basketball jersey numbers that opened his safe in the museum basement—103042—but with no success here. I input the six numbers that opened Squeaky Painter's safe—112602—but those didn't activate the Professor's phone. I selected various combinations of his birthdate and address from his driver's license, all without gaining access. The same was true for using digits of his credit card number. After an hour's worth of attempts I was at a loss about how I might break the six-digit number code to activate his phone.

Setting the phone down, I picked up the Professor's business card that had been lying on the table with his driver's license and credit card. I turned it over and again read the name F T Henry inscribed in the Professor's handwriting on the back.

This name meant nothing to me. But why should it? The Professor had many friends and associates I didn't know. However, it was curious to me that this name was written on the back of his business card and placed, along with his credit card and driver's license, in the thin plastic cardholder attached to the reverse side of his phone.

This person must have some special significance for the Professor. Perhaps F T Henry was someone the Professor met at the Civil War conference he attended in Atlanta the weekend before he was killed. Maybe F T Henry was a history colleague from another university. It even flashed through my mind—however only briefly—that F T Henry was, perhaps, the name of the Professor's covert lover. With that thought my curiosity got the best of me. I grabbed my phone to see if I could learn the identity of F T Henry through an online search.

In keeping with how every avenue in my life has been traveled lately, the response I received to my online search for F T Henry was not at all what I expected. Inputting the name F T Henry immediately brought up not the name of a person, but that of a military installation: Fort Henry, in Tennessee. Since now I saw that the Professor didn't place periods after the F and the T, it seems he may not have been identifying the name of a person on the back of his business card, but instead this Tennessee military fort.

The online information revealed that Fort Henry was the location of a major Civil War battle fought between General Grant's Union forces and those of the Confederacy. The fighting took place on February 6, 1862. But why would the Professor have the name of this military fort written on the back of his business card and stashed in the pocket of his phone with only his credit card and driver's license? It must have some special significance to be placed together with his other two important and frequently used cards.

I knew the Professor often carried handwritten notes in his pocket or wallet to remind him of tasks to complete and meetings to attend (and groceries to buy). He was an "old school" pencil and paper guy in many ways. So, it didn't surprise me that the Professor would carry with him something important written on his business card. The problem was in figuring out why a reference to this military fort might be included on the back of his university business card and why the card was stored in this easily accessible place? It was kept there likely to remind the Professor of something, and perhaps—even though it was a stretch—this something would help unlock his cell phone. Knowing the Professor's way of doing things, this could very possibly be his approach.

Keeping this in mind, I re-started my trial of activating the Professor's phone. I began with what seemed to be the most obvious six-digit connection to Fort Henry: the battle date, February 6, 1862. This would read numerically 2-6-1-8-6-2. I slowly tapped those six numbers into the Professor's phone, and in my wide-eye response nearly dropped it!

I couldn't believe what happened. Immediately the phone lit up. I had cracked the entry code to the Professor's phone by using the date of a Civil War battle! Who, but the Professor, would select a phone code like that! And who but the Professor would leave a hidden reminder of that entry code on a business card attached to his phone. He was quite a character!

Peering at the cracked screen, a tidal wave of unexpected emotions rushed over me! What I saw was a gut punch. The image staring at me from the Professor's phone was one of the three photos of pages from Mary Moore's diary I sent to the Professor in Atlanta the day before he returned home early and was shot in his office. This photo of the diary and the other two photos I forwarded to the Professor were, indeed, what Don was fighting to keep from Johnny Painter that night in his office. With the Professor's phone and its photos in hand, Painter would then be able to access my contact information and track me down. This confirms that protecting me from Johnny Painter is what cost the Professor his life! With this realization, overwhelming pain and heartache engulfed me again. Why did I send him these photos?

Friday, June 16, 2017

It's Friday evening and I've done nothing all day. Since activating the Professor's cell phone yesterday and seeing on its screen the photos of Mary Moore's diary, I have been caught in a web of dark sadness.

It took all my emotional energy to finish the journal entry last night. But I felt it necessary to do so, capturing on paper the anguish I feel now. I know I'll never get over the death of the Professor, but also realize I need to work in every way possible to try and move beyond my present emotional state. Continuing my journal writing and work transcribing Mary Moore's story is one therapeutic way of doing this.

With strong hesitancy I unfolded the paper with my name on it, sent from my sister Martha. I had no idea what the contents of her writing would be, nor why she would send me this "Monthly Bulletin" of the Musical Festival, telling details of this forthcoming event. Placing the paper carefully on my table and smoothing the white parchment, I read these words penned to me from my sister:

> *My Dearest Mary,*
> *I trust you are well, feeling the blessings of God's grace to you. I am sorry for the times of silence between us through the years, and I know that as sisters we have not been as cordial and caring for one another as we should. This feeling of recompense has been on my heart so heavily recently.*
> *The War has taken a toll on the county, and also upon our sisterhood. I want to work in rectifying this. I am writing in the hope you will consider my invitation here for you to pay a visit to my dear Alfred and me in middle-June of this year in Boston, to attend the wonderful celebration conducted to advance, as the booklet here*

*says, "peace throughout the land." I
believe we may use this joining together as a time of healing both for us as
sisters and for our dear nation.*

*Tucked within the pages of this
Musical Festival pamphlet are five
10-dollar National Bank Notes to pay
your travel to Boston to join us in this
grand celebration. Please do come. We
would like you also to invite a guest to
join you for this trip. Alfred and I believe this amount will be enough to pay
train fare here for you both. If not, we
will make up the monetary difference
when you arrive. We will also purchase
your return trip tickets when you
depart. Trains are readily available
and fares are greatly reduced for those
traveling by rail to this festival.*

*If you are uncertain about travel
and this event, please view this won-
derful booklet I am sending here telling
about the Musical Festival and sites to
see in and around the city of Boston. It
is such a grand and glorious place, and
it will be even more so during the time
of this musical extravaganza.*

*I see the coliseum regularly in my
routine travels through Boston. This
vast structure has risen resolutely from
the ground over the past months. An
engraving of this magnificent building
is found on the back of the booklet. It
is said that this structure, expected to
hold 50,000 musicians, singers, and
spectators, will be an edifice un-*

*matched in the history of our nation!
I believe that just seeing it would be
worth the trip for you.*

*Dignitaries from many of the United States and world countries will attend. Arrangements are being made for
President Ulysses S. Grant to be here
for at least one day of the five-day festival, and it appears he will join in the
celebration. Oh, dear sister, please do
my heart well and accompany us. Our
house is large, with plenty of space for
you and a guest.*

*Alfred and I have purchased four
tickets for all five days of the festival.
Hundreds, if not thousands, of singers and musicians from around the
world will be here. According to the
booklet, the pipe organ used in the
coliseum will produce a tone "such as
never been heard on this continent, if
on the globe." It would be thrilling to
have you and a companion join us for
the full week of this event, June 15-19.
We can all attend together each day.
Please, dear sister, come stay with us
for a time of joyful reconciliation from
our strife, and partake in a week of
song and instrument as you and I and
the nation heal from what has brought
much sadness and rupture to our lives.*

*Your loving sister,
Martha*

~

After reading this letter, I had to pause and con-
sider deeply the words written and sent to me by
my sister.

~

After writing this entry, I have to pause and consider deeply these words
I just read and transcribed from Mary Moore's diary!

Saturday, June 17, 2017

I spent a restless night pondering this letter from Martha to her sister.
With a cup of coffee in hand, I went back to work with Mary's diary
first thing today. What caught me off guard was a realization in writing
today's date that yesterday marked exactly 128 years since Mary Moore
wrote the words I am transcribing here, and precisely 148 years since the
assassination attempt on the life of President Grant.

Reading past the words penned by Martha to her sister that I recorded in my journal yesterday, it becomes clear that Mary's immediate
response is to disdainfully dismiss her sister's invitation.

~

In writing this account twenty years after it took
place, it is likely there are instances where my
story is told through a softer and more hesitant
tone than what actually occurred so many years
earlier. However, this is not the case here. My sis-
ter's letter, even as I remember now reading it two
decades ago, flabbergasted and angered me! Not
only was it unexpected to receive this sudden stir-

ring expression of remorseful guilt after all these years of separation, but it was humiliating to be invited by her to contemplate travel over these miles to join in a jubilee observance of the South's ravage. Peaceful it was not. It was dreadful to my spirit and harmful to my soul.

I set her letter aside for a time, wanting some distance from it to compose an appropriate response. Re-reading her letter a few days later did not lessen my inflamed indignation toward my sister, but it did give me presence of mind to consider options of reply. Reviewing the contents of the letter still again, I was drawn beyond its disrespectful tone to consider, particularly, the section telling of dignitaries who will be in attendance, especially President Grant.

As I recoiled in anger from the written words of my sister, young Deborah found the accompanying Jubilee booklet fascinating. She poured over its contents and was captivated by the pamphlet's many engravings and stories of locations and buildings in Boston. The attendees would encounter these at the Musical Festival: The State House, Boston Common, a large statue of Benjamin Franklin in front of the City Hall, the Public Library, a tall building called Selwyn's Theatre, a place identified as Faneuil Hall, and many other descriptions were included in the pamphlet, along with engraved illustrations.

I told Deborah about the invitation sent by my sister to visit her at the Jubilee, but without revealing the condescending tone of Martha's letter nor my disgust with it. Deborah was intrigued by possible attendance of President Grant at the festival, which Martha told in her letter and was also indicated in the pamphlet.

A week after the package from Martha arrived, I composed two brief letters of reply. Both declined the offer to visit my sister, but the tone of each was not the same. One correspondence to Martha was harsh. The other was more conciliatory. Not sure which letter to send, I read each again, carefully. I decided to take one more night's sleep and make my decision in the morning. Either way, I would return the five 10-dollar Banknotes. I did not want to keep or to spend this blood money from my sister.

Sleep was slow in coming that night. Anger toward my sister rose within me as the clock ticked toward dawn. It was then, in the darkness, a revelation of writhing retribution came to me that would distill my true deep anger.

Martha was not the only one to whom my certain fury was directed. There was another who deserved my rage even more: The Northern Butcher, Grant. Awake in the blackened room, I saw in my mind his hideous face. It haunted me. Soon that appearance melted into the likeness of Gideon Lee, then brother Samson, Willy Harris, Charlie Wild, and the many other young Franklin men whose blood was spilled and lives ended by the abhorrent Grant.

Mary's story is so very captivating, but this is all I have time for today. I look forward to finding out Mary's emerging plan for dealing with her anger.

Sunday, June 18, 2017

Two things are clear from looking at the contents of the Professor's cell phone. And neither of them surprises me. The first observation is that the Professor didn't store much information on his phone. It has very few apps. His number of contacts is small, with only a short list of names I don't recognize as being from the university. However, there is a name in the Professor's contact list I do recognize: Johnny Painter. I should delete it. We'll see.

Scrolling further down the brief contact list reveals two other names I recall. The Professor mentioned these names in the notebook I found in his safe: the Smith brothers, Mason and Dixon. As a student of the American Civil War, I keep asking myself, what were their parents thinking in giving the brothers these names?

The second thing that is different about the Professor's phone when compared to my phone and many others is that it holds very few photos. Beyond the three photographs of Mary Moore's diary that I sent to the Professor, there are only a couple dozen images stored on Don's phone. Most are landscape and nature scenes, backwoods country. However, some of the photos saved on the phone are interesting in an odd sort of way. I'm not sure what to make of them.

Several photos on the Professor's phone appear to be the type of town signs seen when driving into a small burgh or borough. These signs read: Ozark, Cass, Brashears, Coal Hill, Harmony, Oark, Swain, Deer, Pottsville, Hector, Ben Hur, and Sand Gap. I'm not familiar with any of these towns, but I do think there was a Civil War battle fought at Pottsville. I'll have to check on this. But I have no idea why the Professor would have pictures of these signs on his phone. Perhaps they are places where Civil War fighting took place.

Along with these town signs are photos of printed and hand-drawn maps. These plats display a few named markers and contour lines showing trails and elevation change. I'll need to do some research to identify where these towns and sites are located.

However, this new Professor-generated quandary will have to get in line behind the others on my list. There is still quite a lot of work to be completed on the diary, questions surrounding April Jones and the two trunks to be investigated, and earlier riddles from the Professor's life waiting to be solved first. Transcribing Mary Moore's journal is at the head of the line. Let's see what I uncover in it this evening.

Envisioning this plan of retribution in the dark of night, my world changed, completely. My tact toward Martha would be entirely different now. Instead of sending my sister a letter stating I will not attend the musical event, my intent will rather be to visit her in Boston and gladly partake in this Peace Jubilee. For in doing so I had a larger more vengeful purpose in mind.

It was now little more than four weeks until the musical gathering in Boston. I needed to send written indication of my decision to Martha soon. That morning, I discarded in the fire the two letters I had written to my sister, both saying that I would not be visiting her. Instead, I penned a short but feigned pleasant reply, telling how joy-ous I am to receive the invitation and that I and Deborah, the young girl taken under my wing, will join her and Alfred for the five-day musical extravaganza.

We will make the circuit by train, and hopeful-ly reach Boston two or three days before the fes-tival begins. The positive message from my heart to Martha was untrue, but not so my acceptance of the trip itself. Even before asking her to accom-pany me, I knew Deborah would delight in joining me to partake in the Musical Festival and see the sights of Boston.

I took my penned response to Martha's invitation to the post-master that afternoon, requesting my letter be sent by rail to Boston as early as possible. While in town I talked with the rail-master about the requirements of making a trip by train to Boston. He was surprised to hear of my desire to travel that far north, but he understood my intent when I said it would be a visit to my sister and that Deborah Lee would accompany me.

The journey by train would take a full three days, with the need to change trains in two locations: once in Baltimore and the second exchange in the city of New York. Apart from that, the master said there would not be much difficulty in making the passage by rail.

What I did next was uncomfortable for me. Using two of the National Bank Notes sent to me by my sister I purchased two train tickets for the first leg of our trip. The rail-master also told me that Deborah and I, paying a few dollars more, could secure a sleeping section on the train, if needed. However, looking at his time schedule, the rail-master indicated to me that a sleeping car would not be necessary for this first portion of the trip, from Franklin to Baltimore.

He recommended that I purchase a sleeping car for the next two legs of our journey, traveling at night during a portion of the trip from Baltimore to New York City, and also from the City to Boston. Each section of the trip would require the purchase of further tickets, but the master indicated this would not be hard to accomplish at the two stations where we were to change trains. I thanked him for this information.

We would board the train north from Franklin toward Richmond early on the morning of Thursday, June 10th, and arrive in Boston the evening of Saturday, June 12th. We now had four weeks before our departure.

~

I'm not sure of Mary's plan and sudden change of heart toward making this trip to visit her sister in Chelsea. But unscrambling her intent will have to wait. I'm headed to bed. Tomorrow I'm going to finally begin cataloging objects in the workroom of the museum.

Monday, June 19, 2017

It felt good to be back on campus this morning. I arrived ready to get started recording and storing the many objects that have been waiting for me on the worktable in the museum. Reaching the building, I prepared to insert my key in the outside door lock as I have done countless times before. Today, however, I paused in noticing the small brown box covering a coded keypad on the brick wall next to the museum door.

The Professor often used this keypad for entry into the museum, but he told me it was university policy that he was the only one who would know the access code. There was an identical entry device positioned outside the door to the museum in the hallway of the History Building. But it also was for use by the Professor only, so I never thought much about the museum's coded access feature.

Seeing the entry pad this morning, I wondered if perhaps the six-digit number to unlock the Professor's phone was identical to the code used to open the door to the museum. That would be the Professor's way of doing things: keep it tricky but simple.

No harm in trying. Lifting the box-cover to the keypad, I tapped in the same six numbers used to access the Professor's phone: 2-6-1-8-6-2.

Doing so, I heard the solid deep click of the door, unlocking access. It worked! Amazing! I can now get into the museum without having to search for my key.

Before I went to the storage room to begin work, I tried the six-number access code on the entry device in the hallway leading to the museum. Sure enough, the inside door to the museum opened using those same six numbers. This will be helpful getting inside the museum when I have my hands full and don't want to fish for keys in my purse or pockets. And, if I ever need to remember it for an exam sometime, I'll always recall the date of the Civil War battle of Fort Henry!

I enjoyed getting reacquainted with the objects I'd laid out on the table in the workroom. I began my morning by tagging an identification code on the two trunks that had initiated this unbelievable journey some five weeks ago. They were still as heavy as I remember. I slid the trunks aside and later took them to the basement by way of a hand-truck and the museum elevator, and stored them inside the secure storage room on one of the lower shelves near the door.

The numerous schoolbooks were organized into similar subject groupings, and I then recorded the titles, authors, and publication dates on the museum tablet. Many were from the pre-Civil War era, but others were published in the years after that.

I took some time inspecting the two hand-carved wooden chess sets. The pieces of one set were quite a bit larger than those in the other set, but both were finely made, each with a wooden chessboard constructed of dark and light alternating wood squares. I wondered if the person who carved these game pieces also designed and built the two trunks, including the one with the well-crafted false bottom.

The women's clothes were placed carefully, piece by piece, in hanging storage bags designed for this purpose. After recording descriptions of the various clothing items into the database on the museum tablet, I numbered each piece and took them to the basement storage room. It's tedious work, but in doing so I feel I'm handling history. My workday was filled with questions about the past and the people who wore and used these objects so many years ago.

On one trip to the basement, I stopped to check on my gold and silver treasure stored in the two safes. Everything is just as I left it, which is what I expected. But it's reassuring and exciting to see the coins and gold bars that now belong to me! I'm still not sure about my future plans, but I'll need to reach some decision soon.

The number of items to catalog and shelve is growing smaller, but there is still work to do. I'll dive into them tomorrow. I've had enough work and writing for today. I'm headed to bed.

Tuesday, June 20, 2017

The most interesting items I inventoried today were two large, line-stitched blankets. Each cloth was light green in color and folded separately when I removed them from the trunk a few weeks ago. I didn't pay much attention to these pieces of cloth at that time.

Today I made space for these blankets on the large worktable. I carefully pulled back the layers of folded cloth to revel two very light weight blankets each about seven feet square, much larger than I first thought. They seem quite old and delicate, as if they'd been well used, folded and unfolded many times.

The design of each cloth is not at all patterned, like a quilt might be. Instead, the line stitching is sometimes done with black or red thread, which travels over the light green cloth for a few feet and then stops. The stitched thread-line starts again a bit further on, but then continues off in another direction. In other places lines are stitched with blue thread. Irregular patches of light blue cloth are positioned sporadically throughout both large pieces of green cloth. Dark purple Xs and dots are stitched at different locations on each piece. Near these Xs and dots various letters, numbers, or simple line symbols are attached. They are quite puzzling.

Both green pieces of cloth contain a hodgepodge of colors and stitching that resemble no pattern I can make out. The same sort of colorful lines are stitched into each blanket, but the two large pieces of cloth are clearly not identical in design.

These blankets will require more time to make sense of them, but that will have to wait. I carefully folded each cloth separately and placed them individually in two sturdy archival boxes. I then numbered each box and recorded the appropriate storage information on the museum tablet, giving the donor's name as April Jones.

I'm making headway sorting through and inventorying objects in the museum workroom. But I'm going to take some time away tomorrow to work on transcribing more pages from Mary Moore's diary.

Wednesday, June 21, 2017

This portion of Mary Moore's account seems to have experienced some water damage or weathering. In places it's harder than others to read her handwriting, so going through it takes quite a bit of time. It's a laborious process to slowly ply the pages apart and work through transcribing the inked words, which oftentimes have bled through the page. Fortunately, the story that emerges is incredibly worth the effort.

> *With a hopeful spirit I have not encountered in Deborah's being since before the death of her brothers, the young girl expressed to me her keen will for us to travel north to Boston and attend the Musical Festival. Neither Deborah nor I had ever ventured far from our home in Franklin. However, I believed that at nearly 17 years of age she would be able to make the trip to and return from my sister's city without much difficulty.*
>
> *Deborah was particularly interested to learn that my sister and her husband were teachers of drawing and likely would be able to assist in*

her artistic pursuits. Her joyous smile and hug of thanks delivered much when I told of my decision for us to visit Martha and Alfred and partake in the Musical Festival in Boston.

At this point in the evening, I was interrupted by a phone call from my friend Jessica. As a fellow graduate student in the History Department, she is doing her summer internship in Knoxville, Tennessee. I hung out with and studied alongside Jessica most of this past year. She called to see how I'm doing, and to ask if she could come visit me on the weekend leading into the 4th of July. Her parents live about 90 minutes from here, and she plans to visit them on the 3rd and 4th of July, before returning to Knoxville.

I haven't had any visitors and few contacts this summer. It'll be good to see Jessica and perhaps talk through some—but not all—of my experiences over the past few weeks. It was nice of Jessica to think of me and want to visit for the weekend.

By the time we finished our phone call it was too late to continue my work with Mary's diary. I'll try to pick it up again tomorrow.

Thursday, June 22, 2017

I've been working through the wide range of objects to be cataloged in the museum. The number of items on and around the table is shrinking day by day. My inventory work with them has been a bit tedious but rewarding. Some of the objects I'm sorting through and cataloging now were given to the museum this past spring, before I began my summer work in the museum. Today was a day to unpack and record into the museum database some of these new-to-me objects.

I began my morning by opening three wooden crates of various sizes. The first container was long (5 feet) but narrower (12" x 12") in its other dimensions. Using the prying end of a hammer, I carefully removed a row of small nails that secured the lid of the crate. There's always an air of anticipation when opening a container for the first time.

The contents here were a surprise. The box held five wood-stock rifles of various lengths, makes, and calibers, along with three handguns. This was a first for me. Not being at all familiar with firearms—other than the one pointed at me by Johnny Painter in the hospital a few weeks ago—I needed help in identifying the specific manufacturers, names, and size of these antique firearms. Since these weapons are being given to our museum, I assumed (correctly) that these guns were used in the Civil War.

The Professor came in handy again. Moving the book collection from his office to the museum's research library a few weeks ago, I remember seeing some publications with photographs and descriptions of firearms used in the Civil War. I was right. Using Moller's book *American Military Shoulder Arms*, Lord's *Civil War Collector's Encyclopedia*, Edwards' *Civil War Guns*, Pritchard's *Civil War Weapons and Equipment*, and a few other resources that once belonged to the Professor, I was able to identify specifically the five rifles and three revolvers stored in this crate and donated to the museum. It's fascinating to see what people know, study, and write books about.

I typed the descriptions and dimensions of the eight firearms into the collection database. After giving them each an accession number, I placed them back in the wooden crate and used the elevator to transport the container to the secure storage room in the basement.

Before leaving for his speaking engagement in Atlanta just prior to when he was shot and killed, the Professor told me he knew the family who donated these three wooden crates to the museum. The Professor, in appreciation, expressed he would send a thank you letter and perhaps go visit them personally when he returned.

This presents a problem. The Professor didn't tell me the name of the donors. So far, I've not been able to see any identifying contact information on or in the three crates, so I'm not sure whom I should thank for these remarkable donations to the museum.

The remaining two wooden crates are smaller in size and weigh quite a bit less than the one containing the firearms. Using the claw hammer, I carefully removed the lid of each remaining crate. The first of these two containers held a neatly folded gray wool Confederate military uniform. Using reference books from the museum's research library, as well as information gleaned online, I was able to identify that the long overcoat in the box was part of a Confederate staff captain's uniform.

The crate also held two sets of matching trousers and two vests. All were in fine shape for being more than 150 years old. I looked over the embroidered sleeve design and carefully crafted stitching on the coat and decided to neatly re-fold the uniform and leave it in this crate for the time being, before recording a description of it in the museum's electronic database.

Crate number three was a bit smaller and even lighter in weight. Opening it, I gently removed two army hats. Using the reference books, I learned that the larger wide-brimmed head-cover is called a slouch hat, and the smaller somewhat floppy cap is referred to as a kepi. Both types of hats were common among Confederate soldiers and officers. At the bottom of the crate rested a leather belt and metal buckle with the large letters CS, as well as a pair of pristine white satin gloves and another set made of soft black leather.

Removing all contents from these crates didn't reveal any donor contact information. I guess I'm at a loss here, but there doesn't appear to be anything I can do about it. Since I'm making headway through the objects on the worktable in the museum, I'm taking off work tomorrow for a long weekend with a much-needed break. Goodbye journal, for the weekend, unless something really interesting comes along!

Monday, June 26, 2017 (morning)

After a much-needed long weekend away from the museum, I'm ready for some serious work there today. Jessica will be here at the end of the week, and I'd like to have this inventory work in the museum pretty much wrapped up by the time she arrives, along with a more solid personal plan in place for the coming fall. After finishing breakfast now, I'm headed to the museum to get started.

The first item I inventoried today was one I'd been eyeballing and thinking about from time to time since the day I first unpacked the two trunks six weeks ago. I remember my curiosity with the three-foot stiff leather tube, which I found contained several intriguingly designed walking canes. I wish I knew the story behind them.

Since I'd opened the leather case earlier, I was familiar with what was inside. The worktable was nearly empty, with plenty of space to set out the five walking canes on the table in front of me. They're so fascinating! One cane is made of smooth dark wood (perhaps mahogany) carved in a continuous spiral from the handled knob to the tip of the cane. Another cane consists of a metallic bronze shaft capped by a multifaceted clear glass head. This handle looks like an antique glass doorknob. A third walking cane is constructed of smooth plain cylindrical wood supporting a golden metallic handle inset with pearls.

The last two canes drew my attention most. One is made of a long bronze cylindrical shaft capped with a wooden lion's head, set with two red-jeweled eyes (maybe rubies). The last cane to come out of the case is made with a heavy dark shaft and a small dog's head for a handle-grip.

This set of five canes is amazing! Even without knowing their story they will find a prominent place in the museum. I do wish I knew more about them, and tales of whom the two trunks belonged to, along with when and where these walking canes were used. This is true for so many objects in the museum.

I typed a thorough description of each cane into the museum database.

Afterward, I carefully tagged the leather tube with its identification before taking the canes downstairs and placing them in the secure storage room in the museum.

I've grown to love this museum and feel connected with it more and more as I've worked here. But I'd also like a break from it. The thought hit me a bit ago that given my summer work in the museum, I likely know more about this place than anyone else in the world. This realization—while startling—does set me up well for a return here to the History Department next year in the fall of 2018, should I want to re-enroll. It's always good to keep my options open.

Coming home this afternoon, I realized it has been a few days since I left my work with Mary's diary. Some pages are stuck together, and the ink has bled between them in places. This makes the reading slow, but I'll see how much farther I can get in it this evening.

During the next few weeks Deborah and I planned and prepared for our trip to Boston. I explained to Deborah that I was somewhat nervous to make this visit. Martha and I were not close. We had little written contact and at this point I had not seen my sister for many years. I could tell this was perplexing for the young girl, who in her mind would give up anything for the opportunity to see her siblings again. This was not the case with me. I didn't want to upset Deborah, but I did want to prepare her for the fact that I knew next to nothing about the world we would be entering soon.

I wasn't able to get through as much of Mary's written account as I would have liked tonight. The weathered condition of these pages really slows my work.

Tuesday, June 27, 2017

I should know by now that my life is filled with unexpected events, sometimes more than one at the same time. The weather today was overcast and heating up near the end of June. So, I decided to drive my pick-up truck to the museum rather than to walk in the growing heat and humidity of central Virginia this time of year. While my truck has been the dependable go-to vehicle since I bought her used four years ago, she does have a lot of miles under the hood. Those miles caught up with us today.

It took a few turns of the key to get my truck started this morning. This is not too unusual these days. However, after driving only two blocks the engine stopped suddenly. Hearing only the rolling of tires on the pavement, I was able to coast my truck to the curb. Fortunately, this happened in a residential neighborhood and not a busy highway. A call to AAA and subsequent tow-trip to a local car mechanic revealed a cracked engine with a charge to replace it far more than the vehicle is worth. Sadly, my dear red pick-up truck completed her last mile this morning.

Under other circumstances I would have freaked out realizing my vehicle had died. But that didn't happen today. Actually, I've been thinking about possibly trading in my truck and purchasing a new vehicle with some of the money that's now mine stashed in the safes in the museum basement. I've been looking around online at cars to maybe buy, and I'm also considering taking time off next year to travel. More and more I've been thinking about hitting the road! The situation with my truck today just stepped up the car-buying decision.

Instead of working on the diary this evening, I spent time looking online at vehicles. If possible, I'd like to purchase one before Jessica gets here Friday. From my online searching I've narrowed it down to two possibilities, both small SUVs.

I walked to the museum this afternoon and did something I still have a hard time believing. From the lower wall safe in the basement, I removed $25,000 cash. This is more money than I make as a Teaching Assistant in the History Department in a year, and likely more than I'll need to buy one of these vehicles. But I want to be on the safe side, just in case. After putting five large bundles of bills in my purse, I left the museum and walked back to my apartment quickly, with a few glances over my shoulder along the way. I've reserved a rental car for tomorrow and will start my vehicle-shopping trip in the morning.

Wednesday, June 28, 2017

After visiting auto dealerships in town and taking test-drives, I decided on a new Kia Sportage. Bright red, just like my old truck. The car salesman showed surprise I was paying with actual cash, but my tale of a recent cash inheritance from my grandfather brought a slight sparkle to his eyes. He knew he had a sale.

I returned the rental car. An employee from the company drove me back to the Kia dealership to finish the purchase and pick up my new vehicle. It's really nice, my first new car, ever. I found that buying a vehicle, particularly with cash and no trade-in, goes pretty quickly. Leaving, I was told the official registration and Virginia license plates would arrive by the end of July.

I was back at my apartment with a new SUV by mid-afternoon. I'm glad to get it before Jessica arrives, but it will raise some questions. She knows a lot about me. After living graduate student-poor this past year, I'm sure she'll wonder where I came up with the cash to buy a new SUV. I'll tell her my mom sent me some money that had recently come her way. This may cause even more questions for Jessica, as she knows my mom and I are miles apart in distance, care, and conversation. But I can make the story work.

~

Deborah spent her days pouring over the booklet about the Musical Festival sent to me by Martha. The more Deborah read the more excited she became to make this journey north to Boston. I reminded her that we would need to be judicious in the number of bags carried on the train.

Deborah assured me she would not bring more items than necessary. But she wanted my approval to carry the fine leather satchel she had hand-stitched—holding the festival booklet sent by my sister—a sketchpad with a few pencils, some sheets of white paper, long pointed sharp scissors for her scherenschnitte work, and her Bible. I assured Deborah these would all be fine to bring with her.

Scherenschnitte? I had to look this up. Wikipedia comes through again:

"Scherenschnitte means 'scissor cuts' in German, and is the art of paper cutting design. The artwork often has rotational symmetry within the design, and common forms include silhouettes, valentines, and love letters. This artistic tradition was founded in Switzerland and Germany in the 16th century and was brought to Colonial America in the 18th century by Swiss and German immigrants who settled primarily in Pennsylvania."

I remember seeing some small-framed examples of this type of paper cutting in an antique store in Philadelphia a few years ago. I had no idea this art form had a name, and that it was German. It makes sense that the name scherenschnitte was not passed on to me, however. It's a word few people I know can even pronounce!

Scherenschnitte and pencil sketching were two artistic skills Deborah enjoyed and excelled in. Being sinistral, Deborah sometimes had difficulty in her scissor work. But even so, Deborah's paper

cutouts were recognized within the Franklin community for their liveliness and quality. Deborah passed many of her days creating fine scissor-cuts displaying silhouette portraits of friends, animals, and nature scenes.

Deborah learned these artistic skills from Jane Vogel, a woman whose descendants had come to Franklin from Germany by way of generational travel through the Shenandoah Valley. It did not surprise me that Deborah desired to bring along her white paper and scissors, as well as her pencils and sketch notebook, to occupy her time with these creations while traveling on the train.

This is a good stopping place for now. With the excitement of the car-buying day wearing off, I'm tired and going to bed.

Thursday, June 29, 2017

I worked this morning in the museum and took the rest of the day off to get ready for Jessica's arrival tomorrow. There's not much to arrange in my apartment, but I do want to step back a little bit from the vehicle-related events of the last couple days and go over in my mind a plan for how much about the Professor I want to reveal to Jessica. What do I tell her and stay silent about regarding the last few weeks?

No talk about what I found hidden in the bottom of one of the two trunks donated to the museum by April Jones. Nothing specific shared about the conversation between the Professor and Johnny Painter that I overheard in Don's office, and especially not the treasure I found hidden in the two safes in the museum basement. Jessica is a friend, but not that good a friend. I also want to find out from her what plans she has for returning or not returning to school in the fall. I'm still unsure if I'll stay or go, but I need to make that decision soon.

Friday, June 30, 2017

Before Jessica arrives, I'm storing some items in one of the two safes in the museum basement. These include Mary Moore's diary and the other three books that were hidden in the bottom of the trunk. Along with them I'll put this journal that contains my transcription of Mary Moore's diary and the account of events in my life that I'm recording here. I want to make sure they are out of sight during the time Jessica is at my apartment. I don't want her stumbling upon them.

I doubt she would snoop through things in my apartment, but I don't want to take that chance. I've gathered these items and I'm headed to the museum to take care of this now. Jessica should arrive in a couple hours. I'll pick up my journal writing after she leaves.

Tuesday, July 4, 2017

It's the 4th of July, but I have no celebration plans. Jessica left here for her parent's house yesterday. I went to the museum this morning and took out Mary Moore's diary and my journal. There's a lot about the last few days I want to record.

It was good to see Jessica and talk about my experiences this summer. I shared with her some of what has gone on in my life, but I kept well hidden those portions I didn't want to reveal. We talked a lot about her life and work in the museum in Knoxville.

She was especially blown away by the description of my encounter with Johnny Painter and his gruesome death in the hospital hallway. Jessica isn't sure she could have handled the situation as well as I seem to have done.

We both shed a few tears when sharing stories of the Professor. I didn't reveal to Jessica anything about the Professor's "dark side" that I've learned this summer. For a number of reasons, it was best to not go there in talking with her.

The strangest part of our weekend happened in a conversation about the Professor. Over a bit too much wine one evening, Jessica asked me a curious and unexpected question: "Were you and the Professor involved with each other in ways more than just a teacher and student? We always wondered about that. You're attractive, smart, and available. Was there more to your relationship with Don than just the study of Civil War history?"

I hesitated a moment before answering, more from surprise at the question than time needed to form a response. "Of course not!" I exclaimed, "My relationship with the Professor was completely professional. Nothing ever went on between us!"

"Oh, so you had a relationship," she quipped, emphasizing and drawing out the word "relationship." "I bet that was interesting! Anything you care to tell?"

"That's not what I meant, Jessica, and you know it!" I retorted, "Nothing inappropriate ever went on between us."

"So then, you're saying that what went on in the 'relationship' between you and Don was 'appropriate.'"

"That is not what I'm saying! Quit twisting my words," I replied, as I playfully flipped a finger-full of wine from my glass in her direction.

"But what did you mean when you said, 'We always wondered about that.' Who do you mean by 'We'?"

Leaning back in her chair, Jessica feigned a soft whisper, "The female graduate students in our class, all four of us other than you. Some thought yes and others weren't sure. We saw you and the Professor together, a lot!"

"We just wondered if we were missing out on something," Jessica said, as her playfully hushed voice trailed off.

"But, maybe, just maybe, you've convinced me tonight there was nothing going on between you and the Professor," Jessica offered with a wink and giggle.

After a short pause, Jessica picked up the conversation, "Since the Professor didn't make a pass at you—or any of us that I know of—and he never indicated being in a 'relationship,' with anyone," showing quote marks with her fingers around the word 'relationship,' "Do you think he was gay?"

I then told Jessica about finding the Christmas card signed by some-one named Maggie, and a Hawaiian travel "wishing you were here" postcard from Kaela in his desk when cleaning it out. "I don't think he was gay, but as I said, he never approached me in any inappropriate or sexual way! Yes, we talked a lot because of my Teaching Assistant posi-tion, and even went to lunch a few times on campus, but the Professor never made a pass at me."

What I didn't tell Jessica is that there were times this last year when I wished he had. Our conversation about the Professor ended there that night.

Jessica wanted to see what work I've been doing in the museum this summer. I still have a few items on the worktable to record and store in the basement, so on Saturday we stopped by to look at the Civil War ob-jects I've cataloged recently. I also wanted to show her the storage room in the basement, but of course not the contents of the two safes set into the back wall.

She was particularly interested in looking over the two green blan-kets with line-stitching that I cataloged last week. Her focus of study at the university—and work at the museum in Knoxville this summer—is 19th- century textiles, but she was stumped as to what these large cloth pieces were. Jessica was familiar with the making of "crazy quilts" from that era, and these large pieces of green cloth did display characteristics of that unique quilt style, but she'd never seen anything like these two cloths.

As we were in the basement looking around at the many storage con-tainers, I saw the low gray metal file cabinet that had been beside the

Professor's desk in his office. Jessica had seen it many times when meeting with the Professor. I pointed out the file cabinet and asked if she wanted to take a look at what was inside.

Since I hadn't gone through all the contents of the file closely, I wasn't sure about everything in it. We decided to look inside to see what we could remember about the Professor's lectures by examining the photographs and notes in some of the manila file folders. It was a fun hour of reminiscing about our time in the Professor's classes.

As we looked over the files, one stood out to me which probably didn't mean anything to Jessica. I made a mental note of its location: top cabinet, about three-quarters of the way toward the back. I purposely didn't pull this file out right then, but the label on the tab of the folder was printed in block letters: "1851-O Three-Cent Silver." I figured Jessica wouldn't know what this label meant, but being unsure of this I quickly steered her to look at the contents of another file folder in the cabinet.

This 1851-O Three-Cent Silver file caught my curiosity. It may hold information regarding the tiny United States coin the Professor told me about just days before he was killed, offering that it contained hidden symbols leading to Confederate treasure. I'll come back and get the file sometime now that Jessica has left. Maybe it will lead me to more valuables!

One thing Jessica and I talked about this past weekend was her plan for the future. Given the uncertainty of the History Department here and because of her successful work at the museum in Knoxville this summer, the museum there has offered Jessica a very nice paid position for next year (and maybe longer). She accepted the full-time job offer given to her last week.

This seals my decision. The administration has granted each of the graduate students in the History Department a leave of absence, so it seems the decision to take a year away and explore a new location of the country would be a nice change for me. I can return here to school after that, if I want to.

I'm going to wrap work up in the next couple weeks and then submit my formal application for a leave of absence until Fall Semester 2018.

With this settled, I'll then hit the road for an extended SUV trip to a place in the country I've always wanted to visit—Seattle, Washington—to live there until I decide if I'll return to the university as approved, or maybe head out somewhere else.

By then I'll have completed work deciphering Mary Moore's diary and likely introduced it to the public. Who knows what life will be like for me after that? With the gold, silver, and cash available to me in the basement of the museum, I could have a pretty fun year ahead.

Wednesday, July 5, 2017

I drifted off to sleep last night to the distant explosive sounds of 4th of July fireworks. Those blasts were nothing, however, compared to the shock wave of what I learned from reading Mary Moore's written account this morning and making a hurried trip to the museum this afternoon.

With our day of departure for Boston, June 10, close at hand, I took it upon myself to make my most important arrangement for the trip. One thing I have been known for throughout my life is the required use of a walking cane. I fell from a horse at age 12, severely injuring my right leg. After nearly a year of healing, the outcome was my need to employ the use of a supportive cane for the remaining days of my life. To make the best of this difficult condition I often purchase and receive as gifts walking canes of unique design, exchanging them for others, periodically, as needed or desired. These canes are a necessary part of my life.

*For this reason, one item that had to travel
with me to Boston was my tubular leather cane
case. I limited my selection on this trip to three
canes. These were my pearl handled wooden cane,
the ornate bronze shaft cane with the red-eyed
jeweled lion's head, and, of course, the one I needed most for this trip: the stout cane with the dog's
head handle.*

I stopped there. My mind was spinning. Mary Moore's description of
these canes reads so much like three of the five canes I accessioned into
the museum collection last week. A pearl handled wooden cane, a red-
eyed jeweled lion's head with a bronze shaft, and a dark colored dog's
head cane, all housed in a stiff leather tube!

There's too much similarity between the walking canes I held in my
hands a few days ago and the words I'm reading in Mary's diary to be a
coincidence. I believe the canes in the trunk donated to the museum by
April Jones are the same ones owned by Mary Moore and written about
in her diary. This is another puzzle piece connecting the contents of the
two trunks to Mary Moore. What has baffled me, however, is why her
cane with the dog's head handle was needed most of all for the trip to
Boston?

*A well-mannered elderly Southern gentleman I
did not know traveled through Franklin in the
early months of the Civil War. This visitor took
residence in Franklin for three days at the boardinghouse owned by Richard and Mary Rebecca
Murfee Barrett. During his visit our paths crossed
a few times. He could easily see that my harsh
limp required the use of a cane. Needing to relin-*

quish some of his possessions due to their cumbersome weight in traveling, the visiting gentleman said he had a walking cane he wanted me to have, one with a two-fold purpose. It was then he handed me a very stout dark colored cane with the handle shaped like a dog's head.

Bewildered by this sudden gift from a stranger, I received the walking cane with much thanks. I then asked the man to please explain to me the "two-fold purpose" of the cane. Offering a wry smile, the white-haired Southern gentleman took hold of the dog's head cane and smartly strode up the road a few paces heartily employing the cane for support with each step over the uneven ground, before returning to me using the cane while walking in the same spry but deliberate fashion.

"This is purpose number one," he offered, "for needed stability, not unlike any walking cane. But now for purpose two."

His next words caught me completely off guard. "This walking cane," the gentleman said, "also contains a hidden weapon."

Motioning for me to come near and examine the cane, the man showed me the dog's head handle up close. What I had not seen until then is that positioned near the handle of the cane was a finger trigger button that when pushed in a desired direction would fire a projectile through the shaft of the cane.

I was flabbergasted. Never having seen a firing instrument such as this I was taken aback by what had just been revealed to me. The Southern gentleman handed me the walking cane weapon.

"An 1858 Remington percussion .31 caliber dog's head cane gun. I have owned it for a couple years, but it is yours now with one stipulation: You allow

*me to give you a thorough lesson in how to prop-
erly employ the hidden purpose of this walking
cane. You may need it one day."*

*Guns, and their use, were not completely new
to me. Even as an unmarried Southern woman, I
was expected to know the use of a firearm. But I
had never before seen or handled a weapon of this
design. The gentleman—whose name I learned
was Mr. Colton Bain—and I walked a short distance behind the blacksmith shop, stopping before
entering the woods. It was there he showed me
the proper way to load, carry, and discharge the
firearm.*

*After directing me through the procedures
for doing so from beginning to end, he watched
carefully as I undertook and completed the steps
for doing so alone. I think we were both somewhat
surprised, however, at the accuracy of my shot as
it struck the middle of the small sapling at which
I was aiming. It was only then he was satisfied to
hand the two-purpose walking cane over to me.*

*The next day Mr. Bain departed Franklin on
the road south. I never saw or heard from him
again. He did, however, leave a small box—
wrapped and secured with a pink ribbon—in
possession of Mary Rebecca, asking her to pass
the package to me after he departed her boardinghouse. Receiving and unwrapping this box I found
it contained one dozen .31 caliber lead bullets, just
the size needed for use in my new walking cane.*

That was enough. I had to go to the museum and inspect the walking
canes there up close. I drove my SUV the four blocks to the museum,
parked in the employee lot, and used the six-digit tap code by the door

rather than my key for entrance. Hurrying through the workroom and down the stairs to the secure storage room, I knew right where to find the leather case with the five walking canes.

Instead of taking the case upstairs, I quickly laid all five canes on a small table. I was more excited than surprised at what I found. All the canes needed my attention, but I was most interested in looking at the sturdy cane with the dark brown dog's head. Holding the cane carefully by the shaft, I examined the handle area closely. If this cane is the one Mary Moore wrote about in her diary, then there would be a firing mechanism button near the handle. And there is!

Unsure in handling a firearm of this design—or of any design for that matter—I thought it best to see if I could learn about this type of weapon quickly through an online search. Using my phone, I typed the words "dog's head cane firearm" into Google and was immediately rewarded with information about this form of weapon and images of a firearm like the cane gun now lying on the table in front of me.

Reading about and looking at the images I retrieved online, I was able to learn that loading and firing the gun was a simple procedure. The handle would unscrew, a lead ball of the correct size placed in the chamber, black powder and a percussion cap secured, and the handle returned back in place on top of the shaft. When needed, the cane shank became the gun barrel. The weapon was aimed and the firing button near the handle then pushed.

I looked closely at the head of the cane in my hand. Sure enough, about six inches down the shaft from the dog's head it was evident that the two sections of the firearm could be separated. Without much effort I was able to unscrew the handle from the shaft. It was easily seen where the lead bullet would be placed within the firing chamber. I was relieved to see the chamber empty. I re-screwed the handle onto the shaft, placed the cane on the table, and dropped myself into a chair nearby. I'm sure this is a day I will never forget.

Thursday, July 6, 2017

Some puzzle pieces in the mystery I'm living and reading now are fitting together. However, I need to figure out how to assemble these various layered fragments to create a fuller picture of the scene around me. Writing things down often helps me sort out information. Here are connections I've made so far, linking objects found in April Jones' two trunks donated to the museum and the writing in Mary Moore's diary:

The diary itself was found in the trunk with the false bottom, donated to the museum by April Jones. However, I don't know how or why these books were hidden in the trunk or even who April Jones is.

The small pamphlet telling about the Peace Jubilee and hidden in the false bottom of the trunk appears in its description to be the same one sent to Mary Moore by her sister Martha and written about by Mary in her diary.

The leather tube with five walking canes—including the one with a dog's head that is also a firearm—found in one of the trunks seems to be described by Mary Moore in her diary as belonging to her.

These pieces, taken together, provide evidence that the life of Mary Moore and the contents of the two trunks now in the museum basement are somehow linked. It's likely, however, that many more diverse fragments need to be assembled before I have anywhere close to a complete picture. Perhaps Mary will give me some clues for moving forward in my search through what I find in her diary this evening.

My plan of retribution unfolded as young Deborah and I prepared for travel to Boston. As I lay in my bed that night those many years ago, the rage I held toward Grant could not be tethered. It would be my life for his. After shooting him with my cane weapon, my escape as a cripple woman would likely be impossible. I knew this as I conceived the steps necessary to achieve justice for

the Sojourners of the South and young men of the Confederacy whose lives were cut short by this heinous Northern general.

Learning from my sister's invitation that President Grant would very likely be present at the Musical Festival furnished me the impetus to attend this event. The dog's head walking cane given to me by Colton Bain some years before would be the centerpiece for my deadly ambition. I would use it to kill Grant, willingly trading my life for his.

Given my circumstance as a visitor to the festival with little prior knowledge of the vast structure where the event would take place, I thought it likely I would not establish the details of how I would encounter and kill Grant until near the time of carrying out this righteous deed. But I was prepared and ready to fulfill my vengeance toward Grant when the rightful opportunity presented itself. And I knew in my heart it would do so! The box of 12 bullets left for me by Mr. Bain would be more than enough needed to achieve my desired outcome, and also provide the opportunity to practice my aim beforehand.

The picture materializing from Mary Moore's diary becomes clearer with each page, but there is still a lot of her diary yet to transcribe. I'm eager to see how events in Mary's life unfold as she and Deborah travel north toward Boston. However, this is enough for tonight. I'm headed to bed, pondering through sleepy wonderings about what story will emerge within the pages of Mary's diary in my days ahead.

Friday, July 7, 2017

I didn't think anything could get in the way of my work deciphering Mary Moore's diary. But I'm wrong once again. While at the museum today, I remembered the file folder labeled 1851-O Three-Cent Silver I came across when Jessica was here last weekend. I should have left it alone for now, but I didn't. My curiosity got the best of me. What I found in that file today, I think, tops all my other discoveries so far.

To end my day at the museum, I went downstairs and retrieved the 1851-O Three-Cent Silver file from the gray metal filing cabinet. I got the file, left the museum, climbed into my SUV, and headed home. After a quick dinner I grabbed the original information about the three-cent silver coin the Professor had given to me just days before he was killed. With this information and the file I picked up in the museum today, I sat down at my dining room table and began sorting through the new material from the file first.

On top was an 8.5" x 11" color photograph of each side of the 1851 coin. These photos helped a lot in seeing details on this small shirt button-sized coin. As I studied the two images, the conversation about the coin I had with the Professor in his office several weeks ago echoed through my mind. I remember we talked about how tiny the coin was in real life, with the date 1851 and the words "United States of America" around the outside edge. Through questions, he led me to describe a six-pointed star with a shield in the center on that same side of the coin.

Turning it over, I described for the Professor how this other side of the coin has 13 stars around the edge and a large C in the middle of the coin. Inside the C is the Roman numeral III, and to the right of that a small O. There is so much packed into this little silver coin! And I remember the Professor's words: "Everything placed within the design of a US coin has symbolic meaning; nothing is included there by random happenstance or for extra decoration." The Professor was right, again.

In the file, along with the two photos of the coin, are hand-written notes and a typed manuscript in draft form, produced by the Professor. It's a firsthand account about 70-pages in length. For this reason, I plan to keep the file contents for myself instead of copying all the pages word-for-word in my journal. I am, however, recapping the Professor's account here, capturing some of the most necessary, intriguing, and sometimes unbelievable highlights of the Professor's typed manuscript.

When Don asked me in his office, "Do you know there are clues to a treasure embedded in the design of a United States coin?" he sure wasn't kidding!

The Professor appears to have been writing an extensive article—or maybe a book—about hidden treasure information purposefully included in the design of the United States 1851-O three-cent silver coin. There's a lot to the story, but I'm writing it here in condensed form. A man named James B. Longacre, chief engraver for the United States Mint in the mid-19th century, designed this coin and is at the heart of this treasure adventure.

The Professor's manuscript contains many details about the life of James Longacre. These features of Longacre's biography are interesting, but I'm not including most of them here. My focus is on the treasure symbols that Longacre, as chief engraver of the United States Mint, included in the design of this small United States silver coin as it went into production in 1851.

In 1850, Longacre was given the charge to create the design for a new denomination of coin—a three-cent silver piece—and present it to Thomas Corwin, United States Secretary of the Treasury. Containing only three cents worth of silver, the coin was intended to be very small in size, not much bigger than a tiny button.

James Longacre set to work diligently on the design of this new coin during the spring of 1850. At the same time as this, a longtime friend of Longacre, John C. Calhoun—noted senator from South Carolina and champion of Southern causes—was gravely ill with tuberculosis. After a long and arduous battle with the disease, Calhoun died on March 31, 1850.

John Calhoun was a firebrand political figure during the first half of the 19th century. He served in several government positions, including United States Secretary of War, United States Secretary of State, and

Vice President of the United States. In 1844, six years before his death, John Calhoun was instrumental in securing for James Longacre the position of chief engraver at the United States Mint.

Here is where the story gets really interesting. Submitting his design for this new three-cent silver coin to Treasury Secretary Corwin, Longacre accompanied it with a letter, dated March 2, 1851. This correspondence contains the following description of this new silver coin's symbolic features: "For the obverse [front of the coin] I have therefore chosen a star (one of the heraldic elements of the National crest) bearing on its centre the shield of the Union, surrounded by the legal inscription and date: For the reverse I have devised an ornamental letter C embracing in its centre the Roman numeral III, the whole encircled by the thirteen stars."

Longacre's description of this three-cent silver coin design is straightforward here, but there's much more to the story that he does not reveal in this letter to Treasury Secretary Corwin.

In writing to Corwin, Longacre describes his design, "I have devised an ornamental letter C embracing in its centre the Roman numeral III." In doing this, Longacre gives no reason why he is including the C or the Roman numeral III, offering only a description of doing so.

It may be the Roman numeral III indicates the monetary denomination of the coin, and the large C stands for "cents," thus together expressing a coin with a value of three cents. But if so, then it seems odd that the letter C, representing "cents," would be by far the most pronounced feature displayed on either side of the coin.

And why use a Roman numeral III instead of the common Arabic number 3? In answer to these questions, documents uncovered by the Professor reveal that these symbols were placed within the design of the coin by Longacre to provide clues to the location of stored treasure—jewels, jewelry, coins, and gold bars—for those with knowledge of the symbolic message this coin contains.

The Professor learned through his research of obscure writings by Longacre that the large letter C placed on the coin had two hidden meanings not revealed in his letter to Treasury Secretary Corwin. First,

Longacre included the capital C in this prominent position on the coin to honor his longtime friend, John C. Calhoun, who was gravely ill and died while Longacre was working on his design for the coin. Calhoun's recommendation was the primary reason Longacre received the position of chief engraver at the United States Mint, and Longacre felt long indebted to Calhoun for his vocal support to receive this sought after governmental and artistic position.

A second reason for Longacre to include the prominent C on the coin is where treasure clues enter the story. This hidden meaning of the large letter C comes clearly into focus when the photograph of the coin is rotated 90 degrees clockwise from viewing it as the letter C. When seen in this pivoted position, the C on the coin is not perceived as the third letter of the English alphabet. Instead, this letter transitions immediately to be seen as a crown or tiara displaying six round gemstones and one diamond-shaped jewel in the center.

In his typed manuscript, the Professor goes on to tell that when viewing the coin from this shifted vantage point, two other important features in the treasure story materialize as well. First, when the coin is rotated 90 degrees from the C-position the Roman numeral III becomes, instead, an image of three parallel horizontal tiers resting below the jeweled tiara.

This is where the O on the coin comes into play. Longacre's writings tell that the O, now seen as resting below the three parallel tiers, indicates the coin was made in New Orleans at the United States Mint. The sideways Roman numeral III and the adjacent O are to be read together and reference the three-story formally designed and architecturally balanced United States Mint Building in New Orleans, which Longacre had full access to as the mint's chief engraver.

The story gets even more intriguing, and the treasure location is explained in detail, but it is now well past midnight and I'm really tired. I'll pick it up tomorrow (actually later today)! I'm going to bed.

Saturday, July 8, 2017

I have errands to run but they will wait. The Professor's manuscript I read yesterday is so captivating, but it needs some explanation! I'm going to finish getting the main parts of it recorded in my journal, even though it may take all day. If it was someone other than the Professor telling the story, and me writing it down, I'm not sure I would believe these things actually happened.

Studying private and long concealed documents and letters sent from James Longacre to various Southern state leaders, the Professor identified discussions in the 1840s and '50s regarding the South's sovereignty and possible secession from the Union. History records that one of the most outspoken supporters of Southern independence and the continuance of slavery in the South was Longacre's long-time associate US Senator John C. Calhoun.

As friends, Longacre and Calhoun worked in tandem through the second half of the 1840s. During this time, gold, silver, precious jewels, gemstones, and expensive jewelry were donated by wealthy Southern families to stockpile in support of a growing movement of Southern states toward separation from those in the North. Calhoun generated donations for this cause through his political speeches and behind-the-scene activities, while Longacre provided a secure location for storage of these valuable contributions. The three-story straight-lined and architecturally balanced United States Mint building in New Orleans, erected in 1838 and completely accessible to Longacre, was the perfect place to safely hide and store the assembled treasures of impassioned Southern separatists. And items of wealth poured in.

Following his approach to business and design, Longacre kept meticulous record-books of what donations were made, and by whom, to this cause of Southern independence. Longacre stored these valuables within a large hidden wall-vault in a nondescript small but secure room in the basement of the Mint Building in New Orleans, to which he was the only one with access.

Spending time in New Orleans and Philadelphia—the latter his home city and location of the primary United States Mint—Longacre arranged to take in monetary and jeweled donations during specific times he was in New Orleans. Within a few years and leading up to the Civil War, documents reveal he was able to amass a fortune within the hidden and secure vault in the basement of the United States Mint Building in New Orleans.

Longacre's ledgers, containing the names and description of donations made by Southern sympathizers, were both beneficial and problematic to possess. Due to the sensitive content recorded in these books, Longacre knew it was imperative the ledgers not be seen by uninvited eyes or fall into the wrong hands.

To help keep these record books secure, Longacre commissioned the construction of two identical heavy wooden flattop trunks. A large white star was painted on the lid of each trunk for identification of ownership. A flowing scripted L was painted in white on the underside of each trunk lid as well. Into the bottom of one trunk Longacre requested the builder include a low concealed compartment. It was here Longacre kept hidden his ledger books of donations made to the Southern cause along with other important papers, providing access to these documents even when traveling.

Wait! This is getting too crazy! Longacre's two wooden trunks, one with a low false bottom, are described in the Professor's writing exactly like the two trunks April Jones donated to our museum. The white star painted on the top of each trunk—although now quite faded—helps confirm them as the same two trunks, one holding the four hidden books.

I'll need to look more carefully to see if the two trunks have a scripted letter L—perhaps also now faded—painted on the underside of each lid. If so, then it's even more certain these trunks are the ones commissioned and owned by James Longacre. But how in the world does all this fit together? Perhaps more of Mary's diary will help me sort through this. But before moving on to explore that question, here's more of the Professor's treasure hunt story!

At this point the Professor was convinced that beginning in the 1840s and continuing years after, a significant hoard of Southern separatist treasure was hidden in the United States Mint Building in New Orleans. The design of Longacre's three-cent silver coin identified the location where supporters of the South could safely deliver their valuable donations, which documents in the Professor's possession indicate they did, quite extensively. But were these treasure items stored in the Mint Building ever used to support the Confederate war effort? If not, were they secretly spirited away some time later? If neither of these possibilities occurred, then could the treasure hoard still be hidden in the basement of the New Orleans Mint after all these years?

Letters and sketches from Longacre, along with his three-cent coin design, provided the Professor with the secret location of these hidden valuables. And nothing recorded in these documents indicate the treasure was ever moved from the building. So, in 1978 the Professor took on the quest to investigate these questions and see if the Confederate cache, or any part of it, was still concealed in the United States Mint Building in New Orleans.

In 1838 the New Orleans Mint began operations. Used throughout the 19th century, manufacturing primarily gold and silver coins, mint operations were curtailed in the early 20th century and ceased coin production in 1909.

In years since, the Mint Building, which currently serves as a branch of the Louisiana State Museum, has been utilized for several purposes. It was once an assay office, United States Coast guard storage facility, Federal prison, and during the Cold War recognized as the best fallout shelter in the city of New Orleans. But, for most of the time between 1909 and the late 1970s the building sat abandoned and dilapidated.

A critical time for the Mint Building was 1965. That year the city of New Orleans was charged by the State of Louisiana to either repair and repurpose the structure, or to demolish it. If the city decided to renovate the building, then the project would need to be completed within 15 years. It was determined that work would begin in 1978 to refurbish and reclaim the structure and identify a role the building could play in the city life of New Orleans.

About this time Professor Donaldson, early in his professional career as a historian, came into possession of Longacre's private papers and sketches detailing the concealed vault in the basement of the Mint Building in New Orleans. With an eye toward searching for treasure, young Professor Donaldson contacted the city of New Orleans and inquired if he could—because of his professional work and interest in Confederate and Civil War history—assist the city in its effort to research and renovate the structure. The city gladly accepted his offer, especially when the Professor expressed that he would do so without charging a fee. The Professor did not reveal, however, his primary interest: searching the building for Longacre's treasure vault.

The next part of his story answers a big question I've had about the Professor. Don spent the summer of 1978 in New Orleans with the people employed on this Mint Building reconstruction project and getting oriented to their plans for overhauling the structure. Very unexpectedly, it turns out that a new graduate from a college in New Orleans, hired to work on this renovation project, was someone the Professor had known many years earlier. This young man recently completed his undergraduate degree in architectural studies and historic preservation and was looking for work in this field. His name was Johnny Painter.

The Professor hadn't been in touch with Johnny for nearly a decade, and Don was surprised to see the young man graduated from college and working on this renovation project. Time flies. Kids grow up. Likewise, Johnny Painter was taken aback by Don's presence at this reconstruction site. Johnny was after a paycheck and professional experience. The Professor was searching for hidden treasure.

A friendship was rekindled in the weeks Johnny and the Professor worked together. They reminisced about experiences growing up in the same small town, and about their time spent coaching and playing on the championship basketball team. Stories and laughs were exchanged. The two even hung out a bit after the workday from time to time, although there was about a decade age difference between them.

With his strong architectural background, Johnny was more the draftsman. He worked with a team composing drawings of what the interior and exterior of the renovated New Orleans Mint Building would look like. The Professor, on the other hand, worked mostly alone and spent his time pouring over original building plans and early photographs of the structure.

Work on gutting the building would begin soon. Time was running out for the Professor. Studying the structural plans and other 19th-century diagrams of the Mint Building, as well as sketches and letters of James Longacre, the Professor was fairly certain he knew the specific location of the vault room. He had walked around and scoped out that area of the basement a few times. It looked promising.

But the Professor needed to find an appropriate opportunity to explore the basement. His search had to be planned for a time when he would most likely not be interrupted. There were lots of contractors and workers in the building most days of the workweek, but nights and weekends were a different story. A visit after dark would be tricky, as any presence in the building at that time would raise suspicion. However, there would likely be no activity in the building this weekend. The interior basement rooms were set to be razed starting Monday morning, so it would be this weekend or never for the Professor to search out the treasure vault.

Saturday was the day. According to Don's typed manuscript, it didn't take long for him to enter the building that morning, reach the basement, and find the small out-of-the-way room he was pretty sure contained the vault. The brick-walled room was empty, with no evidence of a treasure vault. However, instead of exposed bricks throughout all four walls of the room, one interior wall was made of ten-inch-wide wooden slats running parallel to each other and horizontal, floor to ceiling. There was no indication of anything resting behind the wall, but if Longacre's vault was in this room, it had to be hidden behind these wooden wall slats.

The Professor then started the teardown process in this basement room a couple days early. He wasn't sure what—if anything—would be found behind the wooden slats, so he began taking them down carefully one piece at a time. After removing a few long boards from the wall, he could make out the facade of a very large dark-colored safe set into the brick wall. Amazing! He had found a vault, just as Longacre's papers had described!

Locating the vault was both exciting and frustrating for the Professor. Finding the safe encouraged Don that the symbols embedded in the 1851 three-cent silver coin and documents in his possession were truthful and accurate, with the hope that coins, jewelry, gemstones, and other valuables might still be hidden in the safe.

But the Professor was also discouraged by what he found. Don removed enough boards to see the locked vault needed a key—one he did not have. Facing this obstacle, the Professor did, however, have a plan for getting into the vault. But it was not a plan he wanted to use.

The Professor admitted in his writing that what he did next was one of the hardest, and it turns out to be worst, decisions of his life. But running out of time, he figured the only way to gain access inside the safe this weekend would be to involve someone else in the plan as well. That someone would be Johnny Painter.

Johnny Painter was skilled in working an acetylene torch. The Professor was not. He'd never used one. Johnny owned a torch, which the Professor figured would be the most efficient approach to cut his way inside the vault. Saturday night the Professor met with Johnny and told him about the vault he had found in the basement of the building, and the possibility it contained hidden Confederate treasure.

Johnny's eyes lit up. He was hooked, but shrewd enough to want a cut of anything valuable found in the vault. The Professor and John-

ny agreed to a 75/25 split, favoring the Professor, on anything recovered from the safe. This agreement was the beginning of what would be
nearly 40 years of treasure hunting in the backwoods of Arkansas and
throughout the south. But as the Professor wrote in the notebook he left
in his safe in the basement of the museum: It was a partnership, but over
the years became clearly not a friendship. This was especially true, as not
many summers later Johnny demanded the split be now 50/50.

The next day, Sunday morning, would be their reckoning with the
vault. The treasure hunters were short on time before the building renovation began, and this work would start in the basement. The Professor
and Johnny arrived at the Mint Building together in Johnny's van at 9:00
a.m. This was early enough on a Sunday morning to avoid much activity
in the neighborhood, but not so early to arouse suspicion.

For the past few weeks, the building had been a beehive of activity,
with lots of tools and heavy equipment nearby. The Professor and Johnny hoped the site would be deserted on a Sunday morning, and their
plan to gain entry into the vault would proceed smoothly. Both men had
keys to unlock the gate providing access through the 8-foot-high wire
fence surrounding the reconstruction site.

The Professor used his key to open the gate wide. Johnny drove in and
around to the back of the building and parked in a location obscure from
the street. The men removed the acetylene tank and torch and wheeled
it into the Mint Building and down the stairs to the basement. They
wanted to get in and out of the building as quickly as possible, hopefully
with some treasure in hand.

It didn't take long for Johnny and the Professor to enter the room,
remove the wooden slats the Professor had hastily reattached to the wall
the day before, and fire up the acetylene torch. Johnny used the blow-
torch while the Professor served as lookout. Johnny maneuvered through
the safe's front without a hitch, as the ultra-heated cutting device sliced
across the metal with relative ease. Utilizing the hot cutting tool like a
pro, Johnny delivered a 2-foot by 3-foot rectangular hole in the facade of
the vault, as the large heavy steel front-piece fell away with a resounding
crash!

The Professor shined his flashlight into the now gaping hole in the vault. The beam revealed four hefty canvas bags, along with two wooden chests the size of very large shoeboxes. They were all heavy. Not wanting to spend time going through the contents then and there, Johnny and the Professor quickly carried the bags and boxes one at a time up the stairs to Johnny's van, stowing them along with the acetylene torch and tank in the back of the vehicle.

With the canvas bags and wooden boxes secure in Johnny's van, the two men returned to the out-of-the-way vault room. Covering evidence of their heist, the men quickly stowed the large cut-away metal piece inside the empty vault and replaced all the wooden slats to their original position, giving the impression no one had disturbed the room for years, if not decades. The men closed the door to the small room behind them and made their way out of the building. All was going well, so far.

But their adventure that morning was not over. As the van passed through the gate and reached the street, Johnny steered the vehicle to the curb. The Professor jumped out to lock the gate. Doing so and turning back to the van, the Professor saw coming up behind was a vehicle with blue and white markings and bearing the words New Orleans Police Department.

Not waiting for the officers to initiate conversation, the Professor approached the police car before its doors were even open. With a friendly voice he addressed the officers, "Can I help you?"

The two policemen were quick, then, to exit their vehicle, warily wanting to know what was going on at the Mint Building renovation site on a Sunday morning.

The Professor showed the police his driver's license, university ID card, as well as his key used to get inside the fence. Johnny explained that he and the Professor were employed on the Mint Building project and were stopping by to pick up a few things—including an acetylene torch—prior to the interior demolition work that would begin the next day.

Looking at their IDs, the officers were silent and appeared poised to ask the Professor and Johnny to open the back of the van to verify their story. But just then the radio in the police vehicle came alive with a message, telling the officers they were needed elsewhere in the city, immediately! They jumped into action with tires squealing and siren blasting, leaving the Professor and Johnny alone and stunned at the curb.

The Professor admitted in his writing that he had never been more frightened in his entire life. At that point he and Johnny had little idea what, specifically, was in the bags and boxes taken from the vault and resting in the back of Johnny's van. But whatever it was, Johnny and the Professor would have had a hard time explaining it to the police.

The two made their way to Johnny's apartment. It had an attached garage. Driving in and parking the van, Johnny used the electronic remote to close the door behind them. After a long moment of eerie silence, the Professor looked across the front seat into Johnny's wide eyes and slowly voiced the words both men were thinking, "What did we just do?"

Sunday, July 9, 2017

Loose colorful stones, cut gems, thick gold rings and necklaces, sparkling bracelets, and dangling diamond earrings lay in a heap on the kitchen table in Johnny's sparsely furnished apartment. There was even a tiara that looked much like the large C on the reverse side of the 1851-O three-cent silver coin designed by James Longacre. They were from the two wooden boxes the Professor and Johnny had retrieved from the vault.

These treasures didn't take into account the four heavy canvas bags containing gold and silver coins and gold bars. James Longacre had indeed secured a treasure in the hidden vault at the New Orleans Mint. There was no way of knowing if these bags and boxes contained the entire amount collected, or only the treasure that remained from what Longacre took in over the years. But it was a lot, and the hidden vault was, in the typed words of the Professor, "silent now, eviscerated and empty."

With the deed accomplished, the Professor was not interested in staying long at Johnny's apartment or in the city of New Orleans. Don was successful in what he set out to do, and he wanted to return to Virginia as quickly as possible. But two things had to be done before he left.

First, he and Johnny needed to split the cache. The Professor took charge of the distribution. Johnny said he didn't want any of the jewels or jewelry. He had no way of knowing how much they were worth and figured there might be questions and trouble in him trying to sell them. With that, the Professor offered Johnny two of the canvas bags of coins and gold bars as his portion, which Johnny accepted gladly. In one Sunday morning, Johnny Painter had gone from recent college graduate pauper to a wealthy prince, and he was just fine with that.

The Professor told Johnny it was up to him what he did from that point on. But the Professor's strong recommendation was for Johnny to remain completely silent regarding his newfound wealth. Lay low and let time pass before trying to cash in any of it. And do that little by little. Johnny was smart enough about the trouble he could be in with the law if he didn't follow the Professor's instructions and keep his mouth shut.

Loading the Professor's portion of the treasure back into the van, Johnny gave Don a ride to his cheap long-stay motel on the outskirts of New Orleans. This would be the Professor's last night there.

As inconspicuous as possible, the men carried the two heavy bags and two boxes from the van into the Professor's motel room. With the task complete and little fanfare, Don and Johnny said their good-byes. It would be two years before the Professor heard from Johnny Painter again, but that story will be for another time.

The second thing the Professor did that evening was to compose a hastily written letter. In it he indicated that a family emergency had occurred back home in Virginia, and he was needed there right away. He would not be returning to the Mint Building renovation project and offered his appreciation for the opportunity given him to assist in the work.

His sudden departure was not a big problem for the reconstruction team, as the Professor's historical investigation of the building was nearly complete. He left his research documents and writings, along with his letter of departure, in the business mailbox of the project manager on Sunday night.

Early the next morning the Professor headed out of New Orleans. His car trunk was loaded with bags and boxes of 19th-century treasure. Something Don had going for him was his out-of-the-way place for storing these valuables. The secure storage room in the basement of the university museum was theft-proof and fire resistant. This would be the location for the Professor's newfound treasure until he determined his next step with it.

Tuesday afternoon the Professor reached home and drove straight to the museum. Using a hand-truck, he ushered the two remaining canvas bags and two wooden boxes to the storage room in the basement of the museum. His job was, for now, complete.

The Professor's draft manuscript trails off at this point. He leaves no information telling what happened to the treasure items once they reached the museum in the summer of 1978, nearly 40 years ago. The Professor may have sold them, over time, to help support the museum.

It makes a great story. But I'm not sure what, if anything, I'll do with the Professor's manuscript and notes. I don't care about Johnny Painter, but given the Professor's criminal act disclosed in the writing, and involvement by the museum, perhaps it's a spectacular tale best kept to myself.

Monday, July 10, 2017 (morning)

I usually write my journal entries in the evening, but I'm making a switch today. It's Monday morning, just after breakfast, and I thought I'd capture some of my thoughts early in the day. The Professor's story I read and summarized yesterday is just amazing. I should probably figure out some way to make it available to the public.

I would like to know what happened to the jewels and jewelry over the years. I wonder if the Professor kept any of them for exhibition in the museum? Or did he use the Smith brothers—Mason and Dixon—in the sale of these treasures, like he and Johnny Painter did with their gold and silver? I guess that part of the story stays with Don.

The remaining objects to catalog and store in the museum seem so distant now. Only a handful of them still need my attention. It shouldn't take long to record their information in the database, along with a location number, and put them in the basement. But between Don's manuscript that I summarized in my journal this past weekend, and the thrilling story I most recently found written in Mary Moore's diary, my need to catalog these last few objects hasn't been a high priority.

With my decision to take a leave of absence from the university for a year now set, I think it's important to wrap up loose ends here in the museum before taking my newfound wealth and SUV and heading to the Pacific Northwest. I can transcribe the rest of Mary Moore's journal anywhere.

Writing things down helps me sort ideas and set priorities. I need to finish work in the museum. And that's where I'm headed as soon as I get cleaned up for the day.

Monday, July 10, 2017 (evening)

There was one thing I wanted to check out in the museum basement before cataloging the last few objects today. The Professor's manuscript I read this past weekend indicated the two trunks James Longacre had commissioned—one with a false bottom to hide his ledger books—had a scripted capital L painted in white on the underside of each trunk lid. If the two trunks in the basement of the museum have these markings, then it will almost certainly prove they are the ones owned by Longacre, with one trunk used to hide his record books.

I headed downstairs to the secure storage room to check on this. The trunks were easy to locate. Picking up the nearby flashlight, I lifted the lid of the closest trunk. Pushing the switch, a beam of light shot across the lid's underside. Catching the bright shaft was, indeed, a large but faded white capital letter L. A similar well-worn white L was found on the inside lid of the second trunk.

This can't be a coincidence. The wooden trunk that once belonged to James Longacre and used to hide his ledgers of wealthy Southern sympathizers is the same one that concealed Mary Moore's diary and the other three books and is now resting in front of me here in the museum!

As exciting as this confirmation is, I must admit a twinge of embarrassment. Why hadn't I recognized these two white painted letters in all the times I've inspected these trunks? Maybe I'm not as good at my job as I think I am.

It seems I often face more questions when climbing the stairs from the museum basement than when I descend them. It was that way again today. How did James Longacre's two trunks end up in the possession of April Jones? Was this by chance? Were Jones and Longacre somehow related? Were these trunks used purposely by April Jones to hold the objects given to the museum, knowing one of the trunks contained hidden books? Or was it happenstance she owned the trunks and donated them and their contents to the museum without realizing what was hidden in one of them? How do all these puzzle pieces fit? There are so many questions.

Only a few items remained on the table to catalog today. These included an antique sewing kit, two wooden chess sets, and a nice soft leather satchel. After that, my university-contracted summer job of cataloging items for museum storage would be over. And what a summer it has been!

The sewing kit was easy to describe and record into the museum's database: three wooden spools of thread—one each of black, white, and brown—and four small needles, all tucked in a white cotton pouch and wrapped tightly with thin twine. I assigned the sewing kit a storage box identification letter/number and recorded all the necessary information into the spreadsheet.

The two chess sets fascinated me more. I remember unpacking them and seeing that the pieces of one set were larger than those in the other. Picking up a dark-wood king and castle, I wondered who played chess with these, and when and where those games took place? I'd love to know the lively and perhaps secretive conversations these pieces have heard over the years. Perhaps I'll explore these chess sets more if I come back to the university next year.

They'll still be here, that's for sure. And I know exactly where to find them. I loaded their descriptive information onto the museum tablet and gave both chess sets their identification record. They would be stored together in Box MQ-88, if I want to look for them sometime.

The leather satchel was a finely crafted shoulder bag of medium size. I picked it up, stroking the soft brown leather and examining the hand-stitched seams closely. Turning the bag over, four lead pencils rolled out unexpectedly onto the table in front of me. I thought the bag was empty.

Opening it carefully, I found the shoulder bag also held a small sketchbook. Its pages were filled with pencil drawings capturing scenes of nature settings, cityscapes, buildings, and a few of what appear to be statues in outdoors settings. These sketches, consisting of soft and purposeful pencil strokes, were nicely done but didn't seem to be of great artistic significance. It was intriguing, however, to see someone's drawings from probably many years ago.

Closing the sketchbook, I found its front plain and nondescript. I searched the cover for a name, date, or marking of ownership. Nothing was evident. However, close inspection revealed faint pencil writing at the top middle of the inside cover. Moving to better light I could barely make out a name, written in flowing faded script: Miss Deborah Lee. It took a moment for the name to register. When it did, I froze in shock! In my hands was the sketchbook of young Deborah Lee, and possibly the one carried on the train as she rode with Mary Moore to the Musical Festival in Boston.

Tuesday, July 11, 2017

What I found yesterday was a surprising way to end my summer work in the museum. However, I wasn't quite done. Deborah Lee's sketchbook intrigued me. I wanted to do some investigative work with the small drawing pad to try and determine if it was, indeed, the one Deborah took to Boston, thinking that perhaps I could find this out by studying some of its sketches.

After a couple hours with the sketchbook and comparing drawings in it with photographs and etchings of the cityscape and public sculptures in post-Civil War Boston, I was able to identify several similarities. Some of the easily recognized Boston buildings from 1869 that appear in Deborah's sketchbook include the Public Library Building, United States Courthouse, Boston Museum, Park Street Church, and the domed Statehouse.

Included also were very fine sketches of sculptures in Boston depicting Alexander Hamilton, George Washington, and Benjamin Franklin. Deborah was skilled in drawing and it's easy to see that what I'm holding here is the sketchbook she carried with her in Boston. It's another amazing puzzle piece connecting Mary Moore with the two trunks donated to the museum by April Jones.

The worktable that has been the focus of my attention the last few weeks now sits empty. The room no longer contains any objects intended for the museum, or those needing to be returned to their rightful place in the secure storage room in the basement. In one final act of completion I swept the floor, making sure the room around the worktable was clean and orderly. The Professor would approve.

I then headed downstairs to make sure the secure storage room was in fine order for whoever would oversee the museum next. However, I left the cash and bags of coins and gold bars in both safes until I'm ready to leave town. I'll stop and pick them up, return my keys to the museum, and then head out on my extended road trip to the Pacific Northwest. It will be nice to get out of Virginia at this time of year and explore a part of the country I've heard so much about.

Finishing my work in the museum basement today, I had some extra time to pause and look around. It's the first chance I've had to be in this large storage room without a specific task to accomplish. I've been curious to learn what objects are housed in these rows and rows of well-ordered containers. But rather than pull a box off the shelf randomly and explore its contents, I picked up the tablet and began scrolling through the long list of objects housed in the storage room, stopping to see if any descriptions caught my eye.

One piece of information I came across while going through the spreadsheet was a listing of donors who have given objects to the museum over the years. There were many names alongside gifts to the museum, ranging from Civil War maps, books, and weapons to Union and Confederate battle uniforms, women's dresses, and other pieces of clothing from the Civil War and Reconstruction eras. There is such variety and so many things housed in this basement. The storage room is ripe with objects waiting to be shown, and stories from the past ready to be told.

Scrolling through these donor names I didn't see any that were familiar, with one exception. These were the items from the two trunks donated by April Jones that I recorded in the museum database over the past few weeks.

This changed, however, when one name on the donor list caught my eye in a way that was quite unexpected. The entry read, "Gift of Mr. James Longacre." Seeing this name, I wondered if the James Longacre listed here could be a relative of James Longacre who was chief engraver of the United States Mint and keeper of the Confederate jewels, jewelry, coins, and gold bars the Professor and Johnny Painter absconded from the large safe in the New Orleans Mint Building that Sunday morning in 1978?

The name Longacre is not too common. And something that made this entry on the spreadsheet unlike most others is that it contained no description of the gifted objects by Longacre, and no date telling when these donations were made to the museum. The only information included with Longacre's name on the electronic spreadsheet was reference to two consecutive storage box numbers: JB-79 and JB-80. Curious, I headed off to investigate.

What most people don't realize is that museums often put on display only a small fraction of the total number of objects they possess. Most of what a museum owns is kept out of sight, secure and in the dark. Keeping objects away from the light helps to preserve them.

In some large museums the number of objects on display at any one time may be only one or two percent of the total number of items they own. The Professor once told me that our museum has about five percent of its holdings on display at any one time. So, even with that number there are a lot of things stored in the basement.

A finely tuned organizational system is needed to keep track of so many objects in storage. The Professor designed a clear process for recording items housed in the large storage room in the basement. The objects are cataloged through a method of double letters and numbers assigned to each container, which may hold multiple objects, depending on their size, shape, and weight.

This system begins with AA-00 and continues, theoretically, through ZZ-99. However, much of the storage room in the basement is not used yet, so the actual letter and number system currently utilized ends at about the middle of the alphabet: PB-54. The Professor took into account the likely gifting of objects to the museum and their storage in years to come, and thus created this flexible catalog system to accommodate future space needed in the basement.

My search for containers JB-79 and JB-80 was quite direct. It didn't take long to find section J within the storage room and the B row of containers. Searching that row I identified two large metal storage boxes with indicators JB-79 and JB-80 attached to the outside. Taking hold of the first box, I slid it from the sturdy metal rack. It took a lot of my strength to lift and keep the large box steady as I lowered it to the floor. Before opening its lid, I removed the second metal box—equally as heavy—and set it beside the other on the smooth concrete.

With little hesitation I opened the lid of the first container. Again, like with so much unexpected that has happened to me lately, I was not prepared for what I found. The metal box was filled with jewels and jewelry—hundreds of rings, necklaces, and bracelets—many encrusted with what appeared to be colorful gemstones. It was a complete hodgepodge of gold chains, earrings, and loose jewelry.

Opening the second box revealed as many or more jumbled treasure objects of the same type housed in a similar mixed manner. Running my fingers through the two large boxes of jewel-laden objects on the floor, I returned in my mind to my days as a young girl playing with my box of imitation jewelry in much the same extravagant way.

It then dawned on me that the Professor's entry on the tablet, "Gift of Mr. James Longacre," was probably not the recognition of a donation to the museum from a much later relative of the 19th-century mint engraver. Instead, this entry was the Professor's humorous wordplay describing these treasures that Longacre himself had helped assemble. What I was running my fingers through was the treasure—at least some part of it—that James Longacre had worked to gather and hide in the vault in the basement of the New Orleans Mint Building, and which Johnny Painter and the Professor removed from that location in 1978. It's still here—in the museum—in much the same condition the Professor and Johnny Painter "found" it nearly 40 years ago!

This was too much! Not knowing right away what to do with this most recent treasure revelation, I returned the two containers to their rightful location on the storage shelf and sat down to catch my breath. I do know more about this museum than anyone else alive. But I'm not sure how I feel about this fact, and also wonder what other surprising mysteries might still be hiding here in the museum basement.

Wednesday, July 12, 2017

Sorting through the excitement of yesterday, I had a hard time sleeping last night. By sunrise I decided to leave Longacre's treasure "gift" undisturbed for safe keeping in the museum basement. I'm likely the only one who knows its location, and I can come back as a student—and probably work in the museum—a year from now if I want. This treasure has been here nearly 40 years without recognition by anyone but the Professor. It's probably best to return these gems and jewels to where they are now and think through a plan for them in the future. Time will help me figure this out.

August 1 is my anticipated date to leave town. It works well because the lease to my apartment is up at the end of July. With my departure settled, I feel better about where I am now and my plans for the days ahead.

Before leaving Virginia for the Pacific Northwest, I have one final big thing to do. I'm making a road-trip to Franklin, to visit the town where Mary Moore lived and taught school 150 years ago. The world—and certainly the community of Franklin—has changed a lot since Mary was there. But perhaps I'll come across something that sheds light on Mary, her sister Martha, or even Deborah Lee.

My online search didn't show a local history museum in Franklin. But maybe somewhere nearby I'll be able to locate information about these three women or history of the town in the 19th century. I don't know what I might find in a visit to Franklin, but not going there while I'm in the area would make me wonder if I missed something I should know in helping fill out the story I'm uncovering in Mary Moore's written record of events surrounding the attempt on the life of President Grant.

I think a three-day two-night stay in Franklin should be enough time to see if anything interesting turns up in the town. It's about a three and a-half hour drive to get there. Looking at the calendar, I plan to make the trip next Wednesday through Friday. If I find some useful information and need more time in Franklin, I'm sure I can extend my trip. I went online and made reservations at a motel in Franklin. In this small town there's not much choice of places to stay.

Friday, July 14, 2017

Yesterday and today were spent arranging my move. I contacted my landlord, Tim, and said I wouldn't be renewing my lease. He's disappointed, which made me feel good. It's always nice to be missed. I told him I might be back in a year, and that if so, I'd like to rent my apartment from him again. Tim said he'd see what he could do.

I also spent time today with a representative from the university who helped me file my leave of absence form. She was friendly and receptive to the idea of me taking time away, but also encouraged me to return a year from now to finish my degree.

I told her I'd nearly completed my contracted work in the museum. Actually, I'm done there, but want to keep my key to the museum until I'm on my way out of town. I'll return my keys to the museum and the Professor's office when leaving the week after next, probably on Wednesday. She said that was fine. The six-digit keypad entry to the museum could be used instead of the key, but I don't want to take a chance the university might clear the access code before I leave.

Another thing I did today was to investigate how I'm going to safely move more than $200,000 from Virginia to the state of Washington. I don't want to carry it with me on the road. There are only a few banks that have branches in both these distant regions of the country, but I did learn that Chase is a bank with account holder access in both Virginia and the state of Washington. It's the one I'll use. I'll open an account and deposit the money from the safes of Johnny Painter and the Professor here before I leave, and then have access to it when I arrive in Seattle.

This plan doesn't help me with the gold and silver coins and gold bars from the safes. I'll need to take these with me and figure out what to do with them when I get to Seattle, or sell them, as needed, along the way. It's hard for me to imagine that I'm having complications with too much wealth!

I drove to the museum and removed the last $25,000 from the Professor's safe in the basement. I went immediately to the local Chase Bank, opened an account and deposited the entire amount. The bank representative—Ariel—was surprised with my large cash deposit. I explained it was from the sale of a house, and that actually I would be back next week with an even larger amount of cash to deposit: $200,000.

My story was that a couple had moved into the area from California and was buying my house with cash payments. Hearing my story, Ariel rolled her eyes at the west-coast extravagance, but also said that with this and any large deposit of cash—especially $200,000—the banking authorities would likely have some questions for me about where, specifically, the money came from.

Hiding my concern at this news, I told Ariel that I would be fine with them asking me any questions. Saying goodbye, I told her I'd be back next week or so, once the sale of my house was complete. Learning this new information, I may need to rethink the idea of depositing this large amount of cash in the bank.

It's hard to believe, but I haven't opened Mary Moore's diary for more than a week. Paging back through my journal, so much has gone on in my life since Jessica was here on the 4th of July weekend. I left off my transcription as Mary revealed her intent to use the dog's head cane to assassinate President Grant. This evening I'm taking a few minutes to get back into the diary and see what Mary writes next.

Our June 10th departure date for Boston was now two days away. During the past week I practiced my aim with the dog's head cane in the forest outside town. All aspects of loading, handling, and firing the cane went well, in fact so well that with a single determined shot there was one less rabbit in the woods nearby. After the kill, I felt more sorrow for that small animal than I will for the corpse of President Grant!

Our bags were getting packed, arrangements to embark made, and train tickets readied. The rail-master had given us explicit instructions concerning which train to take in our moves from one rail-line to another in Baltimore and New York City.

A few days earlier I had the telegraph operator in Franklin send a message to my sister Martha telling her of our planned arrival time on the

evening of June 12. Martha's return message ex-
pressed her eagerness to see us, and appreciation
for making this trip to Boston.

I intended this to be a one-direction trip for
me. Anticipating that I would not be returning
to Franklin after my arrest or death in Boston,
I made sure the house in Franklin was in good
order with stove wood and foodstuffs well stocked
for Deborah. She was now of age to fend well, and
soon in a place to take over my teaching duties in
Franklin.

I made certain Deborah was well instructed
about landmarks and natural features to watch
for along the trip, and what she might experience
in route. However, doing so I was sure it was
unbeknown to Deborah that she would need to
make the return circuit from Boston to Franklin
by herself.

This gets me back into the diary. Even in this week away, I found myself having to focus a bit more than I expected in order to read Mary's flowing black ink handwriting. It looks like Mary and Deborah are getting ready to leave for Boston, but I don't have the energy or time to go any further with her story tonight. I'll pick it up tomorrow and see if Mary and Deborah get on their way toward Baltimore and beyond.

Sunday, July 16, 2017

I spent the morning cleaning my apartment and packing clothes. I've never lived in a cool and rainy climate before, so I'm getting myself prepared to buy some warmer and waterproof gear once I get to Seattle, especially when winter arrives. I do need to keep reminding myself this won't be a problem, as I will not be living graduate student poor as I've done this past year. Once I get set up in Seattle, I'll see what I plan to do in the year ahead—maybe find a job . . . but maybe not.

~

I remember our departure toward Boston well. Thursday morning June 10th, early, young Deborah and I stood on the platform—bags in hand— as the train heading north arrived precisely on time. I made sure I had my cane case with me, but that morning I used the one with the lion's head and jeweled eyes.

Preparing to take my final step from Franklin, I paused to accept deep in my lungs a departing breath of thick sweet Southern air. The fragrant aroma was my lifeblood, but I was ready to shed it for a more important purpose. A calling awaited me. It was to be my juncture of retribution for my soul and for all those unyielding on, and others resting within, the rich dark soil of the South.

We boarded the train, and the conductor was cordial in showing us our car and seats. At this point there were few others with us, but this changed gradually as we proceeded farther north. I made sure to point out particular towns we passed and short stops made throughout our journey. I wanted Deborah to be aware of her surroundings for the return trip she would need to make without me.

Deborah showed some interest in my mention of notable landmarks along the route, but she was most involved with her artistic handicrafts. Deborah spent hours with her sketchbook, recording images of sights she encountered from the window of the train car. She also used this time in working with white paper and her long-pointed scissors to make scherenschnitte.

She was quite good at this. Within an hour she could employ her scissors to turn a piece of white paper into the silhouette of a well-known person, or a lovely outdoor scene of mountains, lakes, and trees. Of course, Deborah also spent time reading her Bible. All these items she had tucked into her fine leather shoulder bag, which she never let out of her sight.

It's amazing to know that the leather bag and sketchbook Mary describes here are the same ones now resting in a storage container in the basement of the museum. I appreciate having these, but I wish we also had at least one of her scherenschnitte cutouts as well.

This is where I'm stopping for tonight and maybe for a couple days. I'm heading to Franklin on Wednesday morning. I do wonder if the same train station from which Mary and Deborah departed Franklin is still there?

Monday, July 17, 2017

Without even trying, I seem to find myself in the middle of unexpected happenings. This afternoon I went to the museum to put Mary Moore's diary in one of the safes in the museum basement storage room. I'm leaving for Franklin on Wednesday, which will be the first time I've been away for an extended trip this summer. I don't want to take Mary's diary with me, not knowing what I might encounter in Franklin. But I also don't want to leave it in my apartment while I'm gone, especially when I have access to a secure place to store it in the museum.

Going into the museum today brought back so many thoughts from the year behind me. It's been such a difficult yet incredible time, one that's hard to describe with all its major ups and downs. I'm glad I have this journal record, together with my deciphered writings of Mary Moore. Once this diary is released to the public, I'll be the first one to have completely transcribed it, word for word. And what a story that will be!

I consolidated the treasure contents of both safes, including the Professor's handwritten notebook, into the lower of the two safes, the one belonging to the Professor. The top safe—originally Johnny Painter's—is now empty of any gold, silver, and cash. In it I placed Mary's diary. The other three books I found hidden in the bottom of the trunk have been in the top safe since I put them there just before Jessica arrived. I closed the doors to both safes and spun the numbered dials, thinking with satisfaction that by the middle of next week both safes will be empty, and I'll be on my way to Seattle.

Walking up the stairs from the basement a rush of nostalgia wafted over me. This place has been my home for nearly a year. I'm getting ready to leave now, and there's a chance I won't be back until fall 2018... or maybe never. I don't know. I paused and looked around at the empty worktable in front of me.

"I touched a lot of history here," I whispered. "It's been quite a year!"

I decided to take one final trip down the hall outside the museum toward the Professor's office. Doing so, I was reminded of the many times I walked between Don's office and the museum, deep in thought yet invigorated after a conversation with him. It's still hard, sometimes, for me to believe the Professor is gone.

At that moment the urge took me over. I had to see the Professor's office one last time. Even if I do come back to school here next year, things will be different. It's likely someone else will be using Don's office. I wanted to see it once more, to remember the space as I left it.

I completed my walk down the hall, paused at the Professor's office door and then inserted my key. The door opened with the same familiar click. Entering the room it all looked as I left it a couple weeks ago—except for one thing. Lying on the floor of the nearly empty room, a few feet in front of me was a manila envelope that apparently someone had slipped under the office door from the hallway.

Picking up the envelope, the name Professor Thomas Donaldson was written in bold letters across its center. I weighed the decision of whether I should open it. Grasping for direction, I remembered my charge from the university was to distribute to their rightful place all the Professor's things in his office. This envelope was in the Professor's office and evidently belonged to him. His name was on it. He would not be able to open the envelope, so I told myself I needed to take care of this final unexpected piece of the Professor's business. Ethical decision-making can be difficult.

Quickly looking around the Professor's office one final time, I stepped out, shut, and locked the door. With the manila envelope in hand, I hurried down the hall to the museum. Finding a pair of scissors, I cut across the top of the sealed envelope and took from it a single sheet of paper containing a short handwritten message:

Saturday, July 15

Don,

I'm making a quick drop-off stop here before heading back to Guatemala. My delivered items and a note are in the regular spot downstairs in the museum storage room. I'll catch up with you when we both get back from our summer travels.

A.A. Fax-Hunter

This is odd, and for a lot of reasons. Mr. or Ms. Fax-Hunter either has a key to the museum or they employed the entry keypad, which no one other than the Professor is supposed to use. Each of these possibilities has baffled me. I thought the Professor and I were the only ones with access to the museum basement now. And I'm not sure who A. A. Fax-Hunter is and what he or she has recently placed in the museum basement and means by "the regular spot downstairs in the museum storage room"? With all this getting so weird, I was curious enough to investigate.

Leaving a note for the Professor means that this person doesn't know Don is dead. Perhaps being in Guatemala, news of the Professor's death hadn't reached him or her yet. I then headed downstairs to see if I could see anything new in the basement that was left there for the Professor.

A walk around in the storage room looked to be just as I'd left it. Anything brought into this space since I was here last week must have been placed into one of the storage containers. Remembering what I learned from my investigation of James Longacre, I picked up the museum tablet and began scrolling through the list of donors alphabetically. Perhaps the name A. A. Fax-Hunter is included in the listing. Reaching last names beginning with D, then E, and on to F, sure enough I came across the name Arthur A. Fax-Hunter. With it was a corresponding location, container HB-91.

Knowing the retrieval system well, as I do now, it didn't take long for me to find the metal box with the HB-91 location marking. Sliding the container from the shelf, it was not as heavy as those holding the jewels and jewelry I found in the basement last week. I laid the box on the floor and lifted the lid.

Five cloth bundles rested in the box. Lifting them out one by one I set them on a table nearby. Carefully removing the cloth covering of each parcel revealed five finely designed ceramic pots with markings reminiscent of Mesoamerican pottery. This isn't an area of world artifacts I've studied, so at this point I was somewhat guessing.

A folded note was included in the container with the five cloth-covered pots. Opening it, the message read:

Professor,

These are the latest finds in my Guatemala/Belize search. Work is proving successful. I'm searching in new unexplored territory with little oversight and governmental interference.

The pots are Maya in origin, probably from the 3rd century. I wasn't expecting to travel to the States at this point in the summer, but I was able to secure space for these pots and me on a Caribbean hopper, landing near Miami a few days ago. I rented a car and drove here to drop these off for storage. I figure you are still away for the summer. I hope your search proves fruitful as well.

I'm headed back to Miami right away, and then catching a return flight to Guatemala City. I think the area I am working in now will provide a significant cache in the next few weeks. Thanks for holding these until I return in about four weeks. I'll pick them up then, and head out to meet our buyer.

Many thanks!

Arthur

The Professor's "dark side" just grew even darker. This note infers the museum is being used as a holding location for illicit Mesoamerican artifacts, brought into the United States from Guatemala and Belize. It seems Don is allowing illegally gained artifacts from Central America to be stored in the museum basement. I don't know who Arthur A. Fax-Hunter is, but apparently this isn't the first time he's used the museum to hide stolen archaeological objects.

I'm troubled and disappointed with what I'm learning about the Professor and uncovering in the basement. But what the Professor has done is his business. I'm leaving town soon, so maybe it's best I just let this go, at least for now.

There is one thing I did, however. Handling the five pots carefully, I moved each of them over two sections in the storage room and placed them in an empty container (number 51) that I located in section J, row C. Mr. Arthur A. Fax-Hunter will never find these Mesoamerican pots and be able to sell them now. I'd love to see the look on his face when he comes back and opens the HB-91 container where he left them!

I'm perplexed at asking who Arthur A. Fax-Hunter is? It's an unusual name. I still have the Professor's phone. Checking his stored contacts, the name Arthur A. Fax-Hunter isn't listed. I'll search online tomorrow, to see if I can learn anything about this person.

That's enough troublesome uncertainty for tonight. I'm headed to bed.

Tuesday, July 18, 2017 (morning)

It doesn't happen to me often, but it sure did last night! In a way that occurs rarely with me, my sleep was interrupted with a jolt! In my sub-conscious state between asleep and awake, I must have been wrestling with the question that was on my mind all yesterday evening: Who is Arthur A. Fax-Hunter?

Tossing and turning in bed didn't get me any closer to an answer. Finally falling asleep, I woke with a start at 3:08 this morning. Immediately wide-awake, I had a sudden response to my question about the identity of Arthur A. Fax-Hunter, or better said, an interesting conjecture about the name but not necessarily who this man is.

What I mean is this: I believe the name Arthur A. Fax-Hunter is likely a secret humorous pseudonym. Shortening the first name of Arthur to Art and changing a few letters and removing the dash from the rest of the name, reveals the words Artifacts Hunter, an apt name for this individual. I wonder if creating this person's somewhat amusing alias is the work of the Professor? It sure seems like something he would do.

Who Artifacts Hunter is I don't know. But I'm certain it won't do me any good to investigate the identity of this person online using the name Arthur A. Fax-Hunter. With this before-dawn realization, and displaying a slight perky grin at this discovery, I fell back to sleep soundly until being jolted awake by my 8:30 alarm.

Tuesday, July 18, 2017 (evening)

Putting aside the disappointing information I learned about the Professor yesterday, another event in my life did take a positive turn today. This afternoon, I received in the mail something I've been keeping an eye out for the last few days: my car registration and two Virginia license plates. Kudos to the state of Virginia! It's great my plates arrived earlier than I expected.

Locating a screwdriver, I attached the metal license plates to the front and rear of my SUV and stood back in proud attention. Ironically, the plates arrived only days before I'm leaving the state. But I'll display them proudly on my trip to Franklin starting tomorrow and my cross-country travel next week, and I'll keep them in place at least until I set up residence in Seattle.

Wednesday, July 19, 2017

I headed out of town on my trip to Franklin, Virginia this morning. Before going far, I realized the highway took me past the turn-off to the farmhouse where I picked up the two trunks that started this adventure some 10 weeks ago. After an hour of driving, I saw the branch road to the rustic Sullivan property. I decided to pass by the farmhouse now but stop there on my trip back on Friday. My intent for today was to see what I could learn in the town of Franklin.

And this is what I found. My three-hour drive to Franklin was fairly predictable: lots of cars and even more semi-trucks to avoid on Interstate 95. What I did find unexpectedly, however, was the large number of peanut fields growing next to the roadway, especially along Highway 35.

I learned a couple things about peanuts by talking with residents of Franklin. First, peanuts aren't nuts. They are legumes, in the same plant family as peas and lentils. People in Franklin also told me that in Virginia peanuts are planted in May and harvested in the early fall. So, my excursion to Franklin now in July is too early to see the gathering and processing of these legumes.

Still, peanuts are present everywhere in Franklin. A large Hampton Farms peanut butter processing plant is the first thing seen at the entrance to the town off Highway 58. On the edge of Franklin are four huge silos bearing the name BIRDSONG PEANUTS in large letters on the side. Wall murals painted throughout the town show the prominence of peanuts in the life of Franklin.

Before this trip I didn't know that peanuts are such a big agricultural crop in southern Virginia. But this fact about peanuts in Franklin does make an important connection with information found in Mary Moore's written account, telling that the Lee family, more than 150 years ago, made its living growing peanuts.

I probably should have taken the exit marked Historic Downtown Franklin. Instead, I left the main highway on the second off-ramp leading toward the town. My first view after the exit was not what I anticipated. My drive into Franklin provided a three-mile corridor of mostly gray concrete storefronts, featuring fast-food restaurants, the motel where I'm staying, a car dealership, some gas stations, a building supply store, auto parts businesses, a second-hand thrift store, and other various establishments. Not too visually appealing for a visitor.

However, reaching the old town of Franklin aroused a familiar delight. I write this as a young woman who has spent this past year in the South, and who enjoys visiting historic rural communities found throughout this part of the country.

Turning my SUV onto Main Street, I felt peacefully connected to this small-town Southern world. Late 19th- and early 20th-century brick buildings solemnly line both sides of the town's most prominent street. Two and three stories high, these structures stand as stately fixed sentries buttressing one another shoulder-to-shoulder, keeping protective watch over city life passing by.

Many of the building facades feature heavily painted attractive colors, while others display tones of white or gray. Nearly every building has its own set of colorful awnings reaching across clean concrete sidewalks, which in places are well worn and made a bit uneven by time and use. The town is quiet and slow-paced, so very different from the tempo of my life's recent days.

I spent the afternoon getting a feel for the town. A craft boutique, women's clothing store, bank, nail salon, a couple restaurants, insurance companies, an outdoor store, dance studio, and even a gold exchange and coin shop were among the establishments I ventured into during my stroll up and down the streets of Franklin. This town—its buildings and surely its people—is from a time more recent than the days of Mary Moore and Deborah Lee. But then, so am I.

As I made my way through Franklin on this summer afternoon, I was struck with the stark realization that I am estranged from these two women, and I will always be that way. Yes, I was now walking in the town where Mary and Deborah once lived, but we don't share this southern Virginia location together. And as hard as I may try to join myself with these two women from the past, the overlapping layers of our separate worlds will always be somewhat distant.

This disunion between their setting and mine doesn't mean my search for information about Mary Moore and Deborah Lee here in Franklin is pointless. Not so at all. But I need to remember that in doing so—and no matter what I may find about Mary and Deborah—I'll never fully bridge the space that separates their past from my present. Such is the way of history.

Walking this peaceful downtown street today, I did recognize, however, that this main thoroughfare and I do share a similarity. We each are trying our best to negotiate the connective experience linking our own past with our present and future. This was an afternoon for me to step beyond my harrowing and excruciating events of the past weeks. And, what's more, it was my opportunity to reflect freely on my present condition and look forward toward unknown but enticing days ahead.

I enjoyed strolling up and down the few business-lined streets that make up Franklin, Virginia, and pausing for conversation with various shop owners. Many had been in this town for quite some time. Others were newcomers to the community.

What was once the Franklin train station is now closed to passenger service. Rail traffic through the town is limited to freight only. The retired train depot was recently transformed into the town's Visitor Center. This now renovated brick structure was originally built soon after a fire destroyed the earlier rail station on this site, as well as a large portion of Franklin, in 1881.

This is a disappointment. I was hoping to step into the same train depot where Mary Moore and Deborah Lee departed when heading for Boston in June 1869. Instead, the best I could do today was to stand between the rails and look north, imagining a view of their train as it picked up speed toward Baltimore and beyond, so many years ago.

On my way to the motel, I stopped by the community library to search out any books or materials on the history of Franklin. This stop was not too fruitful, as there appears little written record capturing the early years of this town. Overall, it was an interesting day, but with no specific revelations about Mary Moore, her sister Martha, or Deborah Lee. I'll spend tomorrow searching out the historical markers in Franklin, and seeing if I can find any new information or anything that would support the account Mary Moore recorded in her diary.

Thursday, July 20, 2017

Today's search of Franklin was useful for a couple reasons. First, I didn't find anything new about Mary Moore, her sister, or Deborah Lee. While this was a bit disappointing, it did help confirm that I'm not overlooking information that would flesh out the life-story of these women in the early days of Franklin. For this reason alone, I'm glad I made the trip.

Beyond that, what I did find here today supported features of Franklin's past that Mary Moore wrote in her diary. Mary's description of the Civil War coming to Franklin in October 1862, coincides with the city's record of the battle. One of many informative historical landmarks spread throughout Franklin tells the story of three Union gunships maneuvering up the Blackwater River and shelling the town of Franklin that early-October morning, just as Mary described it.

Imagination is needed, however. The waterway today is wide and stately—home to pristine wooden docks and floating lily pads—as it meanders along the edge of Franklin. It bears little resemblance to the much narrower river, where on the morning of October 3, 1862, Confederate soldiers used axes to fell trees across the waterway in their attempt to obstruct Union ships from passing.

One of the historical markers I read in Franklin today also confirmed that Richard and Mary Rebecca Murfee Barrett owned the local boardinghouse at that time. While no records remain to verify his lodging in their hotel, there is no reason to think that Mr. Colton Bain—the Southern gentleman who gave Mary Moore the dog's head cane gun—did not stay two nights in their boardinghouse as Mary recorded in her diary.

All in all, it was a worthwhile two-day trip. Even though I realized in being here that the town of Franklin today bears little semblance to the mid 19th-century world of Mary Moore, it has been useful to visit Franklin and learn these confirmations of what Mary recorded in her diary. They help to validate the facts and experiences she penned.

Perhaps someday soon, when the contents of Mary's diary are revealed to the public, others will venture to this little southern Virginia community and experience for themselves this often-overlooked town that played a newly discovered yet important role in American history.

Friday, July 21, 2017

I like driving. It provides me with time to think. And given how my return trip went today, I need lots of time to process things in my life right now. In the last few days, I've had the chance to see Franklin and imagine an early community where Mary, Martha, and Deborah lived. I honestly didn't learn much new information about them on this trip, but most importantly I was able to corroborate as fact some information Mary recorded.

As I drove north by them, the peanut fields still intrigue me. Perhaps if I come back to Virginia next year, I'll take a drive to Franklin to see the fall peanut harvest. But, after the experience of my trip home today, a return to the area may not be my smartest decision.

Knowing it was just off the highway, I wanted to revisit the farmhouse where this adventure began, the place I met April Jones and picked up the two old trunks. Seeing the turn off road, my plan was not to maneuver my SUV over the rutty roadway my old pick-up truck had difficulty navigating weeks before. Instead, I intended to drive a little off the highway, park, and look across the open field to see if anyone appears to have bought the Sullivan farmhouse and property. If I didn't find any activity, I'd then perhaps make the quarter mile walk to the house and take a closer look around.

Rounding the corner, I headed my SUV toward the farmhouse, planning to find a suitable location to park before the roadway got too rough. But before I even had a chance to stop, my gaze froze. The farmhouse was gone! In its place sprawled a few darkened timbers and blackened stones of a collapsed fireplace heaped atop the rough remnants of its rock foundation. The barn building was still half intact, but all else was now rubbish and ash.

I stopped my car and sprinted over the rough roadway to inspect what remained of the farmhouse. It was a total loss. I stood in disbelief. It was hard to tell for sure as I walked around inspecting the site, but it appears the fire had taken place some time ago.

Little smell of smoke or burned wood hung in the Virginia summer air. It was more than two months since I picked up the trunks from April Jones, and just a few days later visited the empty farmhouse and met Sheriff Bullwright. It seems the fire must have occurred closer to then than to now. I was in shock!

After circling the foundation of the burned farmhouse, I hurried back to my SUV. Fishing through my wallet I found the business card of Sheriff Bullwright and tapped his number into my phone. I wanted to find out what he knew about the Sullivan house fire. He must be aware that it burned down.

Before placing the call, however, I paused and dialed *67 to block my caller information from whomever answered. I do this sometimes out of caution when I don't want the receiver to know who is calling. And for some reason I wanted to keep my personal information private in this case. I'm glad I did, as my conversation with Sheriff Bullwright went downhill fast!

The sheriff was very surprised at my call. He said his office had been looking for me. It turns out the fire at the Sullivan house occurred overnight a few hours after he and I met at the farmhouse on May 16th. Investigation of the fire showed it had been deliberately set.

And that wasn't the worst part. Sheriff Bullwright went on to reveal that two bodies were found in the charred remains of the house, a man and a woman. Neither body has been identified, but it appears both were killed prior to the fire, each shot through the head, as if executed.

Sheriff Bullwright's department wanted to talk with me to find out more about my interest in the property, and if I had any information that might assist in their probe of the killings and the fire. The sheriff couldn't remember my name (which I hadn't given to him that day or today). Since I hadn't volunteered much information about myself, his office had been investigating who I was and how they could contact me.

The sheriff told me I wasn't a suspect. Frankly, I didn't believe him. He clearly wanted to know my name and learn some things about me and my time on the property. His tone and urgent search to find me sounded a lot like I was a suspect! That was my cue, without a goodbye, to end our phone conversation.

I needed to act fast! From some things I said over the phone—and background noises evident as I described the burned farmhouse firsthand—I think the sheriff suspected my phone call was made from the Sullivan property. And it sounded to me that he took my call while driving. He could be close by. A meeting with the sheriff might not end well, at least not for me.

I didn't want him to corner me on the property. I hurried to my SUV, climbed in, turned the key, and hit the gas. With accelerating tires throwing stones and dirt in reaching the main road, I screeched around the corner and headed toward home, hoping to avoid Sheriff Bullwright.

After putting a couple miles between the farmhouse and my SUV, I saw flashing red and blue lights coming toward me from the opposite direction. As the pulsating lights drew closer, I could see what looked like Sheriff Bullwright's unmarked patrol car. Fortunately, the sheriff was probably looking for an old red pickup truck and not a new bright-red SUV.

I tried not to make eye contact with the driver as we passed. A quick glance assured me that Sheriff Bullwright was behind the wheel. His car flew by me doing at least 90 miles per hour. I didn't breathe until I could no longer see the bright flashing lights of the sheriff's car in my rearview mirror.

I made an important decision in the next few miles. Not sure if there's a way for authorities to get past the *67 phone ID block, it's probably best for me to leave town as soon as possible. I don't want to get involved in a murder and arson case, especially one in which I look to be a primary suspect.

Saturday, July 22, 2017

Rather than wait until the middle of next week, I'm leaving town Monday morning. I have a few things to finish. Here's my to-do list:

Take all the gold, silver, and cash from the Professor's safe in the museum basement. Because the bank representative Ariel informed me that large cash deposits would likely be investigated by banking authorities, I've decided not to put the $200,000 in my bank account. Instead, I'll carry it with me. I know it's a risk doing this, but I would rather bring the money with me than be questioned about the source of my large cash deposit by federal banking authorities.

Remove Mary Moore's diary and the other three books from the top safe and get all four of them ready to take with me. Since I haven't inventoried any of the books found in the bottom of the trunk into the museum, then technically they aren't part of the university's collection. (At least I am rationalizing it this way.)

Turn in my apartment key to Tim, and university keys at the administration building. I can't do this until Monday.

Once on the highway west, I'm hoping the authorities won't track me down. Unless Sheriff Bullwright can get past my *67 phone block, he'll have a difficult time getting my name and contact information. If so, then I should be okay, especially since I'm leaving Virginia behind.

Staying until Monday gives me two days to make sure my apartment is clean and I'm ready to go. I'm glad it's furnished so I don't have any furniture to get rid of before leaving town. Most graduate students don't need to move much, other than some clothes and books.

My things will all fit easily in my SUV. What I don't have I can get in Seattle or buy along the way. However, there was one special keepsake I'll make sure is packed. I tucked the clear plastic container with the 1851-O three-cent silver coin securely in one of the few boxes I'm taking with me.

I'm arranging a strange travel plan. But the more I think about it, my approach is the best one to take. Even though I've never seen the western states I'll be traveling through on this trip, and it would seem smart to visit various places of interest along the way, I've decided to try and reach Seattle as quickly as possible. I'll be carrying bags of gold and silver coins, gold bars worth thousands of dollars, $200,000 cash, plus Mary Moore's diary, which is priceless. Once I get to Seattle, I'll feel much better putting this cache in a safe deposit box at the bank.

I spent Saturday evening with my GPS, plotting a trip that will take me on a fairly direct route across the United States. I figure five very long days will get me the roughly 2900 miles from here to Seattle, with a quick mid-day stop for lunch each day. I'll save sightseeing for my year ahead and perhaps travel back to Virginia in the summer to re-enroll in classes next fall.

Sunday, July 23, 2017

This afternoon I made a final trip to the museum. I drove my Kia and parked in the lot, close to the building. Rather than use my key, I tried the six-digit entry pad by the door. It still worked. I guess university security hasn't gotten around to changing the code, or maybe they don't even know there's a number pad that opens the door.

The excitement of starting the trip tomorrow is overriding the nostalgia of this being my last time in the museum, at least for a while. I picked up an empty archival box from the storage closet, which was a perfect size to hold the three books I removed from the safe along with Mary Moore's diary. I brought two other boxes with me. One of the boxes I used to hold the four gold bars (weighing about 15 pounds).

Into the remaining box I put two medium sized canvas bags and one smaller bag of gold and silver coins. I figured this box weighed about 10 pounds. I used a hand-truck to move the three boxes out of the basement and into my vehicle. It helps that the museum is closed for the summer, so there's no one around who might ask what I'm doing with these boxes.

I also took the remaining bag of cash from the lower safe. I made sure the safe was empty, and also checked the upper one to see that it was vacant as well. With both safes cleaned out, I swung the door to each safe completely open to show anyone who visited the secure storage room after me that nothing was inside either safe.

The trip home was, thankfully, uneventful. I did check my surroundings more closely than usual. Reaching my apartment, I brought the three boxes and the bag of cash inside and stored them in a small black rolling suitcase. This I placed with three large cartons of books, along with clothes and the few personal items I'm taking with me to Seattle.

I shouldn't feel this way, but learning some of the illegal things the Professor has done and been involved with over the years has lessened, a bit, the sadness of my departure. I'm now focused not as much on what I'll be leaving behind, but more intent on seeing what excitement the next days bring.

Monday, July 24, 2017

I was up early. I had three things to take care of this morning. Pack my SUV, drop off my apartment key with the manager Tim, and return my keys for the museum and the Professor's office to the administration building. Surprisingly, each of these went quick and smooth. I was ready to go by 9:30 a.m.

Delivering my keys for the museum and the Professor's office provided me with an unexpected benefit. Along with my final paycheck for work done in the museum was a letter from the university vice president informing me that even though I was leaving town before the end of summer term (by two weeks), I was receiving academic credit for my summer internship because of work completed in the Professor's office and the museum. While I did believe I would receive a passing grade for my summer internship, it was nice to have this confirmation letter in hand.

Waiting at a red light on the edge of campus, I took one last gaze at the university in my rearview mirror. With the light then green, I was on my way! I stopped by the bank drive-through to cash this final paycheck, and then traveled west to I-81, then on to I-64 north.

I've stopped tonight in Cincinnati, Ohio, where I'm sitting in my room at the Holiday Inn and making this entry in my journal. The drive today was uneventful, a little over 400 miles. Seattle, here I come! But for now, I'm headed to bed.

Tuesday, July 25, 2017

Tonight, I'm in Des Moines, Iowa. I've sure seen a lot of corn today! This Holiday Inn is pretty much like the one I was in last night. It's not flashy, but it feels good to take a break from driving and have a restful place to sleep. I'll bring my rolling suitcase with the gold, silver, cash, and four books into my motel room each night, along with my other bag of clothes and essentials. The rest of my stuff can stay in the SUV. I think it will be safe.

There are two things I decided to do on this fast-track trip to the Pacific Northwest. First, being on the road all day I'm not doing any work with Mary Moore's diary. Driving so many hours—day after day—will make it hard to concentrate on transcribing Mary's handwritten flowing script each evening. I'll pick up my work with the journal when I get settled in Seattle.

The second thing I'm doing on this trip is to make sure I stop and take a lunch break every day. I'm staying in hotels where I can get a "free" breakfast. I'll skimp on dinner if I'm too tired. But I want to stop, stretch, fill up the gas tank, and have a good noontime meal each day. I'll need the break. I did that today, and along with lunch something happened that was both unplanned and really fun!

I stopped for lunch at a restaurant in Champaign, Illinois. Driving back to the interstate after finishing my meal, I happened to see a sign with the words, "Gold and Silver Exchange." Below it read: "Gold and Silver Bars and Coins Bought and Sold." On impulse, I pulled into a parking space by the building. Why don't I try selling one of the gold coins in my roller bag, and see how much money I can get for it?

This was a crazy spur-of-the-moment idea. I'd never done anything like it. But why not give it a try and see what it's like to sell a gold coin. If I ran into any problems I could make a quick exit out of the store, and the interstate was only a mile away.

Lifting the back hatch of my SUV, I opened and reached inside the rolling suitcase. Feeling the contents of a canvas bag, I pulled out a couple silver dollars and a shiny gold piece. I put the silver dollars back in the bag. The gold coin was the one I wanted. Holding the shiny metal piece in the sunlight, I could easily see the date: 1861. Before the Civil War! It had a stamped eagle and the letters "Ten D." on the back.

I wrapped the coin in a clean handkerchief and put it in the front pocket of my jeans. Not knowing what the gold-selling experience would entail, I was ready to learn. I locked my car and headed inside the Gold and Silver Exchange.

The store was empty of shoppers. I was greeted by a man, balding and looked to be in his late 50s. He seemed pleasant and asked what he could do for me. I told him I had a United States gold coin I was interested in possibly selling. Taking the handkerchief from my pocket and unwrapping it carefully, I laid the gold coin on the counter. The man put on white gloves, as he said he always did this when handling gold coins. He picked the coin up and examined both sides carefully, even inspecting it with a magnifying glass.

The man then broke the silence: "This is a very nice 1861 10-dollar gold piece. I don't see many of these. Just curious, how did you get a hold of it?"

Pausing, I thought fast and stammered out a story that the coin was a college graduation present from my grandfather a few years ago. However, with the recent death of my father I needed to sell the coin. To my surprise, the man behind the counter quietly offered his condolences at the loss of my father, and then hesitantly asked me how much I wanted for the coin. I generated a feigned choked-up response, "Whatever is a fair price, sir. I don't know much about coins."

The coin dealer paused, and then replied, "It's in very good shape, how does $800 sound?"

Those words sounded amazing to me, but I hid my enthusiasm for his offer. Instead, I nodded my approval through sniffles and some false tears. The salesman politely excused himself and stepped away to his safe in the back room, before returning a few minutes later. He told me that to make a sale of any coins at this high value, it was his policy to ask for a photo ID, preferably a driver's license.

I hadn't done this in a while, but for the next few minutes I became Emily Elizabeth Wilson. As my fake driver's license indicated and my SUV license plates confirmed, I was from Virginia. I told the shop owner I was traveling to Montana to see relatives and possibly move there, and I needed cash along the way.

The man made a photocopy of my license, and then counted eight crisp $100 bills into my hand. At that, he passed along another $50, and told me he was sorry for the loss of my father. I thanked him very much, turned and headed for the door. I heard him offer "safe travels," as the door closed behind me. I acknowledged his kind gesture with a brief wave through the glass.

Wow was that ever fun! I did feel sort of bad that the man gave me an extra $50 because of the fake story I told about my father's recent death. But I figure he'll make up for it when he resells the coin. That's the way business works.

My afternoon drive from Champaign was uneventful. Energized by the sale of the gold piece, I wondered as I drove through the miles of corn just how much treasure there is in the back of my SUV. But here I am in Des Moines. The bed is calling. I want to get an early start tomorrow.

Wednesday, July 26, 2017

It was a long drive today. More corn, sometimes as far as I could see on both sides of the interstate. There were lots of road signs telling of interesting places to visit along the way. Wall Drug is advertised every few miles. A place called the Corn Palace sounds intriguing, as does Mount Rushmore and the Crazy Horse Memorial. But I'll wait on these for an extended trip sometime in the months ahead. It's amazing to know that the sale of one gold coin could probably pay for my entire vacation!

I had so much fun selling the gold piece yesterday that I tried it again today. I'm staying tonight at the Holiday Inn in Rapid City, South Dakota, but I stopped for a brief lunch in Sioux Falls. Figuring I would likely get a bite to eat in that location, I took a couple minutes before I left the hotel this morning and used my phone to identify businesses that bought and sold gold coins near the interstate in Sioux Falls. I stopped by one of them after lunch today.

This time I was a bit more prepared. I sort of knew what to expect in the store, and I had my fabricated story about the death of my father better rehearsed. The setting was pretty much the same as the coin shop I visited yesterday. The man behind the counter was similar in age and appearance to the guy in Champaign who bought my 10-dollar gold piece, but he was not nearly as friendly.

I followed my plan of yesterday. This time, however, I was looking to sell a coin dated 10 years earlier, 1851—a 20-dollar gold piece—and wrapped in my white handkerchief. Laying the cloth and coin on the counter, I asked the man if he was interested in buying this gold piece?

His eyes lit up when he saw the coin. Without giving him time to speak or ask me questions, I told him through watery eyes the same feigned account I shared yesterday about the coin being a gift of my grandfather and me having to sell it because of my father's death. This time the man behind the counter was more interested in examining the coin than listening to the details of my tearful story.

After looking the coin over, both front and back, he glanced up at me and said, "21-hundred dollars, firm." I should not have been caught off guard, but I was. It's hard for me to believe this man was willing to hand over $2,100, on the spot, for a piece of metal that I hadn't seen or held in my hand until about 10 minutes earlier.

I dried my eyes and accepted the man's offer. We went through the same process as yesterday in handing over my fake driver's license as identification. I figured this was the best way to try and stay off the grid in case anyone—particularly Sheriff Bullwright who may have had gotten past my *67 phone block—was attempting to track me down.

The coin dealer made a color photocopy of my license—or should I say three color copies of my license. Coming back to the counter, the man told me he hit the wrong button on the copy machine, and it had made three copies of my driver's license, instead of one.

He asked if I wanted the other two copies of my license to take with me? I did. They're now folded and stashed in the back of my journal. I'm not sure what I'll do with them, but I don't want any extra copies of my fake license out in public.

In making three photocopies, the salesman didn't seem too interested that the license was from Virginia. However, after the sale the man did shake my hand and offered thanks to "Emily Elizabeth Wilson" for her business. I returned the gesture as I stashed the 21 one-hundred-dollar bills in my pocket where the gold coin had been only minutes before.

I hurried to my car and was on the street to the interstate within minutes. The drive from there to Rapid City was uneventful. Checking into the hotel and paying cash for my room, I had to laugh in realizing that after three days on the road—paying for gas, food, and lodging—I have way more money in my purse than when I left Virginia. Still showing off a cozy smile, I'm finishing this journal entry and heading for bed.

Thursday, July 27, 2017

Montana is a desolate but beautiful state. Towns simply appear from the landscape, and then dissolve from view just as quickly. I hope to come back here when I can slow down and do some hiking and sightseeing. It seems so open and peaceful.

I sold another gold coin today, but I had a scare shortly after that. Looking at the map, I figured I would have a longer drive this morning with a shorter one this afternoon. My plan would get me to lunch in Billings, Montana, with my stay tonight in Bozeman. This is how my travel plan worked out in the end, but with an unexpected stop before that.

Like yesterday, I used my phone to find a location to sell another gold coin, this time in Billings. After a nice but quick lunch downtown, I found the gold, silver, and coin shop not too far off Interstate 90.

A customer was leaving the store as I entered. Passing, he held the door open for me. My coin to sell here was another ten-dollar gold piece, this one with the date 1860. The conversation went much like the previous two sales. This time, however, the buyer didn't ask how I came to have the coin, so I kept the fictitious story about the death of my father to myself.

The salesman seemed nice, but not much on conversation. His offer was $1,100, which I agreed to without much hesitation. I suppose I should try and barter a bit, but my main goal is to sell the coin with little fanfare and get back on the highway as soon as possible. This I did, but it's where the events of today got a bit unnerving.

Like in the other two sales, the store manager wanted to record some ID with the sale of a gold coin. He asked if I was a local resident, which I told him I wasn't. He hesitated a bit in making the sale when I told him I was from Virginia and just traveling through the area headed west. Pausing and looking directly at me, I could tell he was about to shut down the sale.

Wanting very much to sell the coin, I told the store owner I had no problem with him making a copy of my driver's license, to check my status with the authorities and have the photocopy on file in case some question surfaced later. I hoped that doing this would seal the deal in my favor.

He seemed to be one who might actually check with the authorities on this, even before the sale went through. So, instead of being Emily Elizabeth Wilson for this coin sale today, I handed him my authentic driver's license with my real name and address in Virginia.

Finally shaking his head in agreement and with a smile, the man took my license, made a photocopy of it along with my cell phone number, and we completed our transaction. Leaving the store and driving away I was a little concerned with how this coin sale went down. But seeing those 11 folded 100-dollar bills now on the passenger seat of my SUV helped reassure me that everything would be fine.

I made it to Interstate 90, and all went smoothly—at least for a few minutes. About 15 miles outside of Billings, near the town of Laurel, suddenly flashing red and blue lights appeared in my rearview mirror. I checked my speed, which was beyond the limit, but not much over. It then hit me! Could Sheriff Bullwright have tracked me down?

With the patrol car lights pulsating directly behind me now, I slowed to the right shoulder of the highway, made sure my $100 bills were out of sight, and waited for the patrolman to arrive. In my rearview mirror I could see him talking with someone on his phone.

Now with the officer walking up to the safer side of the vehicle from passing traffic, I put down the passenger front window. He initiated the conversation: "Good afternoon, ma'am. May I please see your license and vehicle registration."

I handed my registration and real driver's license to the officer.

"Do you know why I pulled you over?"

Looking at the officer with a sense of both question and apprehension and trying to put any thoughts of Sheriff Bullwright out of my mind, I said, "Sir, I have no idea why you stopped me. I don't think I was going over the speed limit."

"No ma'am, you were fine within the speed limit. I just have a few questions for you. Were you in the gold and coin shop in Billings a half-hour ago, selling a gold coin?"

Thoughts rushed through my head. What did I say to the man running the coin store? Did I do something wrong? I used my real driver's license selling a coin this time, and I bet that's given my identity away to the Virginia authorities. With some hesitation, I replied, "Yes sir, I was. Is something wrong?"

The officer responded: "Did you notice anyone in the store while you were there? Or anyone coming in or going out during that time?"

I paused a moment. Pushing away thoughts of Sheriff Bullwright, I played out in my mind the scene of my few minutes in the store.

"Not while I was there," I responded, "I was alone. But come to think of it, a gentleman held the door for me when he left the store and I entered. That's the only person I saw in the building, other than the man behind the counter."

"Can you give me a description of the individual you saw as you entered the store?" the officer asked.

"No, not really. I didn't pay much attention to him. I was interested in selling a gold coin I had, and that was most on my mind. However, one thing I did think a bit odd, now that you ask, was that the man I passed was wearing a beret cap and long sleeved somewhat baggy coat on this afternoon in July. Why do you ask?"

"Well, without telling too much, we think the man who left the store as you were coming in is a serial thief. He specializes in stealing gold coins. It seems he has robbed several coin and gold businesses across the country, always asking to see a selection of early United States gold coins.

He's very good at what he does. When the salesperson looks away, even briefly, the thief exchanges one or two of the real gold coins he's looking at with excellent counterfeits, before exiting the store. He wears cotton gloves, as do many handlers of gold coins, so he leaves no fingerprints."

"The coin store owner realized the theft a few minutes after you left the store. He had your name on file from the sale of your coin, and contacted the authorities asking us to do a search for you and see if you had any information that might help in our investigation. I was able to locate you from your license plate number sent to us from the Virginia Motor Vehicles Division. Finding you wasn't too difficult. We don't get many vehicles in this part of the country with Virginia license plates. The store owner said you told him you were headed west."

"He wanted me to assure you that you are not a suspect in the robbery, but he thought that perhaps you might be able to give us some descriptive information about the suspect."

Relieved with how the conversation with the trooper unfolded and that it did not involve Sheriff Bullwright, I told him I was very sorry for not being able to help him more.

The officer thanked me for my time and information and offered me a nice safe day.

He walked back to his vehicle, and I headed down the interstate in mine. A few miles later he passed with a wave, and that was the last I saw or heard from him.

It was only a few hours more to Bozeman, where I'm staying at the Holiday Inn. It was an exciting day involving another coin sale, but this time also a close encounter with a master coin thief and ensuing police chase. I couldn't make this story up! A couple more days on the road and I should be in Seattle. Finishing my journal entry here tonight, I'm going to bed.

Friday, July 28, 2017

I can't believe how long I slept this morning. I guess I needed the rest. On this trip I've been getting up about 6:00 a.m. and trying to be on the road before 7:00. This morning my timing was about two hours later than that, across the board.

The trip from Bozeman to Seattle is longer than I wanted to make in one day. So, I decided to drive a shorter distance today and stay in Spokane, Washington tonight, and then travel to Seattle on Saturday. This makes the trip one day longer than I planned, but other than getting the valuables I'm carrying with me into a safe deposit box in Seattle, I have no deadline to meet.

I decided not to try selling a coin at lunch today. Instead, I planned to grab a quick noontime stop in Missoula and make it to Spokane by mid-afternoon. This would give me time to check into my hotel and then head out to sell another gold coin. I've got it in my blood now. The thrill of selling gold coins, especially the way I'm doing it, is infectious.

All went fine on my drive today. This is a beautiful part of the country. I can't wait to come back here sometime. Interstate 90 through the panhandle of Idaho is spectacular. I'm glad I took this northern route to the Pacific Northwest.

Arriving in Spokane, I checked into the hotel. This makes it Holiday Inn five nights in a row! I brought in from the SUV my personal bag, as well as the suitcase holding the gold bars, coins, cash, and the four books. Since I had a little time before the coin store I planned to visit closed for the day, I decided to be a bit more purposeful in the selection of my coin to sell this afternoon. Opening the suitcase holding the bags of coins, I reached in to remove a handful of gold and silver pieces.

Taking hold of about ten coins and placing them on the table, the sound these coins made together as I handled them rang rich and distinctive. Scanning the dates, the earliest of these coins was a very worn 1842 silver dollar. The most recent was another silver dollar, this one much more pristine and dated 1867. Many of the others had dates in the 1840s and '50s, including a 5-dollar gold piece with a date of 1844.

Since I felt a growing confidence about my experiences selling gold coins this week, I thought I would expand my approach today in Spokane. Sorting through the coins on the table, I picked out the 5-dollar gold piece, but also three silver dollars. Instead of a single sale today, I tried my luck with four coins.

I followed my GPS instructions to the coin and gold store, a fifteen-minute drive. Parking was easy, with many open slots in front of the building. A man and woman—perhaps a married couple in their 60s—was behind the counter. The salesman was just completing a transaction with the only other customer in the store, a man in his 20s, so the woman behind the counter welcomed me with a pleasant, "Hello."

I returned a similar greeting.

Pausing a moment, the woman asked if she could help me.

"Yes," I told her, and continued, "I have some gold and silver coins I want to possibly sell."

Her eyes lit up at the prospect, "We're always looking to buy gold and silver coins. Let's see what you have."

Taking the white handkerchief from my pocket, I unwrapped it and placed the coins on the cloth now resting flat on the counter. She slowly picked the coins up one-by-one, inspecting each of them closely on both sides.

Reaching under the counter, she pulled out a very large catalog, which I assume from the small font and thin pages held information about the current value of every coin ever minted in the United States. While she searched the pages of the catalog for pricing information about the four coins I brought in, I broke the silence with my well-rehearsed story, varying it just a little this time.

I told the woman my father and brother had both died in an automobile accident and that my dad left me these few coins he had purchased as an investment years ago. I was moving from Virginia to Seattle now and needed the money to complete my trip and get settled. I told her through contrived tears and sniffles that I knew my father would approve of my decision.

The woman looked up from her catalog search and spoke softly how sorry she was for the loss of my father and brother. In response I slid the coins off the white handkerchief on the counter and used it to dab my eyes. It must have been convincing, as the woman quickly stepped away and returned with a box of tissues.

By this time the other customer had completed his transaction and exited the store. The man behind the counter was now examining my four coins as the woman continued her inspection of the coin price catalog.

Sliding the large book back under the counter, the woman broke the silence, "Looking at the coins you have here, the dates, mint marks, and condition, we can offer $1,900 for the four coins. Two of the silver dollars are fairly worn but collectible coins. The gold piece is nice and the 1867 silver dollar is a gem. Would that amount be fine with you?"

Before I could respond, the man spoke up, "I overheard your story and I'm also sorry for the loss of your father and brother. How does an even $2,000 sound?"

"It sounds very gracious of you both," I blurted through convincing tears. "That is so kind. I don't know much about coins, but you two seem very nice to do this for me. That money will get me to Seattle, and settled there, until I can find a job. Thank you so much!"

The couple behind the counter smiled and nodded. Little else was said.

I asked if they wanted any identification from me to conclude the sale. They declined, saying that none was needed.

I dabbed my eyes as the woman returned from the backroom and counted out 20 one-hundred-dollar bills. I picked up the money and put it in my pocket. With a hesitant and cracking voice, I thanked the couple again for their generosity and made my way out of the building and into my SUV.

Again, as I did when I left the coin store in Champaign a few days ago, I had a twinge of regret at receiving the extra cash. It was true, however, that my father and brother were killed in a car accident. But that was about 10 years ago, and my father, for sure, did not leave me any valuable coins.

Saturday, July 29, 2017

I can't believe it. I'm in Seattle! Well, close, anyway. I'm staying tonight in Bellevue, Washington, on the east side of Seattle off Interstate 90. The total travel distance from Virginia recorded on my odometer is 3,174.1 miles. A bit long with my lunch and coin sale stops each day, but that's okay. I'm here.

I had another difficulty on the road today, but it turned out okay in the end. On Interstate 90 near the town of Moses Lake, flashing blue and red lights of a patrol car suddenly moved in behind my vehicle. Glancing at my speedometer I could see it pushing 15 miles an hour over the limit. My heart sank. All these miles I'm driving okay until I get to my last day on the road. But I hoped it was a stop for speeding rather than being pulled over because of Sheriff Bullwright's investigation.

Easing to the shoulder as far off the highway as I could go, I turned on the SUV's emergency flashers and awaited my judgment. Again, as I did when stopped by the officer on Thursday outside Billings, I put down the passenger's side window and spoke to the patrolman when he arrived. At his request, I passed along my driver's license and vehicle registration. He took them back to his patrol car and was away for a few minutes.

Returning, the officer was pleasant yet professional. He had run my registration and driver's information through his automated tracking system, which even though I was from out of state showed no recent moving violations. For this reason, he would be letting me off with a written warning instead of a speeding ticket. This caution, along with my vehicle and license information, would be recorded into the State of Washington Motor Vehicles Data Base. He informed me that, "A second warning in the next six months would result automatically in a moving violation and monetary fine."

He finished his conversation with a strong verbal caution for me to watch my speed, even on the open interstate of central Washington. I thanked him for this instruction and giving me only a warning, and we each continued on our way. The rest of the day I was cautious with my speed and thankful this pullover by the officer had nothing to do with Sheriff Bullwright.

It's crazy that I'm arriving in Seattle with lots more cash than when I left Virginia. This coin selling business is fun—and productive. But it's over for a while. I need to focus on finding a place to live and somewhere secure to stash these coins, gold bars, $200,000 cash, the books from April Jones' trunk, and the few other items I'd stored in the safes in the museum.

I've arranged four nights in this hotel, with the approval for more, if needed. Even before leaving Virginia, I searched out various areas of Seattle online, to find a place that might be interesting to live in for a year. Three caught my attention: Magnolia, Capitol Hill, and Queen Anne Hill. But there looks to be quite a few beautiful areas of the city to investigate and choose from.

Since I likely won't be in Seattle for more than a year, a quiet apartment somewhere will be fine. I'm crashing in the hotel this afternoon. I'll begin community sightseeing and apartment hunting tomorrow.

Sunday, July 30, 2017

Seattle is gorgeous, but with a lot of traffic even on the weekend. I guess the two go together. I started out today looking over the three neighborhoods I found online. Capitol Hill was first. It's a nice area, close to downtown with some great views of the waterfront. Apartments seemed a bit pricey, which shouldn't bother me, but they are more modern and trendier than what I had in mind.

I would like to find an apartment in an old, restored house or a renovated former hotel building or church. I'm interested in a place that has recently been remodeled but maintains its classic earlier look. I'll keep

Capitol Hill in mind, but after looking around I headed off to see other parts of Seattle.

Magnolia was next. Nice neighborhoods and it might be fun to live close to the water. Nothing really caught my eye on the first run through. I stopped for coffee and talked with a guy who waited on me, asking what he thought of the area. He said it was pretty laid back, like a lot of Seattle. He also suggested trying the University District, as well as the area around Green Lake. There are so many choices.

My third stop of the day was Queen Anne Hill. Of the three neighborhoods I visited today, it most fit me. There are lots of old houses on all sides of the hill, and the community-feel of various shops, restaurants, and stores at the top of the hill is very inviting. However, I didn't see any places for rent in my short walk through the area.

Now that I'm finished recapping the day in my journal, I'm going to look online at places for rent on Queen Anne Hill.

Monday, July 31, 2017

I started my day with a drive to an area called Green Lake. What a lovely location to have right in the city. I walked the entire 3-mile circuit of the lake, enjoying the clear cool morning and stopping in a few places to check out the neighborhood nearby. This area has my attention, for sure.

From there I drove to the University of Washington. It's nice, but I'm not sure I want to live near a university, at least not right now. Having left one in Virginia a week ago, I don't want to be in that environment right away.

I traveled downtown and spent the rest of the day and into the evening walking the waterfront, Pike Street Market, and throughout the Seattle Center. The Space Needle looks even more impressive in person than it does in pictures, but I decided to take in the view from the top on another day.

I'm so glad to be here. Seattle—with its sounds, sights, and even salty ocean smells—is so alive. I know I made the right choice. I just need to decide where to live in this beautiful city.

Tuesday, August 1, 2017

My move to Seattle was confirmed today. If there's such a thing as higher power providence, I experienced it this afternoon. But maybe my timing was just lucky. Having visited lots of locations in Seattle over the past two days, my gut feeling told me to go back to Queen Anne Hill and check out the available rentals. My online search of the area on Sunday evening showed some possibilities. I wanted to see them for myself.

I looked over five or six apartments on various sides of Queen Anne Hill this morning. Most of them were pleasant, but for a variety of reasons they didn't grab me as the place I wanted to live for the next year. Stopping for lunch at a small café, I ate my turkey sandwich and contemplated life's next steps. I really love this attractive neighborhood, but it looked like I had run out of possibilities for renting a place on Queen Anne Hill.

Green Lake was nice. I thought I'd go back and take a close look at places for rent there. But this is when luck, possibly fate, but definitely good fortune, stepped in.

It was a sunny Seattle summer afternoon, and I decided to take a walk around the Queen Anne Hill neighborhood one more time before going to look at apartments in the Green Lake area. After a few minutes, I noticed across the street a woman staking a "Room for Rent" sign in the front yard of a large stately house. Heading over, I greeted her and asked if, indeed, she had a room available now.

"Well," she paused, "it's really more of an apartment than it is a single room."

I introduced myself and told her I was interested in looking at it, if she didn't mind. I think we were both surprised by the timing of our conversation. I know I was! We chatted as she took me around back to the outside stairs leading to a second-floor entrance.

Climbing the stairs and stepping inside, the space I saw made me smile. This small upstairs apartment turned out to be just what I'm looking for! She and her husband—Mr. and Mrs. Nelson—own the house and live on the first floor. They recently remodeled the basement into an apartment and subdivided the second floor into two separate furnished living spaces.

They are just now completing work remodeling the second of the two upstairs apartments. Looking over this living arrangement, I made my decision to take it on the spot. I would be its first renter. I figured this place wouldn't last long on the market. No sense looking elsewhere if this one suits me!

It's near the top of Queen Anne Hill, on the south side, within walking distance of so much. This includes a Chase Bank where my savings account is located. At $1,800 a month this apartment is a bit more than I paid in Virginia, but it's recently finished and nicely furnished. I need to remember that, within reason, money shouldn't factor into my decision-making. It's my year to splurge, and this is the place I want.

The view is not as spectacular as some houses on the hill, I'm sure, but it's still very nice. Mr. Nelson informed me there was still a little interior cosmetic work to be completed. Some more insulation is required in the attic. The hardwood floor in the closet—original from when the house was built—needs to be sanded and sealed. However, after taking a minute to inspect the closet, I told him that work there could wait until later. Finishing the closet floor is not a high need of mine.

Picky, I am not. I'm just glad to have found a comfortable place to live, and it's so what I had in mind! I signed a six-month lease, with the first option to renew if I choose to do so. Six months for sure will be great! I can't wait to get moved in.

I hit it off well with Mr. and Mrs. Nelson. They seem very pleasant and friendly, but at the same time didn't ask too many questions about my move to Seattle. They did, however, need to know a couple things. First, they wanted a background reference from a prior landlord. I gave them the name and contact information of Tim Roosevelt, who I rented from in Virginia. Second, they wanted to know a family member to reach out to if there was an emergency.

I explained to the Nelsons that this second request presented a problem. I have no family for them to contact. I told the couple the story of how my father and brother had been killed in a car accident about 10 years ago. I then hesitantly explained that this left only my mother and me, and that I've had no contact with my mom for the past three-plus years.

"The last I knew, my mother was living in a religious cult-like commune in southern New Hampshire, growing organic vegetables," I offered and continued, "This rural group lives in seclusion, isolating itself from the surrounding world as much as possible."

"Plus, with it being so long since I've heard from my mom, I'm not sure she's still even living there," I added. "With my mother, you can't be sure of anything. And I'm not certain that the entire spiritual and eco-friendly collective hasn't disbanded or changed location. Sorry, but she's a complete mystery to me."

Sitting in silence for a moment, the Nelsons didn't press me for any more information about my mother or other relatives.

I gave the couple my mother's name in case they wanted to try and track her down now or attempt to do so later. But I also told them that my online searches for information about her in the last few years had not led anywhere. "Since I don't have anyone for you to contact in an emergency, I guess I'll just have to make sure I stay safe," I told them with a halted laugh.

I handed Mr. and Mrs. Nelson $3,600 cash. First and last month's rent. They both smiled and accepted my two-months rental payment with appreciation, which seemed also to end their questions. I had made over $6,000 selling coins on the trip, so handing over that much cash didn't bother me. It was like free money, with seemingly lots more where that came from.

The Nelsons told me that a Seattle lumber baron built the house for his family in 1903. Mr. and Mrs. Nelson have lived in it for the last 41 years. Their three kids are grown and have left the area, but the couple—now in their mid-70s—want to stay in the house. They thought it best to live on the main floor only, and turn the rest of the residence into a bit of a moneymaker by redoing the basement into a living space and subdividing the upstairs as two apartments.

They were just very surprised this last space rented so quickly. Telling me about my current neighbors, there's a young businessman who works in downtown Seattle living in the basement apartment. A retired high school teacher, who is single, rents the other upstairs apartment. He's quiet and travels a lot and is now back east for a few weeks visiting relatives.

I guess it worked out well to have rented this hotel in Bellevue for four nights. I'll be checking out in the morning and moving into my upstairs apartment on Queen Anne Hill. I'm excited! The Nelsons gave me the key and told me I could bring my things in anytime. It's appropriate that today is the 1st of August: the start of a new month and the beginning of a new adventure.

Wednesday, August 2, 2017

Whew, what a day! There were two big things I needed to take care of today. I got them both done, eventually. The first was getting moved in, or at least shifting boxes from my SUV up the stairs and into the apartment. There's space for me to park off the alley in back, right by the stairs. It didn't take too many trips climbing them to carry in what few things I brought from Virginia.

Thankfully, my apartment is furnished so I don't have any large items to buy and lug up the stairs. I'll unpack my boxes tomorrow. I did go to a bedding shop this afternoon and got some sheets, pillows, pillowcases, and a couple blankets. I also stopped by a hardware store to purchase some cleaning supplies and household essentials. I'll figure out more of what I need as I get settled in.

After this I headed to the local Chase Bank a few blocks away. I talked to a representative (Barb) about my trip to Seattle, giving her my new local address and asking what it takes to have access to my bank account after my cross-country move. "There's nothing you need to do," she replied, "as long as you have your account number there shouldn't be any problem accessing your funds." And there wasn't. I'm all set.

I then asked Barb about renting a safe deposit box at the bank. She said the process was easy. All I needed was to show a photo ID—my driver's license would do—fill out a short application and pay the fee, which was $70-$100 a year depending on the size of the box rented. It sounded simple.

But there was a problem. No safe deposit boxes are currently available at the bank. Barb said the boxes are in high demand for some reason, but perhaps one might come open in a few months. When I told her that I really needed to rent a box to keep some valuables in right away, she suggested I try up the street a couple blocks. On the same side of the street there's a small local bank that she knows has some safe deposit boxes. She wasn't sure if any of them are available for rent now, but it would be worth a try. After leaving Chase Bank I headed up the street, scanning business signs for the bank Barb had suggested.

There it was a few blocks ahead. Seeing the bank building, some shops and a restaurant in that direction—but across the street—also caught my eye. Crossing the street and heading toward them I walked past a jewelry store window displaying gold necklaces, colorful bracelets, and expensive watches.

Pausing at the storefront, I opened the door and stepped inside. I asked the lady behind the counter if they bought gold coins, thinking it might be a good place to sell some of mine. The lady was nice in her response, but she told me they buy and sell only jewelry and fine watches, not coins. I was disappointed, but I figure there are probably lots of places for me to sell gold and silver coins in Seattle.

Entering the jewelry store brought with it something I didn't anticipate. Stepping inside the small shop unexpectedly re-charged me with the same rush of adrenaline I've experienced as Emily Elizabeth Wilson, selling gold and silver coins to people who believed my contrived and rehearsed stories about the death of my father and the need to sell some coins. Telling those stories and getting the payment that goes with them is captivating!

I left the jewelry store and walked back across the street to the bank where I wanted to try and rent a safe deposit box. Doing so, I had another spur-of-the-moment idea. Why not be Emily Elizabeth Wilson for a few minutes again this afternoon? Barb said all I needed to show in renting a safe deposit box was a driver's license, and Emily Elizabeth Wilson has one. So that's what I did.

The man at the bank desk was friendly and helpful. Handing me his business card I saw that his name was Daniel James. I told Mr. James that I had just moved to Seattle from out of state and would like to rent a safe deposit box to store some valuables as soon as I could do so. I assured Mr. James I would give the bank my updated contact information and set up a bank account there, once I got settled.

He accepted that. I filled out the paperwork using the name Emily Elizabeth Wilson, showed him my fake driver's license with the same name, paid him $100 (cash) to rent a box—the biggest they had—for a year, and told him I would be back soon with my valuables to put in the lockbox. He thanked me, shook my hand, and that was it!

It was late afternoon by the time I finished these errands and got back to my apartment. I unpacked a few essentials for the first night's stay in my new apartment, before making this entry of the day in my journal.

It's exciting to be here and starting a new adventure. But it's time soon to change gears and get to work with Mary Moore's diary. It will be my focus once I get unpacked and settled, until my transcribing of her story is complete.

Thursday, August 3, 2017

I think it was the baseball player Yogi Berra who coined the phrase, "It's like déjà vu all over again." It's redundant, I know, but I sure had one of those déjà vu experiences today. Unpacking my few possessions was first on the agenda this morning. I bought some plastic hangers at the hardware store yesterday and used them to hang up the limited number of fairly nice things I have in the closet. I stowed the rest of my clothes in the dresser drawers.

One thing I'm missing in my apartment is a bookcase or two. Ironically, this is the piece of furniture I need most of all, as my books, a few clothes, and some kitchen supplies are about all I brought with me. I also want a TV. I figure I can put off making these purchases until I find where best to buy them. Perhaps the Nelsons can help me with that. I'll ask them.

Until then I decided to store my three heavy boxes of books in the closet. The first two containers went in just fine, but as I put the third box on the closet floor, I heard a hollow thud. The sound this box made was different from when I set the first two boxes on the floor.

The vacant-sounding reverberation coming from under the floor in the closet brought back memories of what I heard when tapping the inside of April Jones' trunk in the museum a couple months ago. That space in the trunk contained four hidden books. I wondered now if there could be something concealed in what seems to be a hollow space under the wood floor in my closet?

I moved the three boxes of books back out of the closet. Turning on the overhead light and resting on my hands and knees, I grabbed my phone and turned on its flashlight. Following the intense light I carefully inspected the unfinished hardwood closet floor. Tapping the floorboards periodically, I could make out differences in the sounds produced in various locations.

Feeling with my fingers along the edge of the wood flooring, in the bright flashlight beam I made out the slightly uneven edge of some adjoining hardwood floorboards. Inserting the blade of a sharp kitchen knife into the paper-thin space between two adjacent boards in the closet floor, I pried up a section of wood flooring, about 15 inches square. It lifted up easier than I expected.

Shining my light into the space below the closet floor showed it to be about ten inches deep. Staring into the square opening, my flashlight revealed it to be completely empty. I inspected the space carefully. Nothing was there. Not even cobwebs.

At least that's what I thought at first look. Staying on my hands and knees, I knelt low and shined my light deep into the space between the two parallel wooden joists that supported the closet flooring. This opening toward the rest of the house extended far beyond where the light from my phone could penetrate. But as I experienced when shining the flashlight into the Professor's open safe in the museum basement and was greeted with a brilliant reflection from gold bars weeks ago, here in the space below the closet floor, the light from my phone, shining into the dark extended space, reflected back!

Peering deep into the recess, the beam from my phone showed something shiny resting about 18 inches into the darkness. I was determined to find out what it was. Using the broom I bought yesterday, I grabbed the handle and slid it carefully back into the space and gently positioned the bristle end just beyond the object I could barely see under the flooring. I then pulled the broom back toward me slowly.

An object emerged into the light. It was not the flash of gold bars that caught my eye this time. Instead, what I retrieved from the space under my closet floor was a quart-sized clear glass Mason jar with a metal lid.

Picking up the glass jar, I carried it over to my bed and sat down. I turned the jar completely around and inspected its contents through the glass. There was not much to see. Unscrewing the lid, I removed and carefully unfolded a somewhat brittle piece of white paper that contained the following handwritten words:

My Time Capsule
Monday, March 24, 1913

The Boston Red Sox won the World Series last fall 4 games to 3. One game tied.
Mr. Woodrow Wilson just became President of the United States.

I have a red dog named Rusty.
My daddy built this secret hiding place under the floor of my closet.
It rains a lot in Seattle.
I hope someone finds this jar and reads this paper someday.

Yours truly,
Stephen (I am 8 years old)
P.S. Here is a shiny new half-dollar my daddy gave me to put in the jar.

The writing was clearly done by a child. But even so, it was much easier to read than the flowing handwriting of Mary Moore. The half-dollar in the jar was still shiny. Holding it in the light I could easily see the coin was in nice condition with a date 1913 and an S, indicating the San Francisco mint, just below it. This jar and its contents look to have been hidden in this location under the floorboards of the closet for more than 100 years.

This single silver coin likely isn't worth as much as the hoard of gold and silver I uncovered in the two safes in the museum basement. Yet, it is a special find all its own. I carefully folded the paper and put it back in the jar, along with the half-dollar. Setting the jar on the top of my dresser I wondered about Stephen and the life he lived in Seattle, and perhaps beyond. I'll see if I can learn anything about a boy named Stephen that lived in this house in 1913, once I get settled in. But that search will have to wait until I'm done transcribing Mary's diary.

Friday, August 4, 2017

This morning, I made a return trip to the bank and put several items in the safe deposit box I rented there on Wednesday. I'm glad I selected a large box. Mr. James, the bank assistant I met the day before yesterday, was not working today. I signed the entry log Emily Elizabeth Wilson—which allowed me entrance to my safety box—and handed the bank attendant my key. It was simple and smooth. For my reference, this is what I put in the safe deposit box today:

- 2 canvas bags of gold and silver coins
- 1 bag containing 4 gold bars (each bar weighing about 4 lbs.)
- A bag with $200,000 cash
- 3 books found in the bottom of the trunk (but not Mary Moore's diary)
- The Professor's phone
- Sheriff Bullwright's business card
- The notebook with information about the treasure, written by the Professor and left in his safe in the museum's secure storage room
- The file with information about the 1851-O three-cent silver coin, along with the Professor's 70-page typed manuscript about searching for and finding treasure in the United States Mint Building in New Orleans in 1978.
- The 1851-O three-cent silver coin, in its clear plastic holder.

These all fit in the safe deposit box, just barely, and I feel much better they are out of my apartment and now in this secure location in the bank.

Before putting them in the bank box, I went through one of the canvas bags and took out 20 gold and silver coins. I put these coins in a separate leather bag in my apartment. I'm going to travel around Seattle and try selling these coins, one or two at a time, to various gold and coin businesses whenever I need cash. It's going to be an exciting and easy way to make a living this year. And, I have two canvas bags in my bank box that hold lots more coins when I need them.

It's been a long time since I did any work with Mary Moore's diary. I checked. 20 days, to be exact. Thumbing back through the pages of my journal, it's amazing to see all that's gone on since I last read and recorded the flowing handwritten words of Mary Moore. When I left off, Mary and Deborah Lee were on the first day of their train trip to Baltimore, and then on toward New York City and Boston. It may take some time and focus to get back into deciphering Mary's flowing handwriting, but I'm giving it a return this evening.

~

The train trip north was, for the most part, un-eventful. However, I remember even now, some 20 years later, that Deborah and I sat sadly silent as we observed a multitude of eviscerated buildings left from the War as our train rumbled past. In many places, what were once finely built homes and business establishments now sat in anguished rubble. Tall pine forests that in earlier days smelled sweet bordering the railway line, now lay splintered and decaying along the tracks.

It was often clear the rails had recently been re-laid, after the destruction of war had taken its toll. The lives lost and others ruined, and the tears shed in response, can never be fully num-bered. Even today, decades later, the harsh and ingrained reality of the nation's violent conflict ignites brightly in Southern hearts as an un-extin-guished ember.

Deborah worked on her scherenschnitte as best she could. It was difficult for her to maneuver the scissors through the paper as carefully as she would have liked, due to periodic jarring of the train on the rails. Deborah was more satisfied with the drawings she made. Much of her time was spent at the windows of the train car, watch-ing and sketching sights as we passed.

Deborah and I changed trains in Baltimore. As recommended by the rail-master, I purchased a spot in a sleeping car for the second tract of this three-day trip. This sleeping arrangement as we relocated to a new train car was perfect advice and timing, as it was getting dark when Debo-rah and I boarded the train for New York City. I remember we each slept soundly that night.

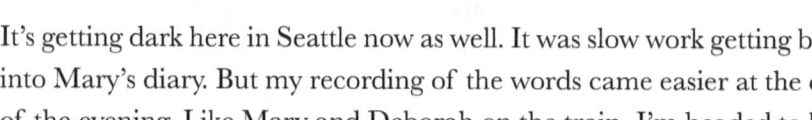

It's getting dark here in Seattle now as well. It was slow work getting back into Mary's diary. But my recording of the words came easier at the end of the evening. Like Mary and Deborah on the train, I'm headed to bed in hopes I will sleep soundly tonight as well.

Saturday, August 5, 2017

My move-in is now nearly complete. I spent most of today shopping for items I need: 2 bookcases, some pictures for my wall, pots, pans, a few kitchen supplies, and a small blue throw rug to cover the rough wood over the secret space under the floor of my closet.

I also made a stop at the grocery store. And I bought a 42-inch TV! It's fun to see the look on people's faces when I lay down multiple $100 bills for what I buy! But these purchases I made today reduced my cash on hand.

My bank account is fine, but it's time for a gold coin sale. It's a fun activity I look forward to. I used my phone to look up some coin and gold shops in Seattle and the surrounding area. There are a lot. I picked out a couple. One I hope will work fine. The second one is a backup, if needed. I plan to start my coin sales in Seattle by selecting two gold coins. But I'll have to wait until next week. Tomorrow is Sunday and the shops are closed.

It's a wonderfully warm August Saturday evening. And it's strange to think that I literally know no one within 2,000 miles. But it's not as if I left a lot of friends behind in Virginia.

I guess I've always been somewhat of a loner. I wasn't an only child, but I might as well have been that way through my teenage years, with my brother and father being killed when I was 13. Mom wasn't much help through those days. But she had her own issues of loneliness and grief to deal with. Mom and I just never clicked. Mothers and daughters are like that sometimes.

Rather than work on the diary tonight, I'm going out to explore the neighborhood. Saturday night in a new city is made for that.

Sunday, August 6, 2017

I had dinner at a café at the top of the hill a few blocks away last night. After dessert I walked down Queen Anne Hill toward the Seattle Center. One of the large water-jet fountains in the park was turned on. Soft colored lights pulsating through the cool spray and the sound of splashing water on the stonework below were refreshing. I soaked in the sensory experience, pinching myself to make sure all this was real.

I struck up a conversation with a couple sitting by the fountain, but before long we parted ways. The walk up Queen Anne Hill toward my apartment was steep and took longer than it did coming down a few hours earlier. But I made it back to my apartment about midnight and fell right to sleep.

I'm doing something this afternoon I haven't done in all my time transcribing Mary's written record. I'm taking her diary outside to work on it there. Summer afternoons are so nice in the Pacific Northwest. Mr. Nelson put a picnic table and bench on the patio by the back stairs. It's quiet, warm, and inviting. Enjoying this setting, I'm looking forward to seeing what Mary recorded in her diary next.

Along with her pencil sketching and scheren-schnitte, Deborah spent time on the train reading her thick black Bible. This was not uncommon for her. At one point on the second day of our trip, Deborah wanted to know if I was familiar with the biblical account of a man named Ehud? I told

Deborah I'd never heard of him, but I asked her to tell me who Ehud was and why his story was in the Bible.

In response, Deborah inquired whether I remembered her telling me how she and her brothers got their names: Gideon, Samson, and Deborah. I told her I did recall that these three names were given by her parents—Joshua and Ruth—in naming their children after Hebrew judges recorded in the Bible's Old Testament, all of them in the book of Judges.

Deborah was pleased and surprised that I remembered this story. She then told me that Ehud was another Hebrew Judge whose account was told in the biblical book of Judges. She went on to explain about Ehud.

Deborah recounted the tale from the Bible in quite dramatic fashion. Ehud was an Israelite leader identified in the book of Judges—Chapter 3—as the person who carried a large extortion payment from the people of Israel to the hated and oppressive Moabite king, Eglon. This tribute money was handed over by Ehud to Eglon at the king's summer palace in the city of Jericho.

After bringing the money to King Eglon, Ehud tricked the king's attendants into giving Ehud a few minutes of private conversation with Eglon. Doing so, the left-handed Ehud extracted a hidden double-edged dagger strapped to his right thigh and plunged it deep into the midsection of King Eglon. With this, Ehud killed the Moabite king in retribution for his actions toward the Israelites, and escaped beyond the city walls before the attendants realized that Eglon was dead.

Ehud and his then assembled Israelite army regarded the killing of King Eglon as a call to action. In so doing, Ehud gathered a fighting force that slayed 10,000 Moabites and the Israelites took back their land.

Deborah finished her account, reciting that after this overthrow of the oppressive hated leader, "The land had peace for eighty years."

I thought this to be a somewhat strange tale for young Deborah to dwell on and tell me about. Yet, it was in keeping with other stories about Hebrew judges, which were some of her favorites and served as motivation for her parents choosing names for Deborah and her two brothers.

This is an odd story, but a good stopping spot for this evening. The black Bible I found in the bottom space of the trunk is now locked away in the safe deposit box. If not, I'd go get it and read the story of Ehud and Eglon for myself. I'll get to that sometime.

Monday, August 7, 2017

Today was the day to get my cash supply restocked. I did this, but sure ended up with way more than I bargained for. After getting dressed and ready for the day, I scanned my phone for the location of the two coin stores I had in mind to visit this morning. I was hoping to stop at only one, but I had a back-up location ready if there was a problem with the first one.

I retrieved the small bag of gold and silver coins from my top dresser drawer, and pulled out two that would be my points of sale today. I selected two 10-dollar gold pieces: one dated 1856 and the other 1858.

The coins were very shiny with little wear. I could feel my anticipation of a sale build.

The map on my phone got me to the first coin store just fine. The business looked well-kept from the outside, but I could also see that it presented a situation I hadn't encountered in my previous coin sales: no easy access parking. In each place I'd stopped to sell coins on my cross-country journey there was plenty of parking in a lot nearby. Here, in downtown Seattle, parking was limited to garages or to the street.

After driving around a bit, I found a parking spot by the curb a couple blocks from the coin shop. This was fine, but it was also where my real adventure began today. Walking down the sidewalk to the store, I felt my front jeans pocket to make sure my white folded handkerchief and the two gold coins it contained were still in place.

Sure enough, they were there. Entering the coin store, a few customers were browsing and peering into glass cases at the many coins for sale. I modeled their actions for a few minutes, looking intently at the coins resting beyond the glass. A man behind the counter asked if he could help me find anything, to which I replied, "Maybe in a few minutes. I'm just looking for now, thanks."

This was my delay tactic. I was hoping that the people in the store would leave soon, and I could have the coin dealer to myself, to recite to him my standard hard-luck story about the death of my father and the need to sell my gold coins. And that is what happened after about 10 minutes. I was then the lone customer in the store.

I approached the man behind the counter and asked if he was interested in buying two old United States gold coins. He said that he might, but would certainly like to see what I had for sale. With that, I took the handkerchief out of my pocket and laid it on the counter, unfolding it and placing the gold coins on top. The excitement of the sales process was coming back to me now!

The man was silent as he examined my first gold coin—the one dated 1856—carefully, front and back, before laying it on the white handkerchief. The second coin he examined was the one that grabbed his attention.

Before even touching this second coin, the salesman reached below the counter and took out a pair of white cotton gloves. Putting them on, he then spent the next few minutes using a small magnifying glass to scrutinize the coin. After looking it over several times, front and back, the man raised up and stared at me intently for a few seconds before asking, "Young lady, do you know what you have here?"

To his question, I gave the man my standard line of response: "I don't know too much about coins."

"Just so you know," the man breathed out, "this 1858 coin is worth about $14,000. Where did you get it? Gold like this is very difficult to come by, especially brought in by someone I don't know off the street."

Before I could answer, the man said that buying this coin would require some paperwork and a bank transfer of funds. "I don't keep that kind of money in my safe."

After he finally paused, I haltingly told the man my story about the death of my father and the need for me to sell the coin to pay for his expenses. But in my flustered condition I could tell I didn't do a very good job convincing him.

My immediate thought was to pick my two coins up and leave the store right away. I needed some time to sort out what to do with this coin worth $14,000! Finally, I blurted out, "I'm not sure I want to sell it right now, after all. Maybe I'll come back later after I give it more thought."

He shrugged at my response but eyeballed me carefully. He did go on to say, "That's your call. Coins like this don't come around too often, so I would be interested in buying it if you ever do want to sell it."

The man then reached below the counter and pulled out two sides of a hard clear plastic 2" x 2" container that could be snapped together. He asked if he could put this gold coin into the plastic holder to keep it from being handled and scratched. I agreed and offered to pay him for the coin holder. The shop owner told me there was no charge for it, but to keep him in mind if I ever did want to sell the coin.

Before I made my exit, the man offered to pay me $1,100 cash for my other gold coin. I told him I would think about it and maybe come back later. I headed for the door and made my way outside. That conversation didn't go too well, but I did find out that I'm even richer than I thought!

I still wanted to get some cash. The salesman said the one gold coin was worth $1,100, and that would be a good amount for today. I drove to the second store, which was a bit outside the downtown area and had a parking lot with only one other car parked in it.

Pulling my SUV into a parking space, I entered the coin store and held the door for a man who was leaving. Stepping a bit past the threshold I noticed a white cotton glove on the floor by my feet. Picking it up and thinking that the man I just passed had perhaps dropped it, I stepped back outside.

The man I had held the door for, who looked to be in his 50s, was taking his cap off and getting into the driver's seat of the car next to mine. I yelled at him and asked if he had dropped the white glove I waved in his direction. He shook his head and mouthed the word "No." Backing his car away from the store quickly, his tires screeched as he raced from the parking lot, barely missing my parked vehicle.

I thought this behavior odd, staring at the man's car as it roared away. It was a white Lexus with a Washington license plate. I wasn't certain of the plate's first three letters—possibly JNB—but the last four numbers were 4315.

It then hit me! Passing that man as I entered the coin store, I noticed he was wearing a long-sleeved coat and a dark cap. It didn't register with me then, but it did now. He was dressed much like the man that exited the coin store in Billings, Montana, and had exchanged fake United States gold coins for real ones before hurriedly walking out and driving away.

Turning and rushing into the coin store, I asked the man behind the counter if the guy who just left had looked at some early United States gold coins? He had. I immediately told the salesman to check closely the coins the customer had examined, to see if those the man returned were, indeed, the same coins he was given to inspect.

His gasp said it all! "No," he screamed! "Two of these are fakes!"

I told the salesman to call the police and tell them your store has been robbed. I will explain all this in a minute, but say to the police the man's car that sped away was a white Lexus with a Washington license plate that ended in 4315, and may have started with the letters JNB. The store owner immediately dialed 911 and reported what I had just said.

The man ended his call and told me that officers were on the way. Physically shaking, he was very curious to learn what was going on. How did I know the man had just robbed him? As I was about to tell him my story, the front door opened and two officers rushed in.

Their timing was perfect to hear what was going on! The store owner identified himself to the authorities and turned to me. "She seems to know more about this than I do. Let's hear what she has to say."

The officers then looked at me warily. Asking for my story, I began, "First, before I explain what's happened, are the police following up on the white Lexus? You find that car, and I believe you'll find your coin thief."

The officers assured us the license plate information for the Lexus was now in their search system and that all "rolling officers" in the vicinity were informed to be on alert for this vehicle. After that, "Now Miss, please tell us what's going on."

I spent the next 10 minutes unpacking my experience near Billings, Montana 11 days ago, when I was stopped on the interstate after being in the coin shop there. I explained that I had some coins I wanted to sell and was going into the store to see what price I could get for them. Entering the building, I briefly passed a customer who I later learned had stolen coins from the shop.

I didn't get a good look at the man then, but I did see him more clearly as he left the store here today. He's in his 50s, with grayish dark hair, about six feet tall and 180 pounds.

Finished hearing my story, the officers and the shop owner took down my cell phone number. I showed them my real Virginia driver's license, not the one with the name Emily Elizabeth Wilson. I told them about my recent move from Virginia and I gave the police and shop owner my Seattle address.

There wasn't much else I could do to help. The officers and store owner thanked me for the information and told me they would be in touch if a follow up was needed or they arrested a suspect. I would likely then become quite involved in the case.

As the policemen were leaving the store, one of them got a phone call. Taking it, he motioned for me to wait. Completing the call, the officer explained that the Seattle police had just found the white Lexus. It had been stolen in West Seattle a couple hours ago and left a few blocks from the coin store. No driver. The police were checking for fingerprints. Maybe they will find some leads there. With that, I headed back to my SUV and made the decision to make one more stop before going home.

I still wanted to make a sale. I retraced my drive back to the first coin store I stopped at today. Parking my car and re-entering the store, the man behind the counter was surprised to see me. I told him that after thinking about it a bit more, I would like to sell the one 10-dollar gold coin for $1,100. And I will keep him in mind if I decide to sell the other coin that I know now is worth quite a bit of money. The store owner was pleased with the opportunity that might come his way sometime.

Going to his safe in the back room and returning, the man counted out 11 crisp $100 bills. They felt good in my hand. He did want to see some ID. I showed him my authentic Virginia license, but told him I had recently moved to Seattle. He took my cell phone number, made a copy of my driver's license, and I gave him my new address on Queen Anne Hill.

"Nice area of the city," he said after seeing my zip code.

As I turned to leave, the man politely said, "And one other thing, Miss. I'm sorry about the death of your father."

I turned back and thanked him with a sincere smile before heading again toward the door. Exiting the shop and reaching my car, I unlocked and opened the door. Shaking my head and slipping into my car, with a short smile I whispered to myself, "That's really funny. I guess the story about my father dying was more convincing than I thought."

Today was quite a day. I now have some cash that will carry me for a while without making a trip to the bank. And I have a gold coin worth

$14,000! I'm going to bed, but tomorrow and in the days ahead I plan to spend more time with Mary Moore's diary. Hopefully, I won't have too many interruptions.

Tuesday, August 8, 2017

After finishing shopping and some errands around town today, I'm jumping into work on Mary's story this evening. I've been waiting all day to find out what happens next in her adventure.

Our second and final night on the train was not as peaceful as the first. Each mile north took me closer to an unsure reunion with my sister. Sleep was hard in coming and brief when it finally arrived.

I had not seen Martha since the day she said goodbye and left our little town of Franklin in 1840, nearly 30 years before the events I am describing here. And I had never met her husband Alfred, nor knew much about him.

Excitement and tension grew during our 3rd and final long day on the train. Something else grew in that time as well: crowds of people. Most carried bags and luggage, and others with musical instruments. I recall there were men and women traveling, some carrying what appeared to be stringed instrument cases, and others bearing various sized brass horns. Even now, some 20 years later, I remember seeing two men strain while loading a large percussion drum onto the train, only a few miles from our destination in Boston. Clearly, they were headed to play a part in the Musical Festival.

The gregarious scenes captivated Deborah as events unfolded on the train at various stops along the way. I'm glad these drew her attention. I was lost in thought about seeing my sister and in the next few days taking steps toward fulfilling my vengeful reprisal toward President Grant.

It was growing toward dusk as our train passed through an increasing number of large redbrick buildings, signaling we were surrounded now by the city of Boston. I was somewhat at a loss. Not sure that after 30 years I would recognize my sister, I wondered if she felt the same of me. My concern grew even more abrupt as Deborah and I disembarked the train into a stirring morass of bodies and bags hurriedly making their way from the train platform toward their sundry destinations.

It was then I heard through the din of the crowd the clear call of our names, "Sister Mary and Deborah, this way!"

Searching through a greatly obstructed view as I etched my way between colorful women's bonnets and men's dark hats, I caught glimpse of a woman possessing the visual echo of a sister I knew years ago. Our eyes met. I raised my hand in acknowledgment, as Deborah and I slowly made way toward Martha through the vast cross-rushing crowd.

My heart raced faster with each step. Reaching my sister, she gathered me toward her in sincere embrace. My arms—but not my heart—replied in kind, although I believe Martha was truly convinced of my joyfulness in the two of us seeing each other again. After letting go of her grasp, Martha stepped back and introduced Alfred and I presented Deborah. We all smiled at one another in welcome, and then followed Alfred as he made his way to their carriage tethered in a stable nearby.

My immediate thought was that Martha had aged. This was true, but so had I. She was now a full-bodied and mature woman, seemingly with years of life experience harbored between her skin and soul.

Deborah and I were tired and, fortunately, our hosts knew it. By the time we reached their home in Chelsea it was well into dark. We assured Martha and Alfred that our needs for nourishment had been met on the train, as we had eaten apples, bread, and cheese, which would tide us over until morning.

Mary and Alfred's house in Chelsea was indeed nice. They had done well for themselves. Deborah and I were each given a room in the upstairs portion of the house, with instructions for us to sleep soundly and let Martha know of any needs we may have. We each said our goodnights, and in response to the tiring travel events of the day quickly embraced the stillness of the Chelsea night that surrounded us.

Well, Mary and Deborah are now in Chelsea. That's enough work on the diary for now. With luck, I'll soon embrace the stillness of the Seattle night that surrounds me.

Wednesday, August 9, 2017

With Mary and Deborah now with Martha and Alfred in Chelsea, let's see what path Mary's story takes next.

~

The following morning was Sunday. Martha and Alfred indicated they often attended services at the nearby Congregational church. Winnisimmet Church in Chelsea was grander in size and ornament than the small plain wooden Methodist church in Franklin, where Deborah and I visited regularly.

Though not far from their house, we traveled to Winnisimmet Church by carriage. This was very helpful to my leg.

The church of Martha and Alfred was nearly filled with parishioners that Sunday morning. It was built from white granite stone with arched windows and beholding a tall thin spire and surrounded with a wooden picket fence and an assortment of leafy trees. Martha and Alfred indicated that this large number of church attenders was not common for a Sunday, but seemingly nothing in the vicinity of Boston was common on this Sunday morning leading to the National Peace Jubilee and Great Musical Festival.

The minister of Winnisimmet Church was Mr. Albert H. Plumb. He delivered the sermon that day. Reverend Plumb was middle sized in stature, holding fine manners, and clearly well trained in biblical understanding. Quite eloquent, his fiery delivery of the Lord's Book was punctuated with example and admonition to continue following a rightward path of life and perform good work in service of others daily.

But his words from the pulpit, as a Northerner, rang hollow to me. Deborah and I had just completed travel through miles of Southern destruc-

tion, much of which I believe these citizens of
Chelsea and many Northerners had never seen or
encountered first-hand.

The sights and smells of death still permeated
the soil of the South even then, some five years
after the War's end. The pathway of right life that
Reverend Plumb called his parishioners to follow
was not the one I saw inflicted upon the Southern world wherein I lived and traveled. Nor did
I view it as an example of Godly living toward
others, which was preached that Sunday morning.
And now I was in Boston, seemingly to celebrate
these Northern atrocities through music and song
with a sister I did not know. I felt a hypocrite and
would myself have been so if not for the grander
purpose for which I had come.

After the church service ended, Alfred took us
on a short carriage tour around the central area
of Chelsea. There was a distinct bustle of activity,
as Martha indicated that the town—even though
situated across the waterway from Boston—was
readying itself for the festivities of the week
ahead.

I think it was not Martha's purposeful intent
to do so, but she was still culpable in its outcome.
As we rode through Chelsea that afternoon, one
could not help but notice the tall white granite
column supporting the sculpture of a soldier
sentry standing at the top. Young Deborah inquired its commemorative purpose, thinking it
was placed to honor those young men of Chelsea
who fought with George Washington in the War
for Independence years before. Instead, Martha
revealed—with a slightly prideful tone—that this
soldier-topped column had been commemorated
in city-wide celebration only two months before, in
April, to honor the 167 Chelsea men who died in
the nation's most recent conflict.

I could tell these unexpected words from Martha caused Deborah to stiffen in crushing abhorrence. No memorial was raised in memory of her now dead brothers and the other young men of Franklin and the South. Her responsive gaze took on a countenance that was steely, harsh, and distant, one I had never seen in the face of this young girl.

Thursday, August 10, 2017

I had a hard time getting to sleep last night. Deciphering and recording these pages from Mary's diary yesterday, I tried to place myself in the shoes of both Mary and Deborah. This becomes one of the great hardships but benefits of studying history: "empathetic historical projection," the Professor called it. This is the need and ability to consider deeply life and times beyond oneself, to view the world within the context of how others lived it in the past, in an attempt to make history come alive.

It's clear that no one is able to accomplish this projection of self into another time and place fully. We are each caught in our current layer of life and location. Yet, attempting to do so develops within us an empathetic skill that helps us understand history, and is beneficial to our lives individually and to humanity as a whole. I can still hear the Professor's voice, so often imploring his students with these ideas about recognizing the benefits and value of our encounters with history.

The remainder of Sunday was spent at the home of Martha and Alfred. Deborah had softened in spirit by the time we reached their residence. After we arrived, Martha took the young girl by her side and inquired about Deborah's interest in drawing and her scherenschnitte work. Before I

knew it, Deborah had retrieved her leather satchel and was showing both Martha and Alfred her sketches and intricate paper cut designs. The two drawing instructors were impressed with her abilities, and they encouraged Deborah to continue in her artistic efforts.

Martha asked Deborah if she would like to take a trip through Boston the following day, before the festival began on Tuesday, to see and to sketch some of the parks, sculptures, and architectural sites of the city. Alfred would act as their carriage driver. Deborah responded in emphatic approval and with much thanks.

I informed Martha and Deborah that it would be difficult for me to make my way in and out of the carriage at various stops through the city with my leg condition and cane, and that I would like to use Monday to rest in preparation for the travel and festivities of the week ahead. Martha understood this need, and she looked forward to having time for the two of us to talk with one another during the days to follow.

In conversation that afternoon, Martha revealed to Deborah and to me that news had arrived assuring visitors that President Grant would be attending the Musical Festival on the second day, Wednesday, June 16th.

The four of us spent the afternoon and evening in polite conversation. Martha inquired about life and my teaching within the community of Franklin, while she shared her and Alfred's experiences in this northern city. They seemed both pleased and content in these surroundings. Our interactions with each other were not strained, but clearly evidenced that our lives, in so many respects, were very different from one another.

*Deborah was mostly silent throughout the
evening. As far youngest of the group, her reser-
vation was not viewed as odd or of sullen spirit.
Neither she nor I revealed to our hosts much of
her life story and about the death of her brothers
in the War. She desired to keep this information to
herself.*

*The day ended not too late, and with discussion
of the sightseeing and sketching trip planned for
the next day. While excited to have this artistic
opportunity in Boston, Deborah did seem tired
and excused herself a bit early to end her evening.*

This seems a good place for me to end my evening as well. I'll pick up the
story of Mary, Deborah, and Martha tomorrow.

Friday, August 11, 2017

This is a great time of year to be in Seattle. The mornings are often
cloudy and cool, but warm sunshine breaks through in the afternoon
ushering in a beautiful blue sky. And, without the dripping humidity of
a Virginia summer! I ran a few errands and did some grocery shopping
at Safeway on the top of the Hill this morning, but the afternoon was
so nice I again took my work with the diary outside to the picnic table.

*The National Peace Jubilee and Great Musical
Festival would begin on Tuesday. Monday was my
day to rest and prepare. Martha and Deborah left
early that morning, with sketchbooks and pencils.
Deborah carried her leather satchel, which was*

similar to the one Martha bore to hold her artist supplies. Alfred guided the reins of the carriage. From the window, I watched the trio disappear into the rush of the morning crowd down the street toward the Winnisimmet ferry, and a day ahead moving throughout the sights and sounds of Boston.

My heart felt uplifted a bit that Martha and Deborah had similar interests. They seemed, for the most part, to enjoy one another's company. At this point I thought it likely that in two days hence, Deborah would need my sister's friendship and assistance to make her way to the train and then back to Franklin alone. Thinking that I would be dead or imprisoned, I could no longer be of help to her.

My mind was turning now to the task for which I had made this long trek north. I was not fearful of what lay ahead and had abandoned such thoughts some time ago. I was now more concerned with learning how to successfully carry out my plan of retribution toward the president, when having no knowledge of the place wherein I would deliver to Grant the necessary gift from my dog's head cane. Tomorrow I would need to view the surroundings inside the Coliseum carefully, in preparation for fulfilling the need to trade my life for that of the Northern Butcher, amongst the backdrop of thousands of revelers joyous in music and song.

In the solitude of my room, I removed from the hollow leather tube the sturdy dark brown cane with the dog's head. I gripped the inviting fine-textured handle, considering deeply its precisely designed two-fold purpose. Examining all features of the supportive weapon, both inside and out, I recalled the moment I received it from the distinguished Southern visitor to our community

*as he passed along to me the premonition, "You
may need it one day." Yes, indeed—Mr. Colton
Bain—two days from now, in the direction toward
the President of the United States, is planned the
moment of its retaliatory revelation.*

*Later that afternoon, Deborah, Martha, and
Alfred returned from their travels to Boston.
Deborah was in high spirits telling me of her
experiences seeing and sketching many of the sites
and sculptures she had learned about through
engraved prints published in the Musical Festival
bulletin that Martha had sent to us in Franklin
weeks earlier. Deborah had brought the booklet with her to Boston. The young girl was most
proud of her drawings of the State House, Faneuil
Hall, and the sculpture of Benjamin Franklin,
which Martha and I both agreed were all quite
nice.*

It's amazing to me that Deborah's sketches of places in Boston that
Mary describes here in her diary—along with her hand-stitched leather
satchel—are now resting in the secure storage room in the basement of
the museum in Virginia. This is going to make a great story and museum
exhibition someday!

*The four of us did not stay up late that Monday
night. We wanted to be well rested for the following day, beginning the Peace Jubilee and Musical
Festival. It would be filled first with a carriage
trip to the recently erected Coliseum in Boston,
and an afternoon seated amongst what was an-*

ticipated to be singers and musicians numbering in the thousands, all joined in an event of jubilant celebration.

My heart was torn in this. My own purpose for celebration was not found in what we would encounter in the Coliseum tomorrow, but rested in what would occur in my life and that of President Grant at the Musical Festival the following day.

Saturday, August 12, 2017

I slept later than usual this morning. It must have been by chance that I had a hard time waking up here on Queen Anne Hill on a Saturday, as my Saturdays are now no different from any other day of my week. But, getting up late today likely happened because I'm not sleeping well, with lots of thought-filled time awake in the darkness of my bedroom.

I'm finding it increasingly more difficult to separate my life here in Seattle from what I'm finding in Mary's diary. More and more I'm carrying within me this story of Mary, Martha, and Deborah, even when I'm not actually reading and recording what the diary contains. I guess that's reasonable, as my diversions from Mary's diary these days are few and far between.

One distraction from work on the diary came to me today through a phone call from Jessica. I wasn't expecting to hear from her. Jessica didn't have much news to share about life in Knoxville, but she did want to know how I'm doing and what I've been up to recently, and if I'm enjoying life in Seattle.

The phone call was a bit difficult to navigate. I didn't have much I could tell her about my time in Seattle. I've done little lately other than transcribe pages of Mary's handwriting, and that's work I need to keep to myself right now. Also, I couldn't tell her about my experiences selling gold coins and my involvement with the coin thief and the Seattle police. Those stories are off limits with Jessica as well. Maybe I should look into getting out more. Summers here are beautiful.

It won't be long and I'll need to make some decisions about what to do with Mary's diary, the other three books from the trunk, and the story that has emerged from them. I can see from the diminishing number of pages in the diary for me to copy that I'm moving closer to the end. It looks like Mary's record of events that occurred at the Musical Festival in Boston begin next.

I have no idea how Mary's diary account will end. History records that President Grant finished his term of office in the spring of 1877 and died in 1885. From this I know that Mary's effort to end the life of Grant was unsuccessful that June day in 1869 in Boston. But I'm curious about what unfolds in the assassination attempt, and happenings in the lives of Mary, Martha, and Deborah after that.

I also need to figure out how I want to reveal Mary's incredible story to the public. I guess all this provides motivation for me to get going on finishing work with the diary and moving on from there.

There was no need to rise early in Chelsea on that Tuesday morning. The Musical Festival was not to begin until 3:00 in the afternoon each day. However, with the expectation of great crowds lining to utilize the ferry crossing to Boston, as well as those surrounding and inside the Coliseum, and the need because of my limp to position the carriage as close as possible to the massive building, we decided to partake an early lunch and depart the house of Alfred and Martha late in the morning.

The number of people waiting at the Winnisimmet ferry port and crush of those on the streets was indeed astonishing. This grew even more so as we rode closer to the Coliseum. The Musical Festival bulletin sent to me by Martha, which Deb-

orah carried in her leather satchel, said that the building would hold 50,000 persons. I believe this number was not an exaggeration.

Martha conveyed to us during our carriage ride that the Coliseum was the largest covered structure ever built in the United States. This description appeared true as we encountered it. Colorful flags were flown from various staffs positioned around the exterior roof area of the Coliseum. Lustrous red, white, and blue banners were draped from the eaves. Standing throngs surrounded the wooden building, gazing at the sights in both awe and admiration.

I was grieved. The scene of this grandiose structure and assembly of vibrant humanity inter-mixing before my eyes that day was something I could never have imagined on my own, yet recog-nizing their purpose for doing so cut deep into my soul. This was not a celebration of peace and the promotion of unity for the nation. It was a festive extravaganza of Northern victory and consequent Southern ravage.

The Coliseum was a mammoth structure. It looked very much like the engraving placed on the rear cover of the Festival bulletin Deborah car-ried in her satchel. Slowly directing the carriage through the overly crowded streets, Alfred was able to reach the Coliseum and leash the horse and carriage into a stable not far from the build-ing. With my severe limp, I very much appreciated this close proximity to the Coliseum. That day I carried my lion's head cane with ruby eyes. For the Festival visit Wednesday, without question, I planned to employ the use of my two-purposed dog's head cane.

There were hundreds of horses and carriages tethered within this enclosed location near the Coliseum. Walking toward the building that day *under unseasonably dark clouds with intermittent rain showers, Deborah told Martha that she once had a beautiful horse named Colonel, and that she loved horses very much. She missed not having one of her own. Martha smiled in reply, saying that she also adored horses and that there looked to be some very nice carriage animals to admire, stabled here this afternoon. Perhaps they could look at some together after the Festival concluded.*

The four of us made our way inside the Coliseum. Beyond being astounded with what we saw when entering the huge two-story structure, I still remember vividly, now some 20 years later, becoming jolted by the overwhelming din of voices reverberating throughout the hall. The broad expanse of humanity, both seated and standing, was something my eyes and ears—and those of all individuals positioned around us—had never before seen or heard.

Ushers directed us to our seats. Because Alfred had purchased four tickets for each of the five days of the performance—Season Tickets, they were called—we were assigned seats in Section D, slip 21. These seats were labeled "Preferred," and located near the middle of the floor seating directly behind Section C, which was reserved for Invited Guests. Because of the condition of my leg, I desired to sit on one of the two side aisles, which we were able to accommodate.

My real goal in attending the Musical Festival this first day was to learn as much as possible about President Grant's visit to the Festival the following day. Between seeing first-hand the interior layout of the Coliseum, talking with Alfred who knew some of the arrangements made for the president's attendance, and experiencing the musical format—which would be similar each day of the Festival—I was able to form a plan to carry out my deadly retribution of President Grant on Wednesday.

The initial day of the Peace Jubilee and Musical Festival was a thunderous afternoon of music and song. Thousands of singers and musicians filled the building with rapturous melodies that stretched the imagination. The pipe organ built for this five-day performance surpassed recognition of the Coliseum itself, with it being regarded as the largest musical instrument of its kind in the world. The resonant sound emitted from the flues and reeds at times shook the rafters of the building and the interior of our being.

The Programme of Tuesday was divided into two parts, which would be the format for each day of the Musical Festival. These were separated by a 15-minute intermission. The audience was presented with band, orchestra, and choir renditions, punctuated with vocal and instrumental solos. These melodies were generally pleasing and performed well, given the thousands of singers and musicians that joined in unison, and—according to Martha—with limited time spent in rehearsal.

Clearly, the audience's greatest response that day was given to the musical offering of the Anvil Chorus. One hundred members of the Boston Fire Department—wearing stark red shirts and positioned across the deep orchestral platform in two lines of 50—each delivered their hammer on an anvil in crashing unison, as directed by the conductor within the playing of Verdi's "Il Trovatore." The loud reverberation of 100 hammers striking down on their anvils in synchronized sound was outdone only marginally by the noise of the audience in frenzied response. Cannons outside the Coliseum were fired at the appropriate moment of the score in precise unison with the musicians and singers, which astounded the crowd and drew their wild ovation.

The Peace Jubilee and Musical Festival ended that day with a full rendition of "My Country 'tis of Thee." More than ten thousand choir voices in unison performed this anthem accompanied by the grand organ, military band, drum corps, and bells. From the corner of my eye, I watched young Deborah faintly mouth the words as the choir sang this hymn. I am certain that when the refrain of the first stanza reached, "land where my fathers died," Deborah replaced the word "fathers" with "brothers." Her eyes edged with tears at this, and her countenance stiffened, displaying the same steely, distant gaze of hardened determination I saw in her during the carriage ride through Chelsea that previous Sunday afternoon.

The first day of the Musical Festival concluded at a quarter-past six. The four of us made our way out of the Coliseum through the massive crowd. Deborah and Martha paused a few times to admire the elegant horses they passed on their walk to the carriage. The trip to Martha's house was slow at the beginning because of the festive throng, but our return ended uneventfully in Chelsea.

Along the way our ride was filled with conversation about the Peace Jubilee and Musical Festival. I tried to be as respectful of the event as possible, and mostly provided Martha the opportunity to tell her impressions of the day. It was clearly a time of marvelous celebration for my sister, and I was content to let her have this joyous moment.

Deborah kept mostly silent. She did seem impressed, however, by what she had experienced that day. Exchanging reflection for expectation,

Deborah expressed a deep curiosity and anticipation for the celebration's next day, which would include a visit to the Musical Festival from President Grant.

I inquired of Alfred what he knew about Grant's schedule at the Musical Festival on Wednesday. One of Alfred's close friends was a member of the Festival's planning committee, and he had shared that a full day of activities in Boston had been arranged for President Grant. He would be arriving by train from Washington in the morning. These events would first include a survey of troops, then a noontime lunch gathering with officials from the city of Boston, and a visit to the Musical Festival that afternoon.

Orchestra renditions would be featured in the first half of the Festival on Wednesday, leading to the 15-minute intermission. President Grant would then be introduced to the audience as the intermission concluded. He would make his way from Section C—on the main floor where dignitaries were seated—to the stage for acknowledgment by the crowd as the chorus sang Handel's "See the Conquering Hero Comes." Reaching this point with the audience standing in adulation, musicians would then deliver a playing of the "Star-Spangled Banner."

Alfred continued. Immediately following this, the Anvil Chorus will perform. Repeating the crashing composition it had delivered at the Festival on Tuesday, this score would no doubt arouse the audience into an unbridled frenzy. It was planned that at this time the gas-lights throughout the Hall would be dimmed for effect.

President Grant would then proceed from the stage down the long center aisle and leave the Hall during this loud anvil rendition. The president's departure would come at a time when the crowd's attention is most likely directed toward musical events on the stage. Departing the main Hall, President Grant and his four-member military entourage would then rest briefly in the reception-room nearby before leaving the building in preparation for his evening activities and a return train to Washington.

These words from Alfred were those I desired to hear. My plan was now formed. It was to be in this location—at the end of the long center aisle with Grant leaving the Hall during the thunderous noise and ecstasy of the Anvil Chorus and with gas-lights lowered—that I planned to deliver my retribution for his slaughter of Brave Sons and Bold Daughters of the Confederacy, gladly giving my life for that of the President of the United States.

Three months work and I'm almost there. The death of the Professor, me being nearly shot in the hospital, finding Confederate treasure, a cross-county coin-selling trip, and so much more has happened in that time. But I'm now on the cusp of learning the outcome of Mary Moore's story about her plan to assassinate the President of the United States, Ulysses S. Grant.

It's getting very late. I'm tired after a long day of transcribing hard-to-read handwriting. For this reason, I'm stopping my work with Mary's diary for today. I plan tomorrow to record her account of the second day of the Musical Festival and what happened there between President Grant and Mary's two-purposed dog's head cane. A lot of days and nights have gone into deciphering the words in Mary's diary to reach this point. I do hope I'm not disappointed with the story I find tomorrow.

Sunday, August 13, 2017

This is how Mary continued.

~

What struck me more soundly than anything else that fateful morning of June 16, 1869, was the presence of Deborah as she descended the stairs from her room. Deborah arrived at the top of the stairway, drenched in morning sunlight, a bit later than she did on the previous days. And seeing her as I did that day provided me with a clear reason for her delayed appearance.

Deborah was radiant. Her clothes were spotless and chaste. She wore the special dress she had purchased for the Musical Festival: a bright white cotton pinafore placed over a light blue dress flowered with pink and yellow daisies. Her hair was done ever so nicely. At nearly 17 years of age, Deborah was a delight to the eyes. It was here, for the first time as she stepped down the stairs toward us, that I saw her reach beyond girlhood to reveal herself as a blossoming Southern woman.

This pleased me so. I rose from sleep that morning knowing this would be my day of reckoning with my two-purposed cane, when I would trade my life for that of the Northern Butcher Grant. But rather than regret my choice to face this event today, I embraced it with determined expectation. And it seemed from seeing her womanly finished preparation that Deborah was looking forward to this day at the Musical Festival as well.

I told Deborah that she looked beautiful as we sat together, and I prepared to make my final trip to the Great Musical Festival. Seeing her from across the room as we left the house, I was pleased to recognize Deborah as a lovely and maturing young woman. I believed she was prepared to fulfill the task ahead, to return to Franklin by train on her own and from there take up the task of school teaching, following in my footsteps.

The carriage trip to the Coliseum was much like the one Martha, Alfred, Deborah, and I had made the previous day. The ferry ride from Chelsea to Boston was especially memorable, with so many people seeking to reach Boston for the Musical Festival. Deborah carried her satchel, which she told me contained her Bible, the Festival Bulletin, her drawing pad, and a few pencils. I had with me my dog's head cane, along with three bullets and firing materials in a small hand-purse.

I am not certain why I brought three firing rounds with me. There would be the opportunity to use only one. But I felt more secure holding extra. My plan was to excuse myself into a private space in the Coliseum once we arrived. There I would load my cane weapon rather than carry it armed to the Festival, where during the carriage ride it might discharge accidentally.

Alfred tethered the carriage near the same spot as the previous day. Walking into the massive building we were again taken aback by the enormity of the structure and the vast sounds emanating from it, even before the Festival began that day. The four of us selected our seats in the same location as the day before.

Once situated, I excused myself and retreated to a more private rear corner of the Coliseum. This crippled woman with a cane went unnoticed by passersby, as I unscrewed the top handle of the cane and carefully deposited into its loading mechanism one of the lead bullets and proper firing materials.

I intended that the lead projectile would soon belong to the heart of President Grant. Securing the two pieces of the cane back together and returning to my seat in the Coliseum, I made sure to keep my hand distanced from the firing mechanism on its handle. My plan was set in motion. I was ready. There was nothing to regret.

The musical programme seemed more unified on this day than the first. But my mind then was not much directed toward instruments and song. I was fixed on my purpose at hand.

I did think it fitting, however, that the final piece performed before intermission was Handel's "Let the Bright Seraphim," from his oratorio Samson. *Here, an Israelite woman calls upon angels to commemorate the biblical judge Samson's heroic suicidal death at the temple of Dagon in Gaza, and triumph over the Philistines. It was at this time that I, too, was calling upon angels as I prepared to commemorate and bring retribution for the death of my dear Samson, his brother Gideon, and the many other heroic Southerners who bravely gave their lives in pursuit of freedom and dedication to the Confederacy.*

We reached the intermission. Now was my time. Deborah indicated that she needed to stretch her legs and would like to take a short walk through the building to see some of the spectacular features of the Coliseum and musical staging up close.

A bit surprising to me then, Deborah removed her Bible from the satchel and carried it with her, leaving the leather bag behind on her empty seat next to mine. I saw her walk across the Hall toward the opposite side of the building and was soon lost from view in the boisterous crowd. It was a quick goodbye between us, one I contemplated would likely be my last time to see the young woman. Deborah, however, was ready to take my place. My cane and I were soon headed to fulfill our intended purpose after the intermission was concluded.

Before leaving, I lingered a bit with Martha and Alfred, thanking them again for the opportunity to make this trip. I even drew myself to embrace Martha, believing it would be my final time ever to do so. I then headed up the aisle through the bustling crowd toward the end of the Grand Hall and my soon-to-be meeting with President Grant.

Reaching this location, the gas-lights flickered indicating that the intermission would soon conclude and the audience was to re-take their seats. Mine, on the aisle next to Deborah, would be empty. Deborah, Martha, and Alfred would wonder where I was, why I was delayed in returning, and if some harm had beset me. But in my mind, I expected that soon the reason for my vanishing would be known to them, and to the rest of the world as well.

I should have let my cell phone buzz some more, but I didn't. It was an inconvenient time for this to happen, but my work with Mary's diary was interrupted by an unexpected phone call. This time it was not Jessica.

Contacting me was a detective from the Seattle Police Department, Officer Williams. She indicated that through a partial fingerprint recovered from the white Lexus and some other evidence, the department had identified and taken into custody a possible suspect in the string of coin store robberies. The officer was calling to request that I come downtown tomorrow morning and review a police lineup, to determine if I could identify the suspect.

I told Detective Williams that I wasn't sure how much help I would be. I didn't get a good look at the man I passed in the doorway of the coin shop, even though I did see him in two different locations, but days apart. The detective was quite adamant and persuasive in coaxing me to be at her office tomorrow morning at 9:00 a.m. I eventually agreed to do so. But this request has got me unnerved.

Even though this is a very untimely place to stop work with Mary's diary, I have to leave it for a while. The concentration I need for reading through and transcribing her words isn't in me right now. Instead, I'm headed out for a walk in the neighborhood, to think about what I might encounter and say at the police station tomorrow.

A long walk through the Queen Anne Hill neighborhood this afternoon did me good, helping to clear my head. But I'm still not looking forward to my experience with the police and their robbery suspect in the morning. I just don't want to be involved, at all. There's no telling what might come from this.

I'm at such a thrilling spot in Mary's diary I have to get back to it. Hopefully diving into this work now will help take my mind off the task of viewing a suspect line-up in the morning.

President Grant's participation in the Musical Festival took place just as Alfred had described its planning. As the intermission concluded, Grant was introduced to the crowd. He rose from a green cushioned sofa and made his way to the stage, amidst the vibrant strains of "See the Conquering Hero Comes." The now standing throng—some say numbering a full building of 40,000 and others 50,000—erupted in joyous ovation. A sea of wav-

ing white handkerchiefs filled the Coliseum. At the immediate conclusion of Handel's chorus, the band members performed the "Star-Spangled Banner." This subdued the crowd somewhat for these passing moments.

Following this anthem the Anvil Chorus delighted the multitude beyond measure with its performance of "Il Trovatore," as they had done the day previous. The audience roared in unconstrained enthusiasm as the raised hammers of 100 Boston firefighters crashed down in unison, each registering at the appropriate time upon their intended anvil. As the day before, the sound of cannons fired from positions outside the Coliseum could be heard, and the crowd responded in abundant adulation.

The noise inside the building was deafening, as I wished it would be. The gas-lights were dimmed to a low level amidst the overflowing sound of musicians, singers, and clashing hammers upon the anvils. At this time and with darkened circumstance the crowd directed its attention away from the president and toward the breathtaking musical event unfolding on stage and resonant sound reverberating through the enormous Coliseum. The audience lifted their collective voices in demand for an encore, which the Anvil Chorus rightly performed.

I watched these events from the far end of one of two long side aisles. Peering toward the stage in the shadowy darkness and overwhelming din of music and song, I could make out the hazy appearance of Grant stepping from the stage. With four military men now reaching his side, Grant strode down the center aisle of the Grand Hall, becoming more in view to me with each step. I tried to anticipate the arrival of the president and his men at the end of the main aisle, and have it co-

incide with when I would cross the Hall in behind the final audience row and join him there with my cane set in ready.

The closer Grant came, the more I awaited the moment of our meeting. The center aisle in front of President Grant and the four military men with him appeared empty now. The crowd had taken leave of the president and was caught fully within the noise and activity of the singers, musicians, and resounding anvils. The collective gaze of the audience was directed toward the performance that was taking place on stage.

My timing was perfect. Grant and his four-man entourage reached the end of the center aisle as I came toward him, crossing behind the back row of the audience. There was now no more than 15 feet between the president and me.

Feeling carefully for the trigger-button on the cane handle, I was prepared to raise the support- ive weapon and deliver its deadly blast. Knowing that I would have only one opportunity to do so, I wanted to secure an unobstructed shot.

But someone now stood between the president and me. The two of them seemingly were engaged in friendly conversation. I did not want to risk injury to this person in my line of fire, so I stepped slightly to the side in order to have unimpeded aim at the president.

I could now see that it was a young woman talking with President Grant. Pausing momentar- ily, my eye caught her light blue dress filled with pink and yellow daisies and a fine white pinafore placed over the top. To my astonishment, I real- ized that this girl speaking with the president was Deborah Lee!

My mind raced in thought. Move, dear girl, step out of the way! Complete your words and make distance from the heinous Grant so that I can complete my purposeful revenge for which I planned to give my life. It was my time of retribution for the killing of your two proud and strong brothers, for Willy, Charlie, Colonel, and all the bold men of the South whose bodies are now submitted lifeless to the dark and wounded soil.

Move young darling, my mind called. It is the moment of Grant's death, and likely mine as well. But I will not be much missed. Relinquishing myself to the grave will be worth the cause. Take leave, so that I may have an open shot as I stand to confront the man of my rage. No one here suspects harm to the president, especially from a cripple woman requiring use of a cane.

But you had other plans, my dear. It happened in a flash, as Deborah stood before the president in advance of when I could raise my weapon to fire. Throwing open the black Bible she carried, Deborah suddenly retrieved from its recesses her long sharp-pointed scherenschnitte scissors, before dropping the Bible to the Coliseum floor. There was a momentary shimmer of steel in Deborah's left hand as she lunged the long-tapered scissors toward the chest of the president.

Just before the sharp instrument reached its intended mark, Deborah's extended arm was grasp by one of the soldiers guarding the president. Another military man swiftly threw his dark blue wool shoulder coat over Deborah's head as the nearest soldier quickly grabbed and subdued Deborah with a hand cloth covering her face, likely soaked in chloroform.

Deborah's body appeared to go limp immediately. A soldier placed the now coat-covered Deborah over his shoulder and carried her out the door and away from the building while President Grant was at the same time rushed into the side room by the remaining guards.

The entire scene lasted only seconds. I stood there alone and stunned at what had just taken place. There was no way in my limping condition I could follow and search out those who had taken charge of Deborah.

I remained in shock. Anticipation had suddenly turned to horror. Jolted by what I had just experienced, the sound of musical instruments, singers, and crashing anvils continued to reverberate through the packed Coliseum. Even now, 20 years later, I can still recall the crushing confusion I felt through the cacophony of music, celebratory cheers, and excruciating devastation that surrounded me.

Deborah's Bible lay open and disheveled on the hallway floor. Walking to where the encounter between the president and Deborah had just occurred, I reached down and picked up the heavy black book. Opening it, I was astounded. In the middle of her Bible Deborah had carefully cut out the shape of her scherenschnitte scissors from scores of the book's consecutive pages. In this precise hollowed out space in her Bible, Deborah had concealed her long sharp scissors and brought them with her to the Festival that day with the intention of using them to kill the President of the United States.

It must have taken Deborah quite some time to accomplish this well-planned artistic cutting from the pages of her Bible. Thus, my intent to use the dog's head cane to take the life of President Grant at the Musical Festival was not the only assassination attempt planned days in advance. From what was found within the pages of Deborah's Bible, she clearly had begun making her own arrangements to kill the president long before the two of us boarded the train in Franklin and headed north to Boston.

Wow! What a story! I didn't see Deborah's plan to kill President Grant coming at all. And Mary's diary account doesn't end here. There are still more pages to go. But I don't have the energy or time to go on from here tonight. It's late, and I need to be at the police station downtown tomorrow at 9:00 a.m. I'll pick up Mary's story tomorrow evening. I have so many questions. I hope Mary has answers.

Monday, August 14, 2017

What a day it's been. I'm not sure I even want to think about what went on today, let alone write it down. But I know I should. Over the years I've learned that recording things in my journal, even when I don't want to, is a good way for me to make sense of life. So here I go.

I saw firsthand today why lawyer jokes are often funny but disgustingly true. Having difficulty finding a place to park in downtown Seattle, which I thought might happen, I had to use a parking garage a few blocks from the Seattle Police Department Building. I'm glad I left my apartment a bit early. The person at the information desk pointed me toward the office of Detective Williams, who I was able to meet a few minutes after 9:00 a.m. She was professionally pleasant, but cool and efficient in her manner and conversation.

Alone in her office, Detective Williams gave me some backstory of the case and prepped me for how the suspect lineup would go. By law, she could not tell me much about the man in question beyond what I already knew. But she did reveal that a lot, but not all, of the police department's case against the thief hinged on my ability to identify him. There was some other evidence to go on, but it was limited in scope. This is not what I wanted to hear.

Detective Williams then told me that beyond the two of us in the lineup viewing room, there would be a third person joining us. This individual would be the suspect's attorney. I'm glad the detective readied me for meeting this additional person, but I'm not sure any words would have fully prepared me for this encounter.

Entering the suspect viewing room, Detective Williams introduced me to the lawyer representing the man in question. She was waiting for us. Her name was Ms. Donald. In her late 40s with short jet-black hair and wearing lots of expensive jewelry, she was dressed in business attire most women only dream of owning. This was in stark contrast to my jeans, t-shirt, and running shoes.

Some people are called "bitch" for seemingly no reason. This woman, without question, clearly earned the title. No handshake. No smile. No words spoken. When I entered the room, she delivered a 10-second silent stare at me—or rather, a stare through me—up and down from head to toe. Her demeanor and slow scan of my body made me feel way beyond uncomfortable. It was a lawyer-planned malicious meeting, executed to intimidate me. And I will admit she was somewhat successful.

I so much wanted to be back in my apartment, copying and recording the story from Mary Moore's diary. Actually, I wanted to be most anywhere in the world but in this room with these two women. But here I was. There was literally no escape.

Detective Williams then explained the process of viewing the suspect lineup. Six men of similar appearance would enter the room next door and stand in a line facing the three of us. We would be shielded behind dark glass, which still enabled us to view the six men but restricted them from seeing us. I was to identify anyone I recognized from the lineup. Completing her instructions, the detective asked if I had any questions, to which I responded that I did not. We were ready to begin.

A light was turned on in the room beyond the glass. Soon after that, six men walked slowly in a single line through a side doorway and turned in our direction to face the glass. Displaying mostly blank stares, all the men appeared uncomfortable.

My task was direct. I was called here to try and identify the man I had passed briefly in the doorway of the coin store in Billings, Montana a few weeks ago and then saw more recently getting into the white Lexus while leaving the coin store here in Seattle. Both my sightings of the man I was to identify were fleeting. I remember he appeared to be in his 50s, about six feet tall and 180 pounds, and with gray hair. But all six men in the lineup had those characteristics.

I stared intently at each man behind the glass. Stopping periodically, I moved slowly through a determined view of their faces. Breaking the silence after a few minutes, Detective Williams spoke to me, "No need to rush, take your time."

To this, Ms. Donald, in the first words I heard her speak, snapped, "No talking! The witness is to be completely on her own!" Detective Williams did not respond verbally to this shrill outburst, but she did give the obnoxious attorney a glaring response. Silence followed.

I went back to review closely the faces of the six men. Some features of each seemed familiar, but I couldn't pick out from the group the man I encountered leaving either of the coin stores. I was sure two of the individuals standing in the line did not resemble the man in the Lexus, so I had narrowed the possibilities from six to four. But that's as far as I could go.

Detective Williams again tried to interject some words to calm and reassure me in the viewing process, but the swanky dressed attorney stopped her in mid-sentence, "Williams, you know the rules for a lineup procedure, no encouraging the witness!"

This time the detective shot back more than a glance, delivering a terse verbal response to the distasteful lawyer. I appreciated this retort, but their fiery exchange put me on edge even more.

After giving myself about 15 minutes staring intently at these six men, I was through. Turning to Detective Williams, I apologetically offered, "I'm sorry, but I just can't identify anyone for sure in this lineup. It might be number 2, or maybe 4 or 5, but I'm just not certain."

With that, the meeting broke up quickly. Without saying a word, the attorney grabbed her black leather shoulder bag and left the room.

After the door closed, Detective Williams told me that this was her first encounter with this "disgusting lawyer," and "hoped it would be her last." The detective went on to assure me that I had done fine in the lineup viewing experience, and she appreciated the care I had taken in deliberating over all six individuals.

The police will continue their investigation of a couple other clues, to see if any leads in the case emerge. But for lack of evidence at this point they'll need to release the suspect from custody, at least for now.

The detective was certain Ms. Donald was headed downstairs to file paperwork to free the suspect as soon as possible. This outcome didn't leave me feeling good, but I had done my best. I don't want to accuse someone of a crime, when I'm not sure they committed it.

Detective Williams thanked me for my service to this case, and said the police would contact me if I could be of assistance later. I thanked her and headed out the door and onto the busy downtown sidewalk.

The weather was nice, and I hadn't been in this part of Seattle since a few days after I arrived in the city. A long walk was needed to help me process what I had just been through. I walked at least a mile-and-a-half through the downtown area and beyond before deciding to stop at one of the many waterfront eateries for an early lunch. Hunger was taking over and I wanted time to reflect on my experience this morning. But this is when my day got even stranger.

Being a little before noon, the lunch crowd and vacationing families hadn't yet arrived today. A lot of outdoor seating was available. I took a table just off the sidewalk. It was a nice lunch of fish and chips, and I enjoyed watching people walk by. Nothing was out of the ordinary.

That's when it happened. Finishing my lunch and reading an article on my phone, I glanced up the street. Walking down the sidewalk toward me, now not far away, was a well-dressed woman in her late-40s with short jet-black hair, sunglasses, and carrying a black shoulder bag. I was in shock but held my composure. Keeping my head down, I focused on my phone. No question, the woman who walked past me here was the bitchy attorney I met this morning, Ms. Donald!

But that's not the weirdest part. Alongside her was a man who looked to be in his 50s, about 6 feet tall, wearing sunglasses and a baseball cap covering what might be gray hair. I'm not sure, but he appeared very much like one of the six men I had viewed in the suspect lineup this morning. I don't know if attorney Donald saw me as they walked past my table, but I can't imagine she didn't recognize me. They both strolled right by.

This whole thing gives me the creeps. I had eaten lunch a long way from the police station. What were they doing here? Had they been following me?

I waited a few minutes until the attorney and her companion were down the street before I paid my bill, left the outdoor table, and headed up the sidewalk in the opposite direction.

Catching a passing bus back to my car, I drove from there to my apartment as fast as I could, legally. I'm not sure what to make of seeing these two individuals together this afternoon, such a long way from the police station where I first encountered them. It's hard for me to believe that it was a coincidence this attorney and her familiar-looking acquaintance walked down the same faraway street where I was having lunch. If their purposeful intent was to follow me from the police station, then what was their reason for doing so? That question has some possible answers, which I don't want to think about.

Maybe some work on Mary's diary this evening will help take my mind off the things that happened to me today. And I did leave Mary's account in a very breath-taking place. I do want to find out what happened to Mary—and to Deborah.

I tried to work on the diary a few minutes ago, but I can't. I'm tired. I'm puzzled. And I'm on edge. Was the lawyer from the police station and the man with her following me? Even though Mary's story is at a thrilling spot, my head isn't into it. I'm taking a sleep aid and going to bed. I hope to feel better in the morning.

Tuesday, August 15, 2017 (morning)

I do feel better after a good night's rest. Those sleep meds really did the trick. I crashed! But I'm still perplexed about crossing paths with Ms. Donald and her companion on the street yesterday afternoon. Of course I don't know, but maybe it was by chance that I saw them there. Perhaps the man in the baseball cap was not one of those in the lineup. I could have just seen him that way. The Seattle waterfront is a nice attraction for lunch, and it might be that the two of them wanted to take a long walk as well. Maybe it was just coincidence. It seems odd, but sometimes that's how the world works.

After sleeping well, I'm ready for some time with Mary's diary this morning.

The anvil chorus was now reaching the conclusion of their performance. As the final crashing notes were being completed and before the gas-lights were raised, I used my dogs-head cane to walk the darkened aisle back to my seat. Deborah's satchel rested on the floor by my feet. In the shadows of the Hall, I slipped Deborah's Bible, unnoticed, into the leather bag.

Martha touched my arm, relieved to see me return. She inquired about Deborah. In silence I shook my head, indicating I did not know where she was.

A moment later the gas-lights fully returned, and the afternoon programme resumed. When it did, the choir voices and musical instruments, loud and strong in their resonance and reverber-ation, were overwhelming to me. Loud musical performance was not what I desired now.

After a few minutes I expressed to Martha that I would like to get some cool air outside the Hall. I used my cane as best I could in retracing my steps up the side aisle to the back of the Coliseum, making sure my fingers did not engage the still loaded weapon. There I found a bench with a bit of fresh breeze. I sat down for a few moments of reflection and thought.

Resting on the bench, my mind cleared. I realized that my foremost act was to find Deborah. What had happened to the young girl? Where might they have taken her? She seemed so small and frail, carried over the shoulder of the large soldier guard and quickly out the door.

I had no idea where I might look for Deborah, but I used my cane to hobble through the promenade in hopes of perhaps seeing some indication that might lead me to her. There was none. Grant had escaped wrathful punishment. Deborah was gone. The deafening sound of song and instrument was all that remained.

After a few minutes I went back inside the Hall and made my way to sit down with Martha and Alfred. They were perplexed by Deborah's absence, wondering why she was delayed in returning to her seat after the intermission.

I remember little of the second half of the afternoon musical programme. My mind and crushed spirit were directed elsewhere. At the conclusion of the performance, I stood in unison with thunderous applause and amongst the surrounding throng that exited the Hall.

Doing so, I picked up Deborah's satchel, slipped its soft leather strap over my head and rested it on my shoulder. It was not too heavy. I told Martha and Alfred that I would care for the bag and return it to Deborah when we found her. But in my heart, I knew she would never again make use of the leather bag and its contents. The crowd surrounding us flowed into the Coliseum plaza.

The three of us walked toward the stable where the carriage was tethered. Martha offered that perhaps Deborah, because of her love of horses, had been drawn to the stable and spent the latter half of the afternoon there. Alfred agreed, and believed that Deborah, easily lost in the crowd, would likely meet us at the carriage. I remained silent in my reply.

There was growing commotion as we drew closer to the stable. We could see people running toward the center of the area where the horses and carriages were tethered. I heard a voice shout, "Assistance, please! Someone's been injured!"

Another person we passed coming toward us advised that a young girl was seen unconscious, lying under a carriage. We rushed toward the scene, but my limp slowed movement through the bustling throng.

Alfred went ahead and arrived first. By the time I drew near the standing and murmuring crowd in the stable, Alfred had turned to face me with a distraught downward gaze. There was at first silence between us. Then Alfred spoke, "It's Deborah. I'm sorry. She's been killed here in the horse stable, died of a broken neck."

Alfred continued, "No one has admitted seeing the accident occur. But those here believe Deborah likely had been playing with the horses when one of them reared up and knocked her down. She either fell and hit her head or was killed by a hoof strike. No one is sure."

Alfred tried to keep me from reaching Deborah. But I maneuvered past him as best I could. Deborah lay before me on the ground. The horses and carriages in the area had been drawn away, leav-

ing space for a medical attendant and us to reach the body of young Deborah. She looked to be more asleep—at peace—than she did of death.

Her white smock was somewhat soiled by what she had encountered in the stable. However, it, nor her blue daisy-filled dress, were torn or disheveled in any way. It appeared almost as if she had been laid in a state of repose here in the stable, rather than killed by a horse's hoof and flung to the ground.

We all stared at one another in silence. This may be their belief, but it was not a horse's attack that had killed young Deborah. I knew the true story, but I kept it to myself.

The doctor confirmed her death was due to a broken neck. The coroner arrived to view Deborah's body and the scene surrounding it. Given the circumstance of where she was found, and the evident cause of death being a broken neck, the medical examiner indicated that no further investigation of the girl's demise would be made. Deborah's body could be removed from the stable and prepared for burial.

I insisted that Deborah would be buried in the South, back in her home of Franklin. And that is what I did.

There are a few pages left for me to record from Mary's diary. But it's mid-afternoon and there's something I want to check out now. I need to take a break, and a walk through the neighborhood will do me good.

One of the four books I found in the bottom of the trunk that I've not looked at closely is the black King James Bible. I honestly didn't have much interest in it. I figured that I already knew what it contained, and the other books captivated my interest more. However, now that I know the story from Mary's diary, I'm curious to see if this Bible could possibly be the same one that belonged to Deborah and was used to conceal her scherenschnitte scissors. It seems to fit with the rest of the story that's come to light. I'm going to take a walk to the safe deposit box at the bank and see the Bible for myself. It would be amazing if this is Deborah's Bible, with its many scissor-silhouette pages cut out.

My walk to the bank was both pleasant and exciting. It's only about 15 minutes from my apartment. Reaching the bank I went to the appropriate customer service table, signed in as Emily Elizabeth Wilson, and gave the woman my key, which she used alongside her master key to open my safe deposit box. As customary, from this point the bank attendant left me alone with the contents of my deposit box. Everything appeared to be just as I had left it, which was not a surprise.

Opening the safe deposit box, I did a couple things. First, I put in the box the gold coin worth $14,000 that had been in my apartment. It needed a safer location. Second, I carefully removed the black Bible. I had decided that rather than peruse it while in the bank, to instead bring the book back to my apartment. I put the Bible into the bag I brought with me and called for the bank attendant to come and finish locking the box, which she did. Returning my key to me, we said our goodbyes and I left the bank.

It was difficult to hold off looking at the Bible, but I didn't open the bag until I reached my apartment. Seated at my table, I took the Bible from the bag. Gently plying the first few pages brought me to the book of Genesis, but this didn't reveal anything unexpected. A deeper dive into the Bible was needed.

Still seated at the table, I set the Bible on its spine. Eyeballing about where the middle of the book was located, and with a thumb on either side of this mark I slowly folded back both sides of the Bible. I had exposed the book of Psalms, but also much more than that.

My suspicions were confirmed! Lying open in front of me, pages of the Bible to my left and those to my right contained identical cut out sections of what looked to be a pair of long pointed scissors. This is incredible. Deborah had cut out page after page of the Bible to create a space to conceal her scissors. It reminded me of the scene from the movie *Shawshank Redemption*, when Warden Norton discovers the cut-out pages of Andy Dufresne's Bible, in which Andy had hidden his rock hammer.

No question. This was Deborah Lee's Bible, the one she carried with her to the National Peace Jubilee and Great Musical Festival and used to hide the instrument she intended to employ in killing the President of the United States.

Another piece of the story is verified! But many questions remain. I still don't know how these books ended up in the concealed compartment of the trunk? To whom did the two trunks belong? And why were they given to the museum? There always seem to be more questions! But I can't wait to share this story, and the objects related to it, with the world.

Wednesday, August 16, 2017

I'm going to transcribe more of Mary's story this morning. But I also want to do something today I haven't done for a while. Taking a break from writing, I plan to go sell a gold coin or two. Not that I need the money now. I just miss the experience. It's been ten days since I made my last coin sale. I hope I haven't gotten out of practice in my storytelling. But before I try my hand at this again, I'm going to delve into more of Mary's diary. I can't believe Deborah is dead.

~

*A black funeral carriage brought Deborah to an
undertaker in Boston. Alfred knew this man and
employed him to preserve the girl's body and prepare it for the train trip to Franklin.*

*Martha, Alfred, and I were shocked and dis-
heartened by the death of Deborah. The two of
them understood and supported my desire to
bring Deborah back with me to Franklin for
burial, which I appreciated very much. They as-
sisted me in making these arrangements late that
evening to secure her body for the journey south,
leaving the next morning.*

*Reaching the house of Alfred and Martha quite
late at night, my task at hand was to pack for my
return to Franklin. I was at a loss here. I had no
need of Deborah's clothing effects, to bring them
back to Virginia with me. I asked Martha to dis-
pose of Deborah's clothes, perhaps in a way that
would benefit someone in Martha's circle.*

*I did, however, want to bring with me Debo-
rah's leather satchel and its contents. I had carried
it with me from the Musical Festival, and I would
make sure it reached home safely. Returning to
my upstairs room to gather and arrange my own
things for the train trip home in the morning,
I was greeted with a sad surprise. Lying on my
pillow was a white folded paper. My name was
neatly written in flowing letters across the front.
Opening the page, I read these words:*

> *My Dear Mary,*
>   *Thank you so much for your caring
> of me in these years since my father,
> mother, and brothers were taken from
> us. Without you I would have nothing.*

You have been very kind and generous to me. I am sorry I will not be here to take your place as teacher in our Franklin schoolhouse in years to come, as I sense you have been preparing that place for me.

Please forgive me in this act of retribution against the president for the deaths of Gideon, Samson, and Colonial. I miss them all so very much. This trip to Boston provided me opportunity to plan and hopefully—today—carry out this act of justice for the killing of my brothers and the many other men of the Confederacy whose souls now rest in the rich Southern soil. My once flood of tears has dried and turned to reprisal.

The Bible story of left-handed judge Ehud, which we talked about on the train, has been my vengeful inspiration toward carrying out the killing of President Grant. I plan to give my life for his. May it occur through this righteous deed I am performing here that, as Ehud carried out the stabbing death of oppressive King Eglon, our land of the South will have—as the book of Judges chapter 3, verse 30 records—blessed "rest fourscore years."

I will miss you.

Your Loving Friend,

Deborah

Wow! I need to stop here and let this sink in. Why is this story not already part of the historical account of the United States and the life of Ulysses S. Grant? I can't wait until it will be.

I went to my dresser and pulled out the small bag of gold and silver coins from the top drawer. The neighborhood seems safe, but you never know. I should probably look for a better place in my apartment to stash these coins. Shaking a few of the coins out on the table, I picked out a gold coin that caught my eye. It was a 5-dollar gold piece, dated 1855, and looked to be in nice condition. It sparkled in the sunlight.

I took a folded white handkerchief and carefully slipped the coin inside. I put it in the familiar front pocket of my jeans. Grabbing my phone, I looked up the location of coin stores in the area. I selected one in south Seattle and, following my GPS, made my way there.

Parking in the nearby lot and entering the building, I could feel my anticipation for a sale build. There were no customers in the store. The man behind the counter was friendly, and wanted to know if he could help me with anything. Quickly falling into my storytelling routine, I disclosed, with a few tears and sniffles, the familiar tale of my grandfather giving me this gold coin as a graduation present a few years ago. I needed to sell it now to help pay for my father's funeral.

The man behind the counter told me first that he was sorry for my loss. He then went on to say that he was always interested in seeing any gold coins and might consider buying it depending on its date and condition. I pulled the handkerchief from my pocket and laid it on the glass counter, unwrapping the coin carefully. He whistled lightly when he saw it, as he put on a pair of cotton gloves and picked the coin up for close inspection.

After a few times looking over the coin, front and back, he laid it on the handkerchief. "That's a fine gold coin," he offered. "Yes, I'd be interested in buying it. How would $800 sound?" I told him that I didn't know much about coins, but that the offer would be fine and much appreciated.

He picked the coin up and immediately put it in a clear plastic holder. Before heading to the back room to get cash from his safe, the salesman told me that he would need some identification from me. He had noticed my vehicle's Virginia license plates. I told him I had just moved to Seattle and would give him my local address in the Queen Anne Hill area and cell phone number in case he needed to contact me. He appreciated that. With this much information required, I decided not to be Emily Elizabeth Wilson for this sale.

The man then headed to the back room. He returned a few minutes later with payment for my gold coin. It felt good to again see eight one-hundred-dollar bills counted out in my hand. He wished me well and offered his condolences for the loss of my father, but this time the man behind the counter didn't pass along any extra cash. I thanked him very much and exited the store. It was such a fun and productive way to spend a Wednesday afternoon.

My trip home was fairly quick—especially in Seattle traffic—and uneventful. Now that I'm done with my journal entry about selling another gold coin, I'm going to go up the hill for dinner out. I think I can afford it!

I decided to try a new spot to eat this evening, not too far from my apartment. The food was great. But as I was finishing my meal something happened that has me perplexed and even a bit unnerved. My phone buzzed indicating I had received a text. The sending number was someone I didn't know. Given the message, I'm not 100% sure the text is meant for me, but I'm pretty certain it is: "Hey Gold Coin Girl. When you're selling, I'm buying. Text this number back, if you're interested."

Setting my phone down, I tried to think back through the people who know, or could know, both my phone number to send me a text and that I have sold gold coins recently. I counted eight:

1. The owner of the coin store in Billings, Montana, whose business was robbed just before I entered. I gave him a copy of my driver's license and phone number.
2. The state trooper I spoke with about the robbery, after he stopped me on Interstate 90.
3. The owner of the coin shop in Seattle whose store was robbed by the man who dropped his glove at the doorway just before I arrived.
4. The police officers that investigated the robbery.
5. The other coin store owner in Seattle, who told me my coin was worth $14,000 and later bought my 10-dollar gold piece for $1,100.
6. Detective Williams of the Seattle Police Department
7. Ms. Donald, the bitchy attorney, probably knows this information about me.
8. The coin store owner that bought the 5-dollar gold piece from me for $800 this afternoon.

I guess there are more people who know my phone number and gold selling than I thought there were. But I have no idea which of these people may have sent this text. It's been a long day. I'm going to bed.

Thursday, August 17, 2017

I'm still thinking about the text I received last night. This is probably why I'm up so early this morning. It's dark outside, 4:00 in the morning, but I'm wide-awake. I'm not going to respond to the text, but I am curious who would send it to me. Most of all this morning, I want to find out what happened to Mary. There are only a few pages of her diary left for me to read and record in my journal.

*Martha understood that I would need to leave
for Franklin the next day. This was necessary in
order for us to have a funeral service for Deborah, and that she would have rest in the Southern
ground as soon as possible.*

*Alfred had arranged that Deborah's body be
placed in a funeral car on the train, and it would
be transported through the same two stops—the
cities of New York and Baltimore—we had made
on our trip to Boston a few days earlier. He paid
for my tickets all the way to Franklin, as well as
the fee for transporting the body of Deborah. I
told Alfred I appreciated his generosity very much.
I did not sleep well that night.*

*Early the next morning Martha and Alfred
delivered me to the train depot. We said a tearful
goodbye. But I will admit today, some 20 years
later, that I shed far more tears for Deborah than
I did in my goodbye to Martha. It was the final
time to ever see my sister.*

*I do not remember much of the return trip
to Franklin. It was, however, lonely. There were
times I thought of the cold lifeless body of sweet
Deborah, but I tried to move those thoughts away
from my mind quickly.*

*My contempt for Grant was then even stronger,
but I also knew I had missed my opportunity for
reprisal. I did ask myself, however, through the
years until his death, how much Grant thought of
and wondered about the young girl that came so
close to taking his life.*

I had removed the lead bullet from my dog's head cane when I returned to Martha's house the day Deborah was killed. For the return trip to Franklin, I traded the use of my weapon cane for the one with the lion's head holding red eyes.

The stationmaster in Baltimore had sent a telegram ahead, saying that they would be unloading a body upon our arrival to Franklin on Saturday evening. In doing this, I had also requested that the stationmaster contact the Methodist minister in Franklin, Reverend Warren, asking for him to meet me at the train station when I arrived. He was waiting for me on the platform as the train pulled into the depot in our little community.

The next day was Sunday. Anyone who would come to a funeral service for Deborah would likely be in attendance at the Methodist church on a Sunday morning. For this reason, the reverend and I decided that we would hold a short remembrance service for Deborah directly after the morning church meeting. This we did.

That Sunday morning was muggy, as many June mornings are in Virginia. On Saturday, two of the gentlemen from town had dug a nice burial site for Deborah's body near the church. Women had picked and arranged some very colorful flowers to place on top of her grave. There were 36 members of the Franklin community attending our church that morning, including some children. All of them stayed to pay their respects for the life of Deborah Lee.

The reverend spoke a few words about the fine young woman Deborah had grown to become. He told of the help she had given to me in the schoolhouse, and of her sincere love and care for wounded animals and birds. Reverend Warren also shared in remembrance of the entire Lee family and the hardships they had endured. Those in attendance agreed with and appreciated the sincere words offered by the minister.

The reverend then delivered two passages from the Holy Scriptures. Citing the book of John, chapter 14, verses 1 through 3, he read: "Let not your heart be troubled: ye believe in God, believe also in me. In my Father's house are many mansions: if it were not so, I would have told you. I go to prepare a place for you. And if I go and prepare a place for you, I will come again, and receive you unto myself; that where I am, there ye may be also."

And from the book of Ecclesiastes, chapter 3, verses 1 through 4, he continued: "To every thing there is a season, and a time to every purpose under the heaven. A time to be born, and a time to die: a time to plant, and a time to pluck up that which is planted: A time to kill, and a time to heal: a time to break down, and a time to build up: A time to weep, and a time to laugh: a time to mourn, and a time to dance."

This was a time to weep and mourn. Tears were shed, and afterward we sang the hymn "At the River" together. The small group hugged one another, shared a few thoughts about Deborah and the entire Lee family, and slowly dispersed toward our homes.

It was a time of love and fond memory, mixed with sadness. Later that day the men laid Deborah's body in the solitude of the sacred Southern soil and covered it with the beautiful flowers. It was Deborah Lee's time to fly away and embrace the rest of her family in heavenly glory.

A few years after this, in a bookstore in Washington, D.C., I came across a large hardbound volume written by a man named Patrick Sarsfield Gilmore. This book was titled History of the National Peace Jubilee and Great Musical Festival: Held in the City of Boston, June, 1869, to Commemorate the Restoration of Peace Throughout the Land. *I purchased the book and brought it home.*

As I wrote earlier in this account, Gilmore's volume about the Musical Festival in Boston is an unrighteous fallacy. It is a celebratory tribute to ongoing Northern tyranny and the whitewashing of Southern slaughter and destruction. I'm not sure why I've retained this book over the years, except to help keep alive Deborah's determined spirit of retribution.

This ends my account of the daring yet unsuccessful attempt to kill the President of the United States, Ulysses S. Grant, on June 16, 1869, in the city of Boston, Massachusetts. I trust that someday, after I join Deborah and her family in the glories of heaven, it will be revealed to the light of history.

I am recording this formal document so that the story of Deborah Lee's dedication, courage, and her heinous death at the hands of Grant's men will not be forgotten. May the record of her bravery challenge and inspire the lives and actions of those who follow after us.

Sitting in stillness I can't believe I've recorded all the pages of Mary Moore's story. It's taken me just over three months to make this complete copy of her writing. I want to continue with some personal reflection about this diary, and also consider what I should do with it now that my copying of it is complete. But before I do this, I need some time away, to think.

The sun is now up and the weather this morning looks clear. I'm going to do something I've thought about several times but haven't done in my short time in Seattle. I'm headed to the Space Needle!

Why do strange things keep happening to me? I couldn't make this story up. It was such a nice walk down Queen Anne Hill to the Seattle Center this morning. The sun was out, but the morning air still felt cool. On the day I moved in, Mr. Nelson told me the view of Seattle from Kerry Park—just a few blocks down the hill toward the Seattle Center from my apartment—was spectacular. And he was right! From this park the panorama of downtown Seattle and the water and distant mountains is breathtaking.

It was about a 50-minute walk to the Space Needle, including my stop at Kerry Park. Arriving at the Seattle Center, it was easy to make out the many refurbished structures, sculptures, and fountains within this park area that was part of the 1962 World's Fair. The Space Needle is the central attraction remaining from that event.

A line of people was waiting to buy tickets for the 43-second elevator ride to the observation deck and a fantastic 360-degree view of Seattle, Puget Sound, and the surrounding mountains. But my elevator trip and panoramic look at these sites will have to wait. My morning turned crazy soon after I got in line to buy a ticket.

There were about 15 people in the queue ahead of me. I could sense others were forming in a row behind me, as well. Standing in any line, even at the grocery store, is not one of my strong suits. I got fidgety. Turning around nonchalantly and scanning those individuals waiting after me, I was caught off guard. About 15 people back, I'm sure, was Ms. Donald—the disgusting attorney. I was shocked! And I'm certain the same man in the baseball cap and sunglasses I saw with her on Monday was standing in line next to her today.

I didn't want to stare, but he sure looked like one of the men in the police lineup. What were they doing here? It couldn't be a coincidence that they were in line with me, could it? They must be following me!

Immediately, I turned back around. Unsure what I should do at that moment, I quickly decided there would be other nice mornings to visit the Space Needle.

Just then the line of people ahead of me moved forward. I shuffled slowly along with them for a few paces, but then broke off and headed fast down the sidewalk away from the Space Needle. I didn't want to be conspicuous, but I had seen enough.

What's happening here? Seattle is a big city. This is crazy! I rounded a building and stopped to catch my breath. Looking over my shoulder, no one appeared to be following me.

Peering around the corner, I could see the line of people slowly making its way to the elevator entrance of the Space Needle. I was unable to make out Ms. Donald and her companion with the baseball cap, but they could have already moved ahead and out of sight. I wasn't going to stick around to see for sure.

Taking a zigzag route out of the Seattle Center, I headed in the direction of my apartment. I couldn't see anyone following me, but I didn't want to take that chance. It was an uphill climb and the weather had warmed considerably by the time I reached my apartment. I needed a shower to cool off and clean up.

I'm staying inside my apartment for the rest of the day, finishing now this descriptive entry in my journal and seeing what's on TV. I'm trying to keep Ms. Donald and her baseball-capped friend out of my thoughts. I've had enough excitement for today.

Friday, August 18, 2017

Even though I'm done recording the story from Mary's diary, I'm still drawn to peruse its pages and re-read the words captured in Mary's flowing handwriting. It's been such a big part of my life these past few months. Picking the diary up and carefully turning the few blank pages that concluded Mary's account, I came across something I hadn't noticed before. There are pages at the far back of Mary's diary that contain light pencil markings. I moved my bright reading light to the kitchen table. A close look revealed four pages near the end of the diary with pencil marks on them. These pages are different from the handwriting of Mary, which was done in black ink.

The lightly drawn pencil lines and shapes are made in a range of colors: red, blue, yellow, and purple. These lines extend across the four pages in various directions. Circular organic blue shapes of assorted sizes, some of them adjacent to lines, were placed throughout the four pages. Letters of the alphabet, numbers, directional arrows, and simple sketched symbols were drawn as well. They're all very confusing.

I wasn't sure what to make of these four pages of colored light pencil marks. My first thought was that I'd never seen anything like them before. But perhaps I had. Something in the back of my mind kept telling me I'd encountered markings like these earlier. But where had I seen such drawings?

After a few minutes of focused attention, their familiarity dawned on me. The pages of Mary's diary I was looking at resembled the two large pieces of green cloth I had unpacked from one of the trunks and placed in the basement storage room of the museum a few months ago. Both green cloths possessed hand-stitched colored thread, depicting lines and symbols much like those drawn here on the back pages of Mary's diary. I remember showing the green cloths to Jessica, and she not having any idea what they were.

This is crazy! I don't know what these two sets of colored markings—those stitched into the cloth and others drawn lightly in the back of the diary—mean, but they seem to be similar in design. This is another research project to work on back in the museum. My life seems to be a never-ending flow of new information leading to more questions.

Saturday, August 19, 2017

I got a text from Mr. Nelson this morning. In it he told me there would be a one-day delay in putting insulation in the attic above my apartment.

Instead of workers doing this job today and Sunday, it would now be Sunday into Monday. I'm really glad he sent the text. In the rush of everything happening, I forgot that Mr. Nelson had told me workers would be installing insulation in the attic this weekend. I needed the reminder.

In a phone call last week, Mr. Nelson said the insulation would be professionally installed and blown into the attic. In doing this work, he relayed that the installers requested access to my apartment, to make sure the vents and heating and cooling systems were functioning properly. He also told me that because the workers would be blowing the insulation into the attic space, they strongly recommended that I be out of my apartment when this work was being done.

For this reason, Mr. Nelson suggested in his text today that I leave my apartment tomorrow morning and return sometime Monday. By then it will be certain the spray insulation in the attic has settled, the vents and air systems are all operating okay, and some other electrical work in the attic is completed. Mr. Nelson has offered to pay me $250 for the inconvenience of being out of the apartment overnight.

It's nice of Mr. Nelson to make this offer, but having to leave my apartment tomorrow and overnight does present a problem. Today is Saturday and I can't get to the safe deposit box at the bank. I have Mary's diary, my journal, Deborah's Bible, and a small sack of gold and silver coins in my apartment now. I don't want to leave these items here, even in my dresser drawer, when workers may be coming in and out while I'm away. I doubt they would snoop around in my things, but you never know. And I also don't want to carry all these with me, if I don't have to, while I'm gone for a couple days. At this point I wasn't sure what to do.

Thinking about this situation for a few minutes, I came up with a cool solution that should have crossed my mind earlier. I don't know why I didn't think of it before now. I'm leaving these books and coins in the hidden space under the floor in my closet, where I found the Mason jar time capsule left there by young Stephen. It's a perfect place, out of sight, that probably no one but me knows to exist. When I leave tomorrow, I'll put some boxes in the closet on top of the blue throw rug covering the rough wooden floor. All will be fine. At least I hope so.

It's Saturday evening and I've come up with an additional plan. Since I need to be out of my apartment for a couple days, why not make the most of it. I've heard that Portland is a nice city to visit. It's a three-hour drive straight south of here. I'm going to leave early tomorrow and spend Sunday afternoon and Monday morning checking out some sights in Portland.

I'm taking a gold coin with me to sell. This will make my trip complete. After doing some online research to identify coin and gold dealerships in the Portland area, I found a location with two coin shops and a precious metals business somewhat close together and just off Interstate 5 near downtown. I'll make a sale Monday morning and drive back to Seattle in the afternoon. This will get me out of my apartment on Sunday and Monday, but also give me a chance to have a nice drive, see a new city, and sell a gold coin. It will be the best of all worlds.

I'm not taking my journal with me. I'm leaving it with Mary's diary, the Bible, and the rest of the coins in the hidden space under the floor of my closet. I'll write about my trip to Portland when I return on Monday. See you then!

Monday, August 21, 2017

I've got so much to write. I'm not sure where to start. It was good to see that all was fine in my apartment when I returned this afternoon. The three books and bag of coins under the floorboards in my closet were just where I left them. It's nice to have at least one thing in life end up as I hoped it would. But rather than jump into the details first, I need to record the story of my Portland trip from the beginning.

The three-hour drive south to Portland yesterday morning was both beautiful and uneventful. It reminded me why I already love the Pacific

Northwest so much. I was told that August and September are two of the best months in this part of the country, and that seems true!

I crossed the Interstate Bridge from Washington into Oregon and made my way south to the heart of Portland, checking my GPS for directions to my hotel. I figured that since I had only one night in Portland I would stay downtown, close to so much. Portland is a beautiful city. The thousands of white and colored lights reflecting on the water of the Willamette River are spectacular, especially at night.

I walked for quite a while through the city and along the river in the afternoon and evening. There is so much to take in. The many bridges stretching over the river are quite elegant. Mt. Hood stood out in the distance. I want to visit it up close sometime. Dinner was nice and I slept well last night. But my real unexpected and unnerving adventure happened this morning.

My early walk along the Portland waterfront was beautiful. After a relaxed breakfast, it was time to sell my coin and then head back to Seattle. My plan was to scope out the three gold and coin stores I had selected, to get a feel for the size and specific location of each business.

I had one 20-dollar gold piece I was hoping to tell a good story about and make a sale. My transaction of a similar gold coin in Sioux Falls a few weeks ago brought me $2,100. I was expecting about the same from the sale of this one.

The gold and silver coins I've looked through from the canvas bags show various amounts of wear. Some are nearly smooth through years of use. Other coins are in pristine condition, as they have been out of circulation and hidden nearly since leaving the mint.

Such was the case for the coin I planned to sell. Its golden hue shimmered brightly in the reflective sunlight. It was one of the shiniest and most well-preserved coins I had seen in the cache, with a date of 1856. I wrapped this 20-dollar gold piece in a new white handkerchief, which was my custom when approaching a sale. My rhyming mantra has become: "Tell the tale, make the sale, leave no trail."

I came to the first coin store on my list. I could tell right away it likely would not fit my needs. It was small, not much more than a hole in the wall. I doubt they would have the cash on hand to satisfy my needs. The second store, specializing in gold coins and bullion, was closed, even though their website indicated it would be open today. I had one more store option on my list. A feeling of disappointment—and getting-close-to-noon hunger—was starting to set in.

The final Portland coin shop I had identified as a potential sales site—a handful of blocks away—held possibilities. I drove around the block, checking out the location. It felt like I was casing the business for a well-executed robbery.

There was quite a bit of traffic in the area. This left few available parking spaces nearby. The store looked to be the kind that might work well for my needs—not too small, and up-scale in its location and presentation. I circled the block once more. Fortunately, this time around I found a parking space just a few car-lengths up the street beyond the front door of the coin store.

I had sold a 10-dollar gold piece with a date of 1856 a few days earlier in Seattle. I got $1,100 cash for the coin, so I was expecting about twice that dollar amount for a 20-dollar gold piece of the same date, and perhaps a little more cash because of the excellent condition of this coin. That amount would make it in line with the money I received from the other 20-dollar gold piece sold in Sioux Falls. It was a great return on a late-morning investment, and the opportunity to tell a good story made the sale even more enticing.

Parking my SUV, I headed for the coin shop. Gripping the door handle, I took a deep breath and entered the store. Like in most of my coin store experiences, I was the only customer. Many coin businesses have seen a drop off in foot-traffic. A lot of coin sales occur at numismatic shows throughout the country or online these days. I would probably have gone the electronic sales route in my previous life, but now wanting to stay as anonymous as possible I like to deal in cash only, if possible.

Two middle-aged men, both a bit round and balding, were talking to one another behind the counter. As I entered, one man greeted me warmly, almost before I had both feet across the doorway. In doing so I was surprised to hear his sprawling southern accent here in Portland.

I wasn't used to encountering a strong southeastern drawl, being away from that part of the country for the past few weeks.

He introduced himself as Mr. Smith, owner of the store, and proudly revealed that he owned coin shops throughout the country. The other man shuffled over to greet me as well. In a brief conversation I found out the men were brothers, originally from Arkansas. This was easily recognized by their similar physical appearance and southern accents.

Both men were highly involved in the gold and coin business. The brother of the store owner was a gold specialist, still living in Arkansas, who traveled the country buying old and expensive United States gold pieces for auction sales. He visited and knew coin dealers throughout the country, especially those specializing in rare—and thus valuable—gold coins.

This man knew a lot about gold coins and those who owned them. He handed me his business card, which I took, respectfully glanced at, and then stowed in my pocket. In hindsight, I should have recognized these bits of information together as a red flag and not followed through with my sales plan.

But I let my guard down and went ahead with the well-used sales story. I asked the men if they were interested in buying a gold coin that had been given to me by my grandfather in Virginia, a coin I needed to sell because of the death of my father. As rehearsed, for effect I slowed my delivery at that point and feigned gaining my composure. Watery eyes were an included sales feature.

There was silent hesitation from the two portly brothers behind the counter. Strangely, as I looked down and reached into the pocket of my jeans to retrieve the handkerchief holding the gold coin, I caught the men glance and subtly nod toward one another in a curious furrowed-brow sort of way. That should have been my cue to leave the store, but I didn't.

In our silence I retrieved the 1856 20-dollar gold piece from my front jeans pocket. I unfurled the protective cloth and laid the coin on a pristine white mat covering the glass counter directly in front of the gold specialist. Both men had put on white cotton gloves prior to inspecting the coin. So far, it was a familiar scene. However, what happened next was unexpected and shocking!

The two brothers stood side-by-side behind the counter. They each took turns picking up the coin and inspecting it silently and carefully under magnification multiple times, front and back. I noticed the store owner's hand shaking a bit as he carefully placed the coin back on the handkerchief.

The brother who owned the coin store broke the silence. His countenance had changed from the warmth of our initial greeting a few minutes earlier. He now looked at me with stern expression and steely eyes.

"Where did you really get this coin?" he asked with monotone directness.

"I told you. It was given to me by my grandfather a number of years ago," I choked. "My father died recently, and I need to sell it to take care of bills and his estate."

The man paused, mulling my words as if giving me time to rethink and change my story.

"Ma'am," he finally replied, "we question that tale for a number of reasons."

His brother, the gold expert, interjected tersely, "Yes, for a number of reasons!" He caught his breath, before continuing, "First, no one keeps a coin of that high quality, and worth more than three-hundred thousand dollars, wrapped in a handkerchief in their pocket!"

My mind reeled at the words, "three-hundred thousand dollars!" Now I was shaking.

"Second," he spat, "for that same reason, no one strolls in off the street to a local coin dealer unannounced on a Monday morning and asks to sell a coin of that value. It just does not happen!"

The man continued, "And third, in my miles of travel and frequent phone and online conversations with gold dealers, I've learned there have been several Civil War-era gold coins sold in various coin shops across the United States and here in Seattle during the past few weeks, all by a young woman of your description with a similar sad-life tale. And, doing so using a couple different names.

He then paused momentarily, before declaring, "Young lady, whoever you are, please tell us, how many times have your father and grandfather died and left you gold coins?"

That was it! My cover was blown. I needed to run, and fast! In one motion I swept the handkerchief toward me with my right hand, making sure to grasp the gold coin inside as I felt it solid within the soft white cloth.

No time to hesitate. I reached the front door in seconds, dashed outside, turned right, and fled up the street. Hurrying, I stashed the handkerchief with the gold coin in the front left pocket of my jeans in the same familiar place it had been when I entered the store a few minutes earlier.

My mind raced. Would the brothers follow me? I suspected so, but I was not going to stick around to find out and then have to answer their questions. Even in my run up the street I remembered the written words Professor Donaldson left in the museum safe telling me that others would be after the gold and would do anything to get it.

Who, besides Johnny Painter, did the Professor single out as perhaps coming after me for my gold? I'll have to go back through the notebook he left in the safe. He told me to take all caution and trust no one when it came to the treasure. Gold has a way of bringing out the very worst in people.

I headed up the street and ducked into a large clothing store. I quickly grabbed four tops my size off a rack and hurried into a nearby fitting room. There I waited, trying on shirts and blouses, but mostly sitting and catching my breath.

It took a few minutes to decide on a plan. I would leave the fitting room, walk around in the store for a few more minutes, and then go further up the street away from the coin store. In an hour or so I would then circle back to my car and, hopefully unseen, make a quick getaway. And that's what I did.

After about an hour visiting stores in the area, I purchased a blue baseball cap and some sunglasses. Putting them on in an attempt to hide my identity, I started back toward my SUV. Seeing my vehicle parked just ahead on the street, I realized the parking space directly in front of it was now open. My drive away would then be less obstructed and not require painstaking maneuvering of the vehicle from tight on-street parking. Things were looking up. It would be a fast getaway from the curb.

Reaching my SUV with keys in hand, in seconds I unlocked the door, got in, started the ignition, and hit the gas. Continuing my good luck, the traffic light at the intersection behind me had just turned red, so I didn't have any passing cars to wait on. It looked to be a quick and smooth exit. At least I hoped so. Grabbing a peek in the rearview mirror, I didn't see either Smith brother. I couldn't tell for sure, but I think I made off without them recognizing me.

I raced my vehicle to the end of the block, cruised around the corner and out of sight from the coin store. I caught my breath and retrieved my phone from beneath the car seat. I drove about ten blocks in a direction I thought would take me to the interstate before pulling into a fast-food parking lot to catch my breath. What had I just done? I hope I got away unseen by the Smith brothers.

There were three things I needed to do right away, and I did them in this order. First, I felt for the handkerchief and retrieved it from the front left pocket of my jeans. Feeling it, I could tell the coin was still in place. I was relieved at that.

Second, I checked my location and set the GPS for a return trip to Seattle. I was not far from Interstate 5, and I wanted to grab some lunch and head north toward Seattle right away.

And third, three hundred thousand dollars! How could that be? A ten-dollar coin of the same year got me $1,100 a couple weeks ago? Using my phone, I went online and typed in "1856 $20 gold piece value." What I found at the site caused me to take out the handkerchief, unwrap the coin again, and inspect it more closely.

What I learned online was that the back side—or reverse—of an 1856 20-dollar gold piece was minted showing an eagle facing left with spread wings, and a shield superimposed in front of the eagle. On the obverse of the coin is an image of Liberty, what looks to be 13 stars overhead in a halo position, and the date 1856 below Liberty.

Situated under the eagle on my coin is an O, showing that the coin was minted in the city of New Orleans. I remember this from the O mint mark on the 1851 three-cent silver coin that led the Professor and Johnny Painter to retrieve the jewels, jewelry, and gold hidden by James Longacre in the safe at the New Orleans Mint.

This O mint mark is what makes the 20-dollar gold coin I have so valuable. The online site said there were only a few thousand of these coins minted. No one knows how many coins of this year, denomination, and mint mark have been lost or melted down over the years. Without the O, the coin would be worth about $2,400. The O mint mark and pristine condition of the coin increases its value to $300,000. My luck with coins keeps getting better all the time!

I carefully wrapped the gold coin back in the handkerchief and tucked it into my front jeans pocket. Fortunately, the rest of my drive to Seattle went smoothly. But there is one thing that emerged in the trip that concerns me, a lot. During my drive I felt the business card I had put in my pocket. It was given to me by the owner of the coin shop in Portland, one of the Smith brothers. I had forgotten about it.

Picking up the card and glancing at it, I almost drove off the highway. The name on the card read, "Dixon Smith, nationally recognized gold and numismatic buyer and seller. Dealer in rare Civil War artifacts." It then hit me. The two men I met in the coin store today were the Smith brothers—Mason and Dixon—that had played basketball on the Professor's team with Johnny Painter nearly 50 years ago.

The Professor wrote in the letter he left in the safe that the Smith brothers are very successful coin and gold bullion dealers. One of the brothers owns coin shops in various US cities, mostly out west. The other travels the country buying and selling gold and silver coins and bars. The Professor and Johnny Painter had been selling coins and bars to the Smith brothers for decades, before the Professor and Johnny were killed. Mason and Dixon Smith also buy and sell unusual and valuable Civil War era objects and have sold quite a few of these artifacts to the museum over the years.

The Smith brothers were rightly labeled by the Professor as rotund characters and quite engaging when you meet them. Don referred to them as "Tweedledum and Tweedledee, characters right out of *Alice in Wonderland*." He went on to describe the brothers as friendly at first, but with "blood on their hands and no remorse in their souls."

They are the people who will want to get gold—particularly the Professor's gold—in any way possible. Don admonished the reader of his letter—me—to stay away from them. Considering what I encountered today, keeping far away from the Smith brothers will be a top priority for me.

After the events of this trip, it feels good to be back in my apartment, writing this journal entry. The drive to Seattle gave me lots of time to think. I've got my plan for the future pulled together, but I'm too tired to write it down here now. I'll get to that tomorrow.

Tuesday, August 22, 2017 (morning)

First thing today I'm headed to the bank. There are three valuable items I'm putting in my safe deposit box: Deborah's Bible that I got out of the box last week, the 1856-O 20-dollar gold coin worth $300,000, and Mary's diary. Since I've finished transcribing this amazing story, I want to move her diary to the safest location available. The bank opens at 9:00 a.m. I plan to be there when the door is unlocked.

I'm glad things went as planned at the bank. The three things I carried there are now in my safe deposit box. With that done, I stopped off at Safeway and did a little grocery shopping. After that, I'm focused on planning my next steps in life. I've tried looking at my current situation and possible future directions from a lot of angles. The plan I've settled on seems the best alternative.

Now that I'm done recording Mary's story about the attempt to assassinate President Grant—and her diary is safe in the box at the bank—my priority is figuring out the best way to make her story known to the public. Doing this, I want to avoid bringing too many questions and any harm my way. I know the diary will receive a lot of scrutiny when it's released. Historians and document specialists will investigate if this diary is authentic.

I'm sure I will be questioned as well. Researchers will want to know why, when finding Mary's diary in the trunk more than three months ago, I've waited until now to reveal it to the world. I'll be asked where the diary has been and what I've been doing with it during this time. Why did I take it to Seattle? Why am I choosing to hand it over now? There will be a lot of unavoidable questions directed at me. But I think I've devised a way around many of the difficult ones.

I've decided to go back to Virginia and re-enroll in graduate school. It's too late to do that this Fall Semester, as classes are beginning there this week. But I can pick up course work again in January as a student in the History Department. Doing this, I'll request a part-time job in the museum. Given my knowledge of the museum and all my experience there this past summer, I'm sure the university will agree to this.

A couple weeks after beginning work in the museum this spring, I'll "find" Mary Moore's diary and the other three books concealed below the false bottom of the trunk. Soon after that I'll tell their story to the world. But no one will know that I actually found these books in this hidden location in the trunk last May.

Bringing the books to light next January should eliminate questions about why I've kept the diary hidden from view all this time. As far as anyone will know, I'll have just then made this discovery of the books in the trunk. I think it's a pretty good solution. It will cover my tracks and keep me from hard-to-answer questions, yet I'll get credit for finding the diary below the false bottom of the trunk.

I will, however, keep the rest of the story to myself. No one will ever know about the gold, silver, and large amount of cash I found in the two museum safes. This will all be mine, coming to me from the Professor.

There is, however, one possible drawback to this plan: Billy Bull-wright. Going back to Virginia will bring me physically closer to the sheriff's investigation of the Sullivan house fire and the two bodies found in the charred farmhouse. But I figure if Sheriff Bullwright had been able to get past the *67 phone block and learn my identity he would have brought me in for questioning by now. So maybe he can't find me or I'm no longer a suspect. Perhaps he's already solved the crime or will do so by the time I get back to Virginia in January. It's a chance I'll take.

Writing this plan in my journal helps me see the entire arrangement as reasonable and doable. I can make this happen!

Given what's taken place in my recent gold selling experiences, along with the strange text message I received a few days ago about selling gold coins, I'm stopping my coin selling for the time being. Beyond that, on my drive back from Portland yesterday I decided it's best to leave Seattle before the Smith brothers possibly track me down or I run into Ms. Donald and her baseball-capped companion again. There are too many people following me or trying to find me. I'm feeling uncomfortable and even a bit scared. I need a clean slate from my pursuers, and I'm heading out of town to get one.

I'm going to stay in my apartment just a few more days. By the end of the week, I'm telling Mr. and Mrs. Nelson that an emergency has come up and I'm traveling back to Virginia. This is true, but what I won't say is that I plan to make two long stops before getting there.

Between now and when I return to Virginia in January, I'm going off the grid. Cash only, and as little use of ID as possible. With $200,000 I have way more cash than I need to make this happen. I want to lose myself and make it really hard to find me.

Traveling through Montana a few weeks ago, I was intrigued by the state's beauty and isolation. In some out-of-the-way town in Montana is where I'm going to live for the next two months: September and October. Then, when the cold weather sets in, I'm off to Texas for November and December. Before leaving Montana, I'll pick an isolated area in Texas where I may want to live for two months. I'll have plenty of time to make that decision in the fall.

In early January I'll set off for Virginia, hopefully renting my apartment from Tim Roosevelt again. From there I'll settle into my university classes and museum work until I make my "discovery" of Mary Moore's journal and the three other books hidden in the secret location at the bottom of the trunk. From there, who knows what direction my life will take. I still have some details of my trip to work out, but as much as I hate leaving Seattle after moving here just a few weeks ago, it's best for me to do this now.

I also think it's a good time to begin a new journal. This one I've written along with a transcription of Mary Moore's diary these past few months will always be unique and special, and for that reason I think it's appropriate to conclude it here.

Since I'll soon begin a new phase of life, I'm closing the story in this journal and will be starting a new one. Before doing that, however, I'm going to end my writing tonight in the way I finish off most of my journals.

I left a few pages blank at the beginning of this journal. I'm going to use them now to write a short lead-in to my record of what's happened in my life during these past three months. Doing this may help me better understand what I've lived through and written in these many pages. This is what I've done in most other journals I've kept over the years, and going back to the start to write the first few pages to finish my journal has become a standard practice for me. It sort of completes the loop of my story.

Looking around my apartment I see two items that have helped me a lot on this journey of life these past few weeks. My "Emily Elizabeth Wilson" driver's license and the key to my safe deposit box are sitting on the table where I left them this morning after returning from the bank.

The safe deposit box key provides security for the valuables that have entered my life recently. The books, coins, gold bars, and cash resting safely in the bank box will likely take me on adventures that even now I cannot imagine. It's appropriate that this important object is a key, as it keeps both secure yet accessible those things that have changed my life and I believe will continue to do so in days ahead.

Being Emily Elizabeth Wilson has given me exciting opportunities to sell coins across the country and rent the safe deposit box here in Seattle. Before that it provided albeit illegal but much enjoyed entry into bars and clubs. It's never let me down.

Turning back to the blank pages I left at the beginning of this journal and using them to recap the story I've recorded here, I think it's fitting to start with a happy recognition of this plastic marker of false identity, describing someone who doesn't really exist, but still with whom we've had a lot of good times together.

With my "Before the Beginning" introduction to this journal now completed and dated Tuesday, August 22nd, I realize I've been at this writing most of the day. It's getting dark, but I'm headed out for a lovely August evening walk in the neighborhood. I bet Kerry Park is beautiful. I'm going there to take in the panoramic view of downtown Seattle at night.

I don't need to do this, but before going out I'm putting this journal, along with my safe deposit box key, under the flooring in my closet. The blue rug I laid over the rough wood floor of the closet a few days ago is a nice added touch. There's the small bag of gold and silver coins in the space below my closet floor as well. I put my Emily Elizabeth Wilson driver's license back in its regular spot in my purse. I never know when it might be needed.

This finishes an incredible story of what is hard to believe I've actually lived through and recorded in this journal during the past three months. I can't wait to share the account recorded in Mary's Moore's diary with the world. To tell the story of my upcoming journey to do that, I'll be starting a brand-new journal right away.

[*About 7 months later*]

Tuesday, March 13, 2018

I hope to burn this journal some day! I'm tired of living in Seattle, which is not the common feel for someone in their mid-twenties, as this city is supposed to be a great spot for Millennials to meet new friends and develop relationships. It's not panned out that way for me at all. I think I've given this city an honest shot at livability in the time I've been here.

The people at work are, for the most part, very superficial. Nothing deep. Everyone has their own problems to deal with, so no one has time for anyone else's difficult life stories. The Seattle weather is too wet and dreary. I was told before I got here it would be that way—especially in the winter—but I didn't think it would go on this long and have such a strong negative effect on me.

I am getting antsy for a move. I'm recording these thoughts here in my journal to be a written reminder of who I am and how I feel at this point in life. I'm writing this in hope of discarding the memory of these dark days in a ritualistic funeral pyre for this journal at some point in the future, when I'm feeling better, and my life is finally fulfilling and all I want it to be.

I just hope that day comes soon. It's time to clean out my closet, discard the things from this apartment that I no longer need, and move on with life. I'm thinking that a sunny city like Phoenix or Albuquerque would be more to my liking. Writing helps in my decision-making. There's really nothing to keep me here, so why not make the move?

Friday, March 16, 2018

This settles it. I'm leaving Seattle. In the time I've lived in this upstairs apartment I just met my neighbor for the first time. As much as I wanted to connect with someone living near me, I'm not sure now it was best for me to do this. He seems like a nice elderly man—probably in his early-70s—and lives in the other upstairs apartment in this old house. He used to teach school but is now retired and travels a lot. I've seen him before, as we've passed each other a few times, but not spoken beyond our short "hello" greetings.

Today was different. He was seated outside at the far end of the picnic table near the stairs up to our apartments. He appeared to be enjoying an unusually sunny day in Seattle this time of year. I arrived carrying a bag of groceries from the Safeway store a few blocks away. I set the bag on the bench to get the house key out of my purse, when he said, "Hello."

I'm not sure why I did this, but I returned the greeting in a self-surprising friendly tone. He asked my name and we then struck up a conversation. After a few minutes I joined my bag of groceries on the bench, and soon my neighbor and I were engaged in more discussion than I've had with anyone since moving here. After nearly 30 minutes of interaction about what brought each of us to Seattle and a little about our interests, the conversation turned dark.

This is crazy to write! He asked if I knew any background information about my apartment. I told him I didn't know what he meant by the question. I wasn't familiar with anything concerning my apartment, except a few general things Mr. and Mrs. Nelson told me when I moved in.

I felt his gaze study me closely, as if trying to decide whether to end the conversation or how I would respond to what he was about to tell me. That should have been my cue to pick up my groceries and climb the stairs to my apartment. But I didn't.

It was then my neighbor told me that a woman about my age who lived in this apartment just prior to me was murdered right here in the alley last August, about seven months ago. That was only about six weeks before I moved in. The killer or killers were never caught. The police think it was a random mugging.

Clearly, the Nelsons never said anything to me about this!

The dead woman's keys and purse were not recovered. Detectives believe it was a case of her being in the wrong place at the wrong time. From the young women's wounds, it appears she fought off her attack and tried to escape down the alley.

She was shot in the back and died at the scene, probably instantly. No one heard the shot, or at least no one reported it. Her body was found, hidden behind a dumpster in the alley, the next day. If that's not enough, my neighbor told me the police said that the woman's apartment—now my apartment—was completely torn apart, as if the killer or killers were searching for something.

The young woman, whose name the elderly man didn't know as he never met her, was from Virginia. He knew this from the license plates of her SUV he'd seen parked in the alley. The woman lived in the apartment only a few weeks—and my neighbor was away most of that time—and she kept to herself.

No one seemed to know much about her. The woman didn't appear to have a job she commuted to. The Nelsons said there were no relatives for them or the police to contact. The young woman's vehicle disappeared at the time of the robbery. The police think the SUV was stolen by whoever shot her, and probably cut up for parts. No trace of it was ever found, as far as my neighbor knew.

The police believe the shooter killed the young woman and afterward took her purse. From it they got her address and house and car keys, and then ransacked her apartment from top to bottom in search of valuables. The authorities thought it odd, however, that a watch and some rings were found in the apartment.

The authorities weren't sure what to make of those things being left behind. But the case is cold now, with no other similar incidents having occurred in the neighborhood. Of course, the lock on my door was changed before I moved in, but all this shocking news today rattles me too much! I am giving Mr. and Mrs. Nelson and my boss at work notice that I'm leaving, and now for sure making my move from Seattle to the sunny Southwest at the end of the month.

Saturday, March 24, 2018

I'm not sure whether to laugh or cry, flee Seattle now or wait another week until my notice to move comes due. What happened to me yesterday turned my world upside down! I've been up all night, reading. Yes, reading a young woman's journal!

Here's how yesterday began. With moving day approaching, I decided to take action. There's not much stuff in this one-bedroom apartment, but there are a few things to pack. Living in Albuquerque—where I'm headed—is not like it is in Seattle, at least as far as the type and amount of winter clothes is concerned. My move is only a week away, so I took Friday off work to attack my closet and discard what I don't need.

In moving some boxes in my closet, my hand caught a sliver from the rough hardwood floor. Using the flashlight on my phone, I examined the floor to find the wooden piece that jabbed my finger. Moving my hands carefully over the floorboards, I was startled to notice that a section of the closet floor shifted slightly.

With a nail file and a kitchen knife, I lifted a section of the wood floor. It came up easier than I thought it would. Shining the flashlight into the opening, I saw a small canvas bag and a journal notebook in the open space under the floor of my closet.

The bag contained about 15 old gold and silver coins. The book turns out to be an eye-opening handwritten journal account of events in a woman's life beginning last May in Virginia and ending here in Seattle on August 22nd. Interspersed throughout her journal is the descriptive story of an assassination attempt made on the life of President Ulysses S. Grant in Boston, in June 1869. This is weird!

A couple things were sandwiched between pages in the journal: 2 color photocopies of a Virginia driver's license with the photograph of a young woman named Emily Elizabeth Wilson, and a key to a safe deposit box in a bank a few blocks from here.

Spooky continues as I read page after page of this journal. The writer's description of things going on in her life at the time the

*journal ends—August 22nd—make me think it was written by the
woman who lived in this apartment just before me. I believe she's
the one I learned last week was murdered in the alley behind my
apartment, and about whom the police are still looking for the killer or killers. In putting pieces of the journal I am reading together,
I wonder if her apartment may have been ransacked in search of
what I found hidden below the floor in my closet and what is in the
safe deposit box at the bank.*

*The woman, whose real name I don't know but she uses the
name Emily Elizabeth Wilson from time-to-time, writes about
killings that took place in Virginia and being on the run because
of a treasure cache of gold and silver coins she has now. She says
that a number of gold bars, valuable coins (one worth $300,000!),
$200,000 cash and some historical books are locked in the safe
deposit box of the bank a few blocks away. One of these books is
a diary that tells the story of an attempt to kill President Grant in
1869. This is crazy!*

Putting my pen down and sliding my journal across the table, my
mind raced. If the story I'm reading in this woman's journal is true,
then there's an incredible treasure at my fingertips. And I need to
make a plan to get it. I'm not even sure how to calculate the value
of what's in the safe deposit box in the bank this woman has written about, but the gold coins alone must be worth way more than
I'll make in a lifetime as a small business bookkeeper.

Calculating payroll numbers for a Seattle dry cleaning business—
what I'm doing now—doesn't pay much. And even with me skimming some significant cash off the top, which the owners know

nothing about, there's no way I'd ever come close to making the kind of money that could be mine from the bank just up the street. I do need to remember, however, that people have died wanting to get it.

Having taken a day off from the dry cleaners to sort through—mentally and physically—what I found hidden under the floor of my closet, and thinking through some options, I have an idea. Even though the woman who lived in this apartment before me is not Emily Elizabeth Wilson, she tells in her journal that she used this name to open the safe deposit box at the bank a few blocks away. She's who I need to be, and that's where I need to go.

Two color photocopies of a Virginia driver's license with the name Emily Elizabeth Wilson were tucked inside the journal I found hidden under the closet floor. With it is a key to the safe deposit box and a small canvas bag with gold and silver coins from the 1800s. I could get out of Seattle with this journal and these coins, which would probably fund me for a while. But it's hard to leave behind what this woman describes is sitting in the safe deposit box at the bank. It could be worth millions!

I'm not sure about these books she describes and the story they contain. I've never been interested in history, and I don't remember much about President Grant from my high school history classes. But if I'm able to get the coins and gold bars out of the safe box in the bank, then I might as well take the books, too. The story told about them in the journal is interesting. And the woman's diary from the 1800s could be valuable. Someone might want to buy it from me.

But to have any chance to get what's in this bank box, I'll need to convince people at the bank that I'm Emily Elizabeth Wilson. My features and hair color are not the same as the picture on the Virginia driver's license, but I think with some effort I can at least come close with the hair. It's worth a try, with so much at stake that could possibly be mine. It would change my life, forever!

I figured out which bank this is by the description of its location in the journal. There is only one other bank just down the street from the Chase Bank on Queen Anne Hill. I've passed the bank where the safe deposit box is located quite a few times. But I've never been inside the building. However, I do know that most small local banks have a similar building layout: an open floor plan in the middle of the room, with offices down the sides and tellers up front away from the doors, and very few windows.

I do have one thing going for me. The woman posing as Emily Elizabeth Wilson was killed in August last year. It's been seven months since she was last in the bank. I'm hoping new people are working there now, having never met Emily or perhaps won't remember her from that long ago.

Emily's journal writing says she visited the safe deposit box only three times after she opened the account. All the trips were soon after she moved to Seattle. The lure of getting a hold of this treasure is too much! It's a chance I have to take.

I picked up some light brown hair dye on a quick trip to Safeway. With a few scissor cuts and some hair coloring and straightening with a curling iron, I'm slowly looking more like the woman on the Virginia driver's license. It's a picture of Emily Wilson from a few years ago, so that helps. People change their hair color and styles all the time.

I've practiced writing the name Emily Elizabeth Wilson a few dozen times. I'm copying as close as I can the name as it appears on her Virginia driver's license. It's taken a while, but I think I'm getting pretty good at it. Hopefully my writing of her name looks authentic enough for me to get access to the safe deposit box.

Tomorrow is Sunday. I'll be ready to go on Monday. After completing my trip to the bank I'm then heading out of town, for good. I told Mr. and Mrs. Nelson that I'm leaving Seattle sometime this week. It works out well, as my six-month lease ends next Saturday, March 31st.

I know there are a lot of risks involved here, but seemingly fabulous rewards if I can pull this off. I put the few things I'm taking with me to Albuquerque in the trunk of my car. There isn't much. The rest I've discarded in a dumpster or left for the next tenant. I'll finish packing my final items tomorrow.

My plan for Monday is to park close to the bank entrance, with an easy getaway, if needed. If any sort of question or problem with me getting access to the bank box comes up, then I'll get out of there fast. I don't want to get caught with a key to a bank box that doesn't belong to me.

I paused at the entrance to the bank, took a deep breath, and reached for the door handle. I chose 12:20 p.m. for my entry. This might be a time when workers with less seniority—perhaps new on the job since Emily Elizabeth Wilson last visited the bank—could be covering for associates who have gone to lunch. It helped that this was one of the regular drizzly and chilly March days in Seattle. The securely tied rain hat I wore didn't seem out of place as I entered the bank.

I figured that between the four books, $200,000 cash, four gold bars, a couple bags of silver and gold coins, and some papers and a few other items Emily Wilson talked about in her journal, I would likely need two large stout-handled grocery bags to carry the contents from the bank box. It turned out I was right.

"Be stoic, nondescript, but pleasant," I repeated silently to myself as I walked decidedly toward the woman at the front desk on the left. Behind her I could see a short corridor that led to a barred door of the well-lit room that contained rows of safe deposit boxes.

It was with her I would need to sign in, tell my box number—which, fortunately, is embossed along with the bank's initials into the head of the key—and present this key for synchronized use with the bank's master key in order to have access to Emily Elizabeth Wilson's safe deposit box. It's all very routine and specified. YouTube explained it all.

"I hope this plan works," I told myself, "because there is no Plan B."

I reached the woman at the desk and our gaze met. The last thing that crossed my mind before greeting her was a terse, "Don't screw this up!" The woman introduced herself as Kathryn Brown. I told her my name was Emily Wilson, and that I wanted access to my safe deposit box.

She responded with a warm, "Sure, we can do that."

As Ms. Brown shuffled through a small alphabetical file-box for the signature card I would need to endorse to gain access into the safe box, I nonchalantly asked how long she had worked at the bank. Kathryn told me she had been at this location for only the last two months.

I smiled at that reply, offering, "Welcome to the neighborhood."

Kathryn Brown handed me the card to sign, which endorsed granted me access to the bank box. Doing so, I quickly glanced at the other three signatures of Emily Elizabeth Wilson on the card, put there when she accessed the box each time last August. Those handwritten names looked a lot like the ones I've made when practicing in my apartment the past couple days.

Taking the pen handed to me by Ms. Brown, I duplicated the name "Emily Elizabeth Wilson" on the next open line of the card. I must say that the name I wrote there looks much like the other signatures on the card.

It worked, because the bank attendant greeted me with a pleasant, "This must be you, Ms. Wilson."

I smiled in response. From there Ms. Brown and I headed toward the room holding the safe deposit boxes beyond the barred doorway.

I handed Ms. Brown the key to my safe deposit box. She inserted it alongside her master key. Turning both keys in sync, the exterior door to my bank box swung open.

"Do you need any help removing the box?" Kathryn asked.

I declined her help, but offered a sincere, "No, thank you."

Kathryn then opened the door to an adjacent viewing room used by patrons when going through material removed from their bank box. I thanked her for providing this access. She then left me alone.

I didn't take time to carry the box and its contents to the viewing room. Instead, I quickly opened the interior metal box and loaded the books, a wrapped package of cash, bags of gold and silver coins, gold bars, and the rest of the box's contents into the two large cloth totes. Scrambling as fast as I could, it took only a few seconds to transfer these items from the bank box to my two bags.

I then returned the now empty safe deposit box to its appropriate location within the rows of similar containers. Closing the exterior door to the safe box, I removed my key, putting it in my pocket.

Picking up the two full tote bags, I found them to be somewhat heavy. But with the rush of adrenaline now pulsating through me, I managed to lift and carry them toward the doorway without much difficulty.

I reached the door of the safe deposit box room, and without hesitation stepped into the central lobby area of the bank. All I needed now was to cross the nearly empty room, reach the glass door of the building, and make my exit from the bank. I was so close.

Just then, Kathryn Brown appeared in front of me from the side.

"I've finished work with my safe deposit box, shut the door to it, and took my key," I told her as I stepped quickly passed the barred door toward the lobby of the bank.

With those words spoken, I was immediately interrupted. Standing with Kathryn Brown in front of me now was a man in his 50s, wearing a dark striped suit, white shirt, and muted tie. Both he and Kathryn wore grim faces.

I caught my breath. There was nothing I could do but face them.

The man spoke first, "Ms. Wilson, we have a problem."

I stared at him blankly.

The man in the suit continued, "When you rented this safe deposit box last August, you advised the bank of your recent move from Virginia. There's been a note in our file indicating that you informed the bank attendant you had recently relocated to Seattle and would contact us with an updated address right away."

The man's voice grew louder, "We've been trying to contact you periodically for the past seven months to gain a current address and phone number. The United States Banking Code does not permit you to hold further access to this box until we get this information for our records. Please update this for us now, or I'll be required to immediately ask you to give up your safe deposit box here in the bank!"

"Well sir," I replied, "I'm sorry about this. I had to get a new phone number soon after I arrived in Seattle last summer, and I haven't needed access to the safe box here in the bank since then."

I continued, "Ironically, just now I took everything out of my safe deposit box," indicating to him, with a slight lift, my two large bags. "I'm moving from Seattle soon and won't be needing the safe deposit box any longer."

With that, and bags in hand, I slid my way around the two bank personnel and headed toward the front door of the bank.

Over my shoulder I heard the man raise his voice, "I'm sorry, Ms. Wilson, but if you are no longer utilizing the safe deposit box, then we request that you sign off use of this box and return your key to us!"

Now near the door, I turned and set down one of my heavy tote bags. Reaching in my front left pocket, I took from it the safe deposit box key and gently tossed it in a high arc toward the man in the suit.

While the key was still airborne, I picked up both bags, turned, and walked briskly out the glass front door. "Focus and walk. Get to the car, get in and get away fast. You're almost free!"

I'm glad I parked where I did. I got in the car and thrust my two large bags onto the passenger's front seat, started the ignition, and hit the gas. Tires screeched as I sped from the bank. I saw the man in the suit look at me through the front door glass, but I was gone before he could exit the building. I was on my way.

One block turned into two, and two into four. With each mile the bank was further behind. And there was no sign, at least yet, of the authorities pursuing me.

I'm on my own and headed toward Interstate 5, south toward Portland and beyond. My goal is to reach sunny Albuquerque, eventually. I don't see anything standing in my way. But who knows what adventures I may encounter before then. Among all the many unknowns surrounding me, at least one thing in my life is certain now—I'm far wealthier than I've ever been or ever dreamed that I would be.

Acknowledgments

I thank Jane Bolin, Dan Bolin, Cay Bolin, Doug Blandy, Shelby Jaedicke, and Miles Ouren for their thoughtful input during my work on this book. I appreciate very much their insights, information, and influence helping to shape this book and my life. Many thanks also to Lori Price for her excellent technological oversight, thoughtful editorial involvement, stellar design skills, and dedicated effort to help see this book to completion.

About the Author

Paul E. Bolin, PhD is a historian of art education, having taught at the University of Oregon, The Pennsylvania State University, and The University of Texas at Austin. He retired from The University of Texas at Austin in 2018. He co-authored (with Doug Blandy) the book *Learning Things: Material Culture in Art Education,* and co-authored (with Ami Kantawala and Mary Ann Stankiewicz) the book *Steppingstones: Pivotal Moments in Art Education History.* Paul lives in College Station, Texas with his wife Jane and cat Tigger, and enjoys time spent with his two daughters, son-in-law, and grandchildren whenever possible.

All correspondence can be directed to author@paulebolin.com. See www.paulebolin.com for related historical content, information on current books, and future publications.

Grand National Peace Jubilee and Musical Festival (monthly bulletin) by George Coolidge, 1869.

www.ingramcontent.com/pod-product-compliance
Lightning Source LLC
Chambersburg PA
CBHW020301200626
46814CB00006BA/2030